# WORKHOUSE LASS

*A Selection of Recent Titles by Una Horne*

# WORKHOUSE LASS

## Una Horne

This first world edition published 2008
in Great Britain and the USA by
SEVERN HOUSE PUBLISHERS LTD of
9–15 High Street, Sutton, Surrey, England, SM1 1DF.

British Library Cataloguing in Publication Data

Horne,  Una
   Workhouse lass
   1. Orphans - Fiction 2. Workhouses - Fiction 3. Women
   domestics - Fiction 4. Poor women - Education - Fiction
   5. England, North East - Social conditions - 19th century -
   Fiction
   I. Title
   823.9'14[F]


   ISBN-13: 978-0-7278-6651-6   (cased)
   ISBN-13: 978-1-84751-070-9   (trade paper)

*All Severn House titles are printed on acid-free paper.*

Typeset by Palimpsest Book Production Ltd.,
Grangemouth, Stirlingshire, Scotland.
Printed and bound in Great Britain by
MPG Books Ltd., Bodmin, Cornwall.

*For Fred, who was a workhouse lad made good and who told me what the life was like in those far-off days.*

# One

## 1863

'**M**ammy!'

Lottie woke suddenly, panic flooding through her whole body. She sat up in bed and stared across the large dormitory filled with beds and sleeping children. The child in the bed only 12 inches from hers began to cry, and a couple more followed suit.

'Quiet!' shouted a stout woman standing in the doorway holding a lantern. 'Any more noise and I'll bray the lot of you.' The room quietened at once until only an odd muffled sob could be heard.

Lottie sank down in the bed, feeling the lumps in the hard mattress against her backbone and skinny shoulders. The bed was wet, she realized with a shiver of foreboding. She would be smacked, or brayed as Matron called it, anyway. Well, she thought, she was used to that. Ever since her mammy had gone to heaven she had been smacked most days.

Matron closed the dormitory door and the room was dark again but for the moonlight filtering in through the high windows. Lottie stared at the bits of sky she could see through the panes. There were stars shining between small clouds. Her mammy was there, she told herself, and she was happy and watching over her little girl.

Lottie couldn't remember very much about her mammy. But she comforted herself with holding on to the small scraps she could remember and added to them in her imagination. She hugged her pillow as her heart slowed back to normal after her nightmare. She couldn't remember what the dream had been about even, only that she needed her mammy. Mammy would look after her; she would make the unnamed thing go away. Even if Lottie couldn't see her, she knew Mammy was there in the sky just like one of those stars.

Suddenly aware that the tiny girl in the next bed was sobbing and the noise was getting louder, Lottie sat up and leaned over towards her.

'Ssh,' she said softly. 'Whisht now, whisht, don't cry, pet. If Matron hears you she'll come back and we'll both get wrong, we'll be smacked.'

'Lottie? Can I come into your bed? Please can I?'

'Howay then, come on,' Lottie replied and a small body climbed in and snuggled under the blanket, not minding the dampness of the sheet. She put her arms around Lottie's neck and Lottie cuddled her skinny little frame to her. Betty had only come into the workhouse a day or two ago and she was only two years old or maybe three. Even the matron couldn't say for sure how old she was, because she had been a foundling. One of the guardians, Mr Robson, who had a greengrocer's shop, had caught her biting into a plum she had taken from the stall at the front of the shop and had chased her into Newgate Street before catching her.

'You little imp!' he had shouted and she had dropped the plum and begun to tremble and wail in fright.

'Shame on you!' a woman shouted at him. 'What do you want frightening a little bairn like that for?'

A few late shoppers, for it was eight o'clock on a Saturday evening, stopped and stared at the woman, the child and Mr Robson.

Mr Robson's face was as red as a beetroot with the injustice of it, for the remarks they made about him were uncomplimentary, to say the least.

'She was stealing my fruit!' he said and then wished he hadn't, for he certainly didn't want to bandy words with people like that. After all, late shoppers were usually folk in from the mining villages and just looking for bargains as the shops closed for the weekend. After something for nothing, they were.

'The lass must be hungry,' another woman observed. 'What's a mouldy old plum to you?'

'Nevertheless . . .' Mr Robson began, then stopped. 'As a matter of fact, I was looking for her mother,' he said stiffly. 'But as there is no sign of her, I'll take her up to the workhouse for the night. Not that I have to explain to any of you. I am a Poor Law Guardian and it is my duty.'

'Oh aye,' said the woman, favouring him with a scornful glance. 'Of course it is.'

He turned away, remembering he wasn't going to talk to these people. Instead, still hanging on to the little girl, he called to his assistant to close the shop while he went up to the workhouse, with its adjacent orphanage.

'It's an infernal nuisance, that's what it is,' he grumbled to Matron when he brought the child in. 'I have better things to do on a Saturday night. But what else was I to do? There was no sign of her mother, or father either. If she has one, that is.'

He handed the child over to Matron, holding her away from him with some distaste, for there was a nasty, dirty smell about her.

Lottie happened to be walking along the corridor at the time, trying not to be noticed, but the woman had a sharp eye. She too held Betty away from her clean apron as she called to Lottie.

'You there! Lottie Lonsdale! Take her and see she is washed and gets a uniform. And mind, I'm putting you in charge of her. Oversee her properly or you'll feel the edge of my belt.'

'Yes, Matron.'

Matron and Mr Robson watched as Lottie took the child and went on down the corridor. 'I'll enter her into the record, Mr Robson,' Matron said. 'There's no need for you to bother. You get off home to your wife and family, they'll be wondering why you're out so late.'

'I will, thank you, Matron,' Mr Robson replied. 'But it was my Christian duty to fetch the lass. Duty comes first, Matron.'

'Indeed, Mr Robson.' She smiled archly at him and the bow beneath her chin wobbled. She shouldn't have mentioned his wife and children, she thought as he turned away. He may have joined her in a cup of tea in her cosy sitting room. Sometimes she could do with a little company in the evenings.

Meanwhile, Lottie had taken the new little girl to the kitchens, where Susan Dunn was washing up the supper bowls at the enormous stone sink. Though Susan was twelve years old, old enough to have recently joined the inmates on the women's ward, she had to stand on a stool to reach the tap. It was just a cold water tap, but there was a large copper boiler to the side of the range and hot water had to be ladled from there.

'Who's this then?' she asked Lottie, as she eyed the little girl. 'I'm not seeing to her mind, I'm done for the day. Just as soon as I finish off these pots.'

'Matron said I had to see to her,' said Lottie. 'Is there any panacklty left? I reckon she's hungry.'

'A bit. You're lucky, I haven't washed the pan out yet. I was just going to put the panacklty in a bowl and put it in the pantry. The night porter likes a snack when he comes on.'

Lottie looked at the child. She was gazing at the bowl with undisguised hunger. She would have to be fed before she was bathed.

'I think the bairn's need is more important than the night porter's,' Lottie opined and Susan nodded agreement as she put the bowl of potatoes, onions and a few scraps of fat bacon on the table and Lottie sat the girl in front of it.

'What's your name, any road?' she asked.

'Betty,' the girl said, through a mouthful of the food she was stuffing into her mouth with her hands rather than the spoon Susan had given her. Lottie brought in the tin bath and ladled hot water into it from the copper boiler and added cold from the tap.

'Well, hurry up and eat your supper. Then you can have a bath and I'll fetch you a uniform from the linen cupboard.'

It was the policy of the Guardians for the inmates of the workhouse to do all the cooking and cleaning for themselves and that included looking after the little ones. In addition, the children had to be taught how to take over all the tasks as soon as they were old enough. After all, they were there at the expense of the ratepayers, and should show their gratitude for their board and lodging by paying some of it back.

After all, they got a free education too, didn't they? It was not so long ago that poor children got no education at all, and even now most scholars at the National Schools had to take their threepence every Monday morning to be taught their letters and figuring.

Lottie knew all about this, because the children were reminded of it every single day.

Lying in bed a short time after being assigned to Betty, her arms around Betty as the little girl's breathing slowed into a sleeping rhythm interrupted only by the occasional snuffle, Lottie was having difficulty in getting back to sleep herself. Her thoughts were going over her nightmare and the unnamed dread that was always in the back of her mind.

It was still dark when she heard the shuffling and occasional cough as the male inmates walked along by the end of the corridor on their way to the stone yard. That meant it must be half past five in the morning already and they were starting their working day. They broke stone with picks and shovelled it into huge barrows, ready to be taken away to be used to mend the roads across the county and even up to Weardale, where roads were being built which stretched right across the dale as far as Tynedale in places where there had been no roads before, just cart tracks or donkey trails.

Betty had settled down at last and was fast asleep, her thumb stuck firmly in her mouth. Poor little soul, thought Lottie, did she remember her mother at all? Did she miss her, as she herself had missed her mother when she came into the workhouse? The tears were dried on to the tiny girl's cheeks and her lashes sparkled in the dawning light. Soon she would have to wake the child up and return her to her own bed or there would be another reason they would both be smacked. Still, it was very quiet at this hour and if she sneaked to the linen cupboard she could get dry and clean bedclothes and change the bed. If she hid the wet sheets in the dirty laundry basket, then neither of them would be smacked.

Carefully, Lottie drew herself out of the bed and ran off down the ward to the linen cupboard at the bottom. As she had thought, the woman responsible for it the night before had left the key hanging in a concealed niche near the door.

Betty reminded her so much of herself when she had been left on the step of the workhouse, not because her mother had deserted her as Betty's had done, but because she had been taken away to the women's ward and Lottie had never seen her again. That terrible night was the earliest memory Lottie had. The figure of her mother had become shadowy after the six or seven intervening years, but the feelings were as sharp as ever.

# Two

'You'll be all right if you are a good girl, Lottie,' her mother had said when she brought her to the Big House. That's what Mammy had called it, the Big House, and Lottie, who was only three, had looked up at the forbidding stone frontage of the place. It was a dark night and she and her mammy had been walking all day and Mammy was breathing with a funny rasp, which frightened Lottie more than the fear of the house. By the time a man came to open the door and let them in, her mammy was slumped against the stone at the side of the door and when she tried to walk over the step she slid gently down in a heap.

Lottie was crying by then and the man caught her roughly by the arm and dragged her into the entrance.

'Shut your noise and sit down there,' he said sharply. And she did, for he was a big man and she was frightened of him. She watched with large, frightened eyes as a woman came and was seeing to her mammy and taking her away, and Lottie never saw her again except in her dreams.

'Your mother has gone to heaven,' Matron said on the day Minnie Lonsdale was laid to rest in a pauper's grave beside all the other paupers. Lottie was taken to the committal and she saw the box in which her mother was, but she comprehended very little of it. But when she went to church in the crocodile of girls dressed in checked dresses and black stockings and boots, the big girl who held her hand and walked alongside her whispered that her mother had not been in the box really, she had gone to heaven. The big girl's name was Edna and it was her job to look after Lottie and take her to the earth closet and stop her messing herself. Mostly she was kind but sometimes she lost her temper and smacked Lottie. 'You do what I tell you or I'll smack you in the gob,' she would say and Lottie would shrink back, for everything in the

Big House was bewildering and frightened her, but mostly she didn't like being smacked.

Lottie talked to her mammy at night, whispering of what had happened to her during the day, and she gleaned some comfort from that. After a while, the picture of her mother she carried around in her head began to fade until it had gone altogether and there was nothing left but the memory of her presence and the feelings it aroused in her.

By the time Lottie was ten, she was working in the linen room of the workhouse at Crossgate. She could sew a neat seam and patch and mend the clothes of the inmates of the workhouse. She also still had the job of looking after the waif who went by the name of Betty Bates, just as she herself had been allotted to the girl called Edna when she first entered the place. Not that Betty's name was really Bates, but she had come to the workhouse as a foundling and the matron, who had the naming of little girl paupers, chose it. The one before that had been called Allen.

'Betty, you'll get into trouble if Matron finds you here. You're not supposed to be in the corridors,' said Lottie as she came out of the sewing room one day and found the tiny girl standing by the door, thumb in mouth. The one o'clock bell had rung for dinner and everyone was looking forward to it, because today it was to be a special dinner, provided by the ladies of the town.

'Don't tell,' said Betty, looking fearfully over her shoulder.

'I won't tell,' Lottie reassured her. She took Betty's hand in hers and fell into her correct place in the hierarchy of the sewing room, behind the grown-up women and in front of the younger ones. 'There will be brawn, maybe, and even cake,' she whispered to the little girl and Betty's eyes brightened. She could say very little as yet, being only three and a bit slow, but she could say Lottie's name and small phrases like 'don't tell', a phrase she used a lot as she wet her bloomers so often still, even through the day.

The orderly lines of children in their blue-checked dresses and black stockings and older women in rough grey serge and their hair knotted back and covered with large caps that came over their foreheads almost to the eyes, were swelled by others from the laundry and scrubbing maids with swollen red hands.

The women were to eat in the same room as the men today because it was a special day. Women looked forward to seeing their men and children for the first time in weeks. Of course, the men would be at tables on one side of the refectory and the women at the other with the children in between, but messages could and would be passed along the lines of narrow tables.

It was one of the days that stood out in Lottie's memories of the workhouse at the junction of Allergate and Crossgate when later, as she turned thirteen, she was sent to Sherburn Hill to Place. All the children thought of Place with a capital 'P', for it meant they would be free of the workhouse and even be earning money for themselves. Place meant a job and lodging outside, where they did not have to answer to Matron or Master or even to the Poor Law Guardians, those men and sometimes women who were the absolute monarchs of the paupers.

'I don't want you to go,' sobbed Betty on the day Lottie carried her bundle out to the door where Mr Green was waiting to take her to his house in Sherburn Hill. It was the longest sentence Lottie had ever heard the girl, who was now five years old, say.

'Betty Bates, you come in now and go to your class,' Matron's voice came from inside. She opened a window to the side of the front door and leaned out to speak to Lottie. 'Be a good girl now, Lottie Lonsdale, don't you be giving our lasses a bad name,' she said and Lottie nodded silently. She might have spoken, but if she did she might have been rude to Matron and she wasn't sure if the woman could bar her going, even now.

'You be good now and learn your lessons, Betty. I will try to see you when I can,' she said instead, her own eyes filling with tears. 'I will, I promise. I'll have a half-day off every month and I'll come to see you if I can.'

She had exchanged one master for another, Lottie thought as she came down the stairs in the house on the end of a row in Sherburn Hill. It was half past five one morning a few weeks later. Mr Green was gruff and barely looked at her when he was barking his orders at her. He watched how much she ate as though she were stealing it from the mouths of his children.

This morning as usual, she went into the kitchen at the back of the house and riddled the ashes in the grate and re-laid the fire. Before she put a lucifer to it, she looked over her shoulder in case Mr Green should see her do it.

'I'm not made of money, you know,' he had said last time he saw her use a lucifer. 'You should bank it on a night and then there'll be a few embers to start the fire away.' Lucifers were to buy from the grocer's cart that came along twice a week, but as an overman at the pit Mr Green got a supply of coal every few weeks. It was tipped in the alley behind the house close to the coalhouse hatch and was to shovel in. The Green boys were too young to do the job: Noah, the eldest, was not yet ten and small for his age. There were always lads who would come and offer to 'put in the coals' for a penny but Mr Green would have none of it.

'I'm not keeping a great lass like you and paying a lad to put in the coals,' he said when she suggested it. So Lottie had to do it, getting the coal in before Mr Green came home from the pit, no matter what else she had to do that day.

Lottie put the kettle on to boil and cut bread and butter for Mrs Green's breakfast. While she waited, she sat down for a few minutes in the rocking chair by the hearth, the one that had been Mrs Green's before she became bed-bound. This was her favourite time of the day, when she had a few precious moments before she had to make Mrs Green comfortable against her pillows and then make a meal for Mr Green coming in from fore shift or going out on back shift. Then the lads were to get up and feed with great bowls of porridge sweetened with sugar and with fresh milk poured over it.

She was just lifting the heavy iron kettle from the fire when there was a cry from the front room that had been turned into a sick room for Mrs Green. Placing the kettle on the hearth, she ran through to see Mrs Green half out of bed, hanging precariously, with only her legs anchored beneath the bedclothes. She seemed quite incapable of righting herself and was moaning pitifully.

'Mrs Green, what are you doing?' asked Lottie in alarm. She hurried around the bed and for all her small stature managed to lift the woman back to the safety of her pillows, where she flopped with her mouth open, her breathing fast and shallow. Lottie grabbed the extra pillow from the chair by the bedside and propped her up a little better so she could catch her breath. Oh, she looked badly, Lottie thought. Mrs Green's skin was blue around the mouth but her cheeks were flushed and her skin was hot to the touch. She brought the woman a drink of water from the pail in the pantry and held it while she took some. Only a few sips, for even that seemed to exhaust her.

Then she wiped her face and arms with a cold flannel.

'You're a good lass,' said Mrs Green.

'Where's my breakfast?' asked Mr Green from the doorway. 'Lottie? I don't pay you to sit about on the wife's bed.'

Lottie jumped up quickly, dropping the flannel and having to bend down to retrieve it. 'I'm sorry,' she said. 'I'll do it now. Only Mrs Green needed me.'

'Aye well, be quick about it,' said he. 'A man shouldn't be coming in after ten hours in the pit to an empty table.'

'Alfred, the lass is doing her best.' The voice from the bed was weak and fluttering.

Mr Green regarded his wife, frowning. 'Mind, you keep out of it, Laura,' he said, but not roughly or unkindly. If he had a soft spot for anyone, it was his wife.

'I'll stay here, Lottie,' he said, 'while you get it ready. I picked some mushrooms on the way home; do them with a bit of bacon. Give us a shout when they're ready.'

Lottie fled to the kitchen and did as she was bid. By the time she was calling the boys down to eat with their father before they went out to the National School, the house was filled with delicious smells. They came down the stairs in a rush: Noah, the eldest, who was nine; Freddie, who was eight; and Mattie, six. Mattie was grizzling again, she saw, his shirt hanging out where his braces met his trousers, his feet still bare.

'Freddie hit me,' he said pathetically to his father. 'I want my mam.'

'Leave your mam alone,' Mr Green ordered. 'Sit down and eat your porridge.' For the boys and Lottie had porridge for breakfast rather than bacon and mushrooms. But it was good porridge, made with real, fresh milk. The two older boys set to with a will and the only sounds were the occasional slurp and that of Mr Green's knife against the plate.

When he finished, he sat back in his chair and looked at

Lottie. 'I want you to go and get the doctor when you've got
the lads away to school,' he said. 'Tell him the wife's badly.'

Lottie looked back at him in some alarm. He must think
Mrs Green was very bad if he wanted the doctor to come
back. He had only been to see her a few days before and Mr
Green grumbled at the expense every time the doctor came.

'Don't look so gormless, lass,' he said. 'Hurry yourself and
get on with it.'

''Is Mam badly?' asked Noah. 'Can I go in to see her?'

'Leave her alone, lad, she wants some peace. If I hear you
bothering her I'll take the belt to you. Now, away to school
with the lot of you.'

Lottie ate the last spoonful of porridge made with the
skimmed milk left after taking off the cream for Mrs Green,
for the boys had used up all the fresh milk. 'I'll go straight
away,' she replied. Grabbing her shawl from the back of the
kitchen door, she ran off down the yard, thankful for the
chance to get out into the fresh air before starting the clearing
and cleaning in the house.

'I think you should ask the Nightingale nurse to call and see
your wife,' said Dr Gray to Alf Green when he had returned
with Lottie and had examined Mrs Green. 'Sister Mitchell-
Howe, her name is. Here, I'll write it down for you.'

'How much will that cost?' Alfred Green asked. 'I don't
begrudge it mind, but I've a lot of expense already what with
having to have a lass to keep an eye on the lads as well as
the wife. Will she not do? She's good with Laura, I'll say that
for her.'

Dr Gray looked at the pitman before him and sighed. The
fellow was an overman and as such must be earning more
than most miners. He was fond of his wife too, he could see
that.

'A trained nurse can see to your wife better than a young
girl can,' he said. 'In any case, she will keep an eye on her
if she visits every day until Mrs Green is over the crisis.'

They were outside in the narrow passage that led from the
front door past the room where Mrs Green lay to the kitchen
at the back. It was Laura Green's voice that decided the issue.

'Lottie,' she said, her voice too weak to penetrate to the
kitchen where Lottie was scouring the porridge pan. 'Lottie!'

'Lottie!' Mr Green shouted and the girl appeared in the passage, looking anxious. She had managed to get the boys off to school before the bell rang and ran to call the doctor and washed and changed Mrs Green before he came and now she was trying to catch up on her work. She was already thinking about the task after the next one and that was to prepare something filling for the lads' dinner when they arrived back at twelve o'clock.

'See to her, can you not hear her calling?'

Lottie hurried into the sitting room where the patient, in trying to reach for a drink, had overturned the cup and spilt water on the bed sheet, which was a clean one, having been changed for the doctor's visit.

When Lottie tried to change her nightgown and sheets, Laura let out an involuntary cry of pain and both men in the passageway heard it.

'I'll help you in a minute, Lottie,' said Mr Green and turned back to the doctor. 'Why then,' he said. 'I reckon we'd best give that newfangled nurse a try. How much do you reckon it will cost me?'

'You'll have to ask her that,' the doctor replied. 'But I think Sister Mitchell-Howe is reasonable. If you just have her coming in twice a day until your wife is over the worst it will do.'

'Mitchell-Howe, what sort of a daft name is that? Well, we'll see what she charges,' Mr Green muttered as he showed the doctor to the door.

# Three

'Dr Gray asked me to call to see Mrs Green,' said the woman who was standing on the doorstep when Lottie answered a knock at the door. She was dressed in a funny hat with ribbons that tied under her chin and an all-enveloping cloak. She carried a bag something like the one the doctor carried but made of some cheap material, not leather. 'My name is Sister Mitchell,' she went on and smiled. She had a lovely, kind smile and Lottie warmed to her, for in her young life she had learned to differentiate between sincere and insincere smiles.

'Sister Mitchell-Howe?' asked Lottie, for that was what Dr Gray had said. She peered up at the woman a little fearfully despite her smile, for the way she was dressed reminded her of the matron at the Big House.

'You can call me Sister Mitchell,' the woman said, smiling again and Lottie forgot her small trepidations, for she had a very pleasant face when she smiled, this newfangled nurse.

'Howay in.' Lottie opened the door wider and the nurse followed her into the house and through to the front room. Her voice was little more than a whisper, for Mr Green had gone to bed and he could get very angry if he was woken. Even little Mattie never spoke above a whisper when his da was in bed.

Lottie was impressed with the nurse's treatment of her mistress. Sister Mitchell took off her cloak and laid it over a chair before donning a large white apron. All her movements were careful and controlled and she managed to change the bed sheets and sponge Mrs Green down causing the minimum of discomfort to her patient.

'Watch now,' Sister said, 'be as gentle as if you were washing a new baby.'

Lottie watched and helped where she could but she was

hesitant and fearful of hurting Laura Green, whereas Sister Mitchell was deft and sure in all her movements.

'Bring Mrs Green some beef tea if you have any,' Sister said, when at last she was satisfied that her patient was as comfortable as possible. Lottie ran to do her bidding. By, she thought as she watched over the pan of brown liquid heating on the bar, she would like to be a nurse when she grew up properly. A proper Nightingale nurse like Sister Mitchell, that was what she would be. Could you be a Nightingale nurse if you were a skivvy from a workhouse and only 4 foot 10? She glanced into the mahogany-framed looking-glass, which hung over the mantel shelf. Her skin was thin and white and her brown eyes peered back at her because she couldn't see a great deal more than a blur from a few feet away and she was small and the looking glass high up. Her cap had slipped down on her forehead and she pushed it up over her unruly hair. Hair so fine and soft that no amount of hairpins would hold it.

The beef tea began to bubble and she hastily lifted it from the bar and poured it into a cup. Her hand trembled and she spilt a few drops on the saucer and had to fetch a clean one and wipe the side of the cup.

'You couldn't be a nurse, you're too clumsy,' she berated herself aloud.

'Is it ready?'

Sister Mitchell had come through and was standing in the doorway watching her. 'Only I have to be getting on and I want to show you how to support a patient so she can take a drink with the least possible distress to her before I go. I'll come back about teatime.'

When Lottie peeped into Laura Green's room, half an hour later, she found her mistress sleeping peacefully. Poor woman, she thought as she gazed at Laura's face. Her skin had a translucent look, though her cheeks were flushed. A pulse beat erratically on the temple Lottie could see. It was hot in the room and the air smelled stale. She hesitated before deciding to open a window for a short while. The window was stiff and resisted her attempts at first, but in the end she managed to open it a couple of inches. Satisfied, Lottie tiptoed out of the room and closed the door quietly.

The whole house was quiet with both master and mistress

in bed asleep. Lottie had tidied the kitchen and now had little to do that she could do without making a noise until the boys came home and she gave them their dinners. Today she had a pan of mutton broth ready and she had baked bread the day before so there was little preparation to the meal. She opened the back door and slipped out into the yard for a breath of fresh air.

She leaned against the yard wall for a few moments, closing her eyes and breathing deeply. Though there was the all-pervading smell of coal and soot in the air, it was cool and there was a slight breeze blowing. After a while she picked up the broom, which stood upended against the wall where the tin bath hung, and started to sweep the yard. It wouldn't do for Mr Green to look out of the bedroom window and see her lazing about. As she swept, she dreamed of becoming a Nightingale nurse like Sister Mitchell. She would grow taller, she would, and she would learn not to be clumsy and she would save up her money and buy spectacles so she could see properly. (How much would they cost? She would have to find out.) But then the colliery hooter blew and returned her to the present. It must be twelve o'clock and the lads would be on their way back from school and the broth wasn't even on the fire to warm yet.

Besides, she thought dismally as she went inside, her thoughts returning to her ambition to be a nurse like Sister Mitchell, she would have to learn to read and write and spell better; subjects the school in the workhouse hadn't bothered a lot with. No, they had concentrated on teaching her to sew a fine seam and clean up after folk. After all, what did skivvies want with reading and writing? They would be sitting in a corner reading when they would never be good for anything but scrubbing floors.

'Where's me dinner?' demanded Noah as he came through the door, closely followed by the two younger ones, Freddie and Matthew.

'It'll only be a minute,' Lottie replied, stirring the broth in the pan to prevent it sticking as she heated it. She lifted the heavy iron pan with both hands and put it down on the iron stand on the table.

'It should have been ready, I want to play with the lads,' grumbled Noah. 'You're supposed to have it ready.'

'It is ready,' said Lottie, as she ladled broth into a bowl and put it before him, then did the same for the others. She started to cut slices from the loaf, giving them each a piece.

'You're not supposed to answer back. You're not my mother, you're just a maid. My da pays you to do it. You're just a workhouse skivvy.' Noah stared at her truculently, before stuffing bread in his mouth.

'A workhouse skivvy,' echoed Freddie and Matthew and they both giggled.

'You have to do what I say or I'll tell my da and he'll send you back to the workhouse,' said Noah. 'Dirty clarty workhouse,' he added.

'Dirty, clarty workhouse,' said Matthew.

'Don't say that, Mattie pet,' Lottie said to Matthew.

'You cannot tell us what to do, Noah says,' said Freddie.

Lottie closed her eyes and bit her lip to stop her angry retort. After a moment she said, 'I am looking after you while your mam is badly. I will have to speak to your da if you're naughty.'

The three boys laughed uproariously. 'My da calls you workhouse!' Noah cried.

Lottie turned a fiery red, more from anger than anything else. But she did not reply for in the moment's quiet after she heard the faint voice of Laura Green from the front room. She left her broth and hurried in to see her, to find that Laura had slipped down on her pillows and was unable to lift herself up.

'I'm sorry, did they wake you?' Lottie asked as she helped her back against the pillows. The woolly bedjacket she wore fell back and exposed her elbows, red and swollen with the disease. The sight filled Lottie with pity as she covered them back up.

'No . . . yes, but I like to hear them,' Mrs Green whispered as though she had no strength to speak louder. 'Only, they'll wake Alfred and he needs his sleep.'

'I'll remind them, they must have forgotten. You know what lads are like.'

'Aye.' Laura sank back on her pillows and closed her eyes, for the effort had exhausted her. 'You see to them, pet, you're a good lass.'

Alfred was already awake. As she came out of the front room he came downstairs in his bare feet, braces dangling by the side of his trousers and a collarless shirt open at the neck. He favoured Lottie with a furious glare before pushing past her to the kitchen. The boys were still laughing and making remarks about 'workhouse lasses' but they fell silent immediately they saw their father, no doubt suddenly remembering they were supposed to be keeping quiet. He belted all three around the ear, one after the other, and not varying the weight of the blow from the eldest to the youngest.

'Hadaway back to school out of my sight!' he snarled, not raising his voice but sounding just as threatening as if he had. Cringing and sniffling and with Mattie holding his ear, the three scrambled for the back door and ran down the yard to the gate. Only when they were out of sight did he turn to Lottie.

'You, you little bastard,' he said. 'You're supposed to be keeping them quiet. You'd best mend your ways or you'll be back in the workhouse along of all the other bastards.' He suddenly thrust out a hand and smacked her across the ear too, so that her head rang and a sharp pain shot through from one side to another, making her teeth chatter. She staggered under the blow and grabbed hold of the chair just vacated by Noah. But it was the insult to her mother that hurt the most.

'I'm not a bastard,' she said as soon as she righted herself and could face him again. 'My mam and dad were married but he died.'

'Oh aye,' Alfred Green sneered, 'O' course they were. You lot all say that. But it doesn't signify, you're still bastards scum, expecting hard-working folk to pay the poor rate to keep you in the Big House. Well, it's time I got a bit back from you and you'll do as I say or I'll know the reason why. Now, if I hear another sound the day I'll be down here and belt the living daylights out of you. Do you understand that?'

Lottie said nothing. A deep resentment burned in her chest but she controlled it, for she knew she couldn't bear to go back to the workhouse and say she had been let go for talking back to the master of the house.

'I said, do you understand?' Alfred caught hold of her front and raised his hand to her, ready to strike again.

'Aye,' said Lottie.

'I cannot hear you, what did you say?'

'Aye, I said aye, Mr Green,' Lottie replied. She burned with a resentment that was stronger than the pain from the blow but she kept her voice controlled and her face expressionless. She had learned to do this over the years in the workhouse when confronted by an unjust authority. But all the time her thoughts were racing. She had to get out of this house. But how could she? There was poor Mrs Green who needed her. And the lads. Young Mattie was not a bad lad, but he was influenced by his older brothers, of course he was. Besides, where would she go? Not back to the workhouse, which she had left with such high hopes. There would be no help for her there.

'If I hear another sound from down here, I'll take the belt to you,' Alfred Green said, still in that quiet, menacing voice he was using so as not to disturb his wife. 'Now, get on with your work.' He stalked back up the stairs and Lottie watched his braces swinging his shirttail, which was hanging out of his trousers.

Lottie turned back to the kitchen and her work. After a while she began to feel a little less despairing and even started to sing as she worked, though very, very quietly. In her young life she had found that despair got her nowhere, she just had to get on with it. But she could dream, couldn't she? She cleaned the kitchen and washed the passage and sandstoned the front step, working energetically and with a thoroughness that had been drummed into her in the workhouse. But in her thoughts she had escaped into the world of her imagination and there she had gone to a proper school and learned to do things and she had friends like Sister Mitchell and she was making something of herself. Maybe not a Nightingale nurse but something else. Like working in a posh shop up by Castle Chare and all the nobs came in and asked for her to serve them.

'Miss Lonsdale is so good, so knowledgeable about the latest fashions,' the bishop's wife said to the manager of the shop, for Lottie had decided it would be a dress shop selling fine silk dresses and bombazines. Lottie wasn't sure what bombazines were, but she had heard them being admired by two ladies who were looking in the window of a shop in Silver Street. One day she might even become the manageress of the shop, even the owner. And she would take Betty on as an apprentice and they would live together in the rooms above the shop and they would have a red velvet covered sofa and . . .

'Afternoon, Lottie, how is my patient?'

Lottie scrambled to her feet from where she had been kneeling by the front step as she applied the sandstone to the sides. It was Sister Mitchell, back already!

'G-Good day, Sister Mitchell,' she said, feeling a pang of guilt, for she hadn't looked in on Laura Green for at least an hour. 'Em, she is asleep I think.' She dropped the scouring stone into the bucket and followed the sister indoors, wondering if she should apologize for leaving the step scouring until so late in the day. It was a morning job but the morning had been *so* busy.

'You see to that, Lottie, I'll call if I need any help,' Sister Mitchell said and watched as the diminutive figure in the over-sized cap and apron hurried out to the back of the house. Poor Lottie, she thought, the lass reminded her so much of her friend Bertha when she was that age.

Mrs Green was awake and moaning softly to herself but when she saw the nurse she smiled slightly, a smile that transformed her worn face. 'Sister,' she whispered. Was her fever lessening? Or was this just the onset of the crisis?

# Four

L ottie sat in the flickering light of a candle that stood in a holder on the bedside table. Outside, rain pattered at the windowpane and the wind blew down the chimney, making the small fire in the grate blow out sudden flurries of smoke. Lottie's head nodded and eventually her chin fell down on her chest as she succumbed to sleep. Her upper body slumped on to the bed and she slept until her usual getting-up time, which was five o'clock.

Her neck ached when she woke and her eyes felt as though there were cinders in them. It was cold in the room, as there was only a tiny red glow left in one corner of the grate; the rest was grey ashes.

'Mrs Green?'

Suddenly awake, Lottie jumped to her feet and leaned over the bed. The candle was gutted and only a pale shaft of moonlight came through the thin curtains.

She touched Laura's forehead with her fingertips: it was cold. Her temperature had broken, praise be.

It was only after she had mended the fire with some sticks from an offcut of pit prop and added a few pieces of small coal so that it flared up, crackling, that Lottie turned back to the bed and an awful suspicion entered her head. Mrs Green had not moved, though her eyes were open. Lottie fetched the candle from the kitchen mantelpiece and lit it at the fire and held it to Laura's face. Laura was gone, passed away, gone to live with the angels. The usual euphemisms raced through Lottie's head. Sometime during the night, she had died.

Her husband Alfred was at the pit and the boys were in bed. Only Lottie had stayed up beside her, in case she needed anything during the night; but Lottie had been exhausted by all she had had to do the day before, for it had been washing day. Still, she had sat on a chair by the bed and sponged

Laura's face and hands at intervals. Her skin was hot and dry and Lottie had to be very gentle so as not to hurt her. But Mr Green had given Laura an extra dose of laudanum before going out and she had seemed to be sleeping fairly peacefully.

Lottie had seen dead people before in the workhouse. She had even helped the old woman who laid them out; had done so since she was eleven. She knew that Laura was dead. But she was only thirteen and she was nervous. She stood by the bed, filled with guilt besides the nervousness. She should have been awake, she knew she should have been awake. Even the paupers usually had someone keeping vigil with them when they died. Poor Mrs Green had had no one.

'God rest you, Mrs Green,' she whispered. Then she went out of the front door and around to the next door, which stood side by side with the Greens'. There was a faint light in the window and she knocked on the door and Mrs Bowron came.

'I think Mrs Green has passed away,' Lottie said, her eyes wide, for she could barely see Mrs Bowron's face in the near dark.

'Eeh lass, I think she might have been gone for a while,' said Mrs Bowron when she followed Lottie into the house and laid a hand on Mrs Green's cold forehead. 'Get Noah out of bed, now, and send him up to the pithead to tell his da.'

Lottie hurried to do her bidding, though she paused by the door. 'I fell asleep,' she mumbled.

Mrs Bowron looked at the girl's white face. Why, she was nobbut a bairn, she thought. 'It doesn't matter, she would have gone any road,' she said, trying to offer some comfort to the girl. 'Hadaway and get Noah.'

But Noah sobbed and cried when she told him and the other boys woke and they cried too, all three huddling together and wailing and sobbing. In the end, Lottie had to put on her shawl and run up to the pithead. The only person she could find at that time of the morning was the engine winder and he was busy with the engine, winding up the cage with tubs of coal. The noise was deafening and there was an overall stink of coal dust and sulphur that made Lottie gag. She had to shout to make herself heard.

'Here's the under manager now,' he said when at last she succeeded in getting her message across. 'Tell him.'

The under manager frowned when he saw her. 'What's up, lass?' he asked. 'Thou shouldn't be here.'

Lottie explained again and he glanced at the clock on the wall of the engine house. 'Send a message, Potter,' he said to the engine winder. 'Best stand outside out of the road,' he advised Lottie. He didn't hold with women cluttering up the engine house.

Potter tapped on the iron casing of the engine with a spanner and again a few minutes later, and an answering tap came. Lottie was diverted for a minute, wondering how those few taps had sent the message for the overman. But still, the fact was the engine noise came louder and the overhead wheel began to whirr and the cage came up again, but this time with Mr Green in it. He dipped his head and stepped out into the yard.

'Well? What's happened?' He sounded irritable and impatient. Evidently the taps had not told him his wife was dead. Lottie had hoped that they had.

'Mrs Green has gone,' she said. She began to shiver for it was, after all, a cold October pre-dawn.

'Gone? Gone where?' Then comprehension dawned and he gazed down at her. His expression didn't change; it seemed to have frozen on his face. Maybe he didn't care that his wife had died, Lottie thought dismally. Did men not cry? Paupers did sometimes, she remembered. Maybe that was the difference between men like Mr Green and paupers. She folded her arms across her thin chest, trying to make them as small as possible so they would be covered by her short shawl.

'I'll come back wi' you,' he said and strode out of the yard, the metal studs in his pit boots ringing on the stones of the yard. Lottie had to trot to keep up with him.

Mrs Bowron met them at the door. The noise of the boys crying was still coming from upstairs. 'I'm that sorry for your loss,' the neighbour began, but he cut her short roughly. 'Aye, thanks Missus,' he said. 'Lottie hadaway up and stop the lads making that racket.'

The next few days, until the funeral, Lottie was run off her feet preparing food and tea for the neighbours and family calling to pay their respects to the deceased. She somehow got through them despite her permanent haze of tiredness, until in the end she was hardly aware of what she was doing, be it slicing bread and butter or cleaning the house from top to bottom before relatives descended on them.

Sister Mitchell called. 'If I can help you with anything, Lottie,' she said, 'I will.' But Alfred Green heard her. Lottie had asked her into the house when she knocked, but now Alf put a firm hand on the Sister's elbow and ushered her out.

'Nay, she can manage,' he said. 'I can't afford to pay nurse's prices now that I have a funeral to pay for.'

'I wasn't asking for pay,' Eliza gasped.

'Just being nosey, were you?'

Eliza's face turned scarlet and she turned on her heel and went back to her gig.

In fact, there was a funeral club with the union and it covered the bulk of the expenses, as both Lottie and Sister Mitchell well knew.

'I meant as a friend. I was not asking for payment,' she repeated, looking back at him from her seat behind the horse, but he had already closed the door on her. He would not have her in the house for reasons she could not fathom.

But at last the funeral was over and the relatives and other guests departed.

'I would help you with the lads, Alf,' said his sister, before going back to Hartlepool. 'But you know I have my own family to see to.'

'Aye,' said Alfred hardly and opened the front door for her. She hesitated.

'I just thought,' she said, 'you know that Whitby jet brooch that Laura wore on her blouses? Well, I bought it for her for when you got wed, if you remember. I do like it and it would be a nice keepsake. And . . .'

'I'm not giving it you back,' said Alfred, opening the door wider. 'You'd best go or you'll miss your train.'

'I just wanted it for a keepsake,' his sister sniffed. She had flushed a bright red and her eyes flashed, but she compressed her lips and marched out into the street.

Life in the house returned to something like normal. Lottie didn't have Mrs Green to see to of course, but she still seemed to be working from early morning until late at night. She fell into bed exhausted at the end of every day. Even when she had an afternoon free, she had to prepare the meal before she left and see to the boys when she got back in the evening. Mostly she went for a walk along by the Wear or if it was a nice day she sat on the riverbank enjoying the sun, but only for half an hour. She simply had not enough time to walk all the way back to the workhouse to see Betty.

Besides, she was so tired, the workhouse seemed miles away. So she sent her a postcard and hoped someone would read it to the little girl.

Once or twice she met Sister Mitchell on her rounds while she was out shopping at the Co-op store, and once, a red-letter day this, Sister asked her back for tea. There she met Sister Mitchell's son, Tot, who was around her own age though still a schoolboy. And she met Sister Mitchell's friend, Bertha, and learned that she had been a workhouse lass like herself, only in Alnwick, which was somewhere in Northumberland.

Three weeks after Mrs Green's funeral, Lottie at last managed to go to the Big House to see Betty. She stood on the step before the imposing front door and pulled on the bell rope and from inside came the familiar jangling of the bell. It was part of her childhood, that bell, ringing out as it did so often just as the daylight faded. It was usually answered by an inmate and the person who had pulled the rope had to wait outside on the step while the inmate went to Matron's office and told her there was a pauper outside wanting admittance, or a vagrant, or sometimes, a woman with a little child. Sometimes it was a little baby, wrapped in rags or sacking or even in a lacy wool shawl and fine lawn. By the time the door was opened, the person who had brought the infant was away, hurrying up Crossgate or diving around a corner.

'We're full!' announced the old woman who answered the door to Lottie, startling her out of her reverie.

'You'll have to come back . . .' The woman stopped and peered at the visitor. 'Eeh! It's Lottie isn't it? Mind, you've not been gone long before you've come back, have you?'

'I've just come to see Betty Bates,' Lottie replied, lifting her chin.

'You'd best come in then,' the woman inmate said. 'She's

in the kitchen. You know where that is, you don't need me to show you.'

Turning on her heel, she walked away and Lottie made her way to the back of the building to the kitchen, which was dismally dark due to the tree branch right outside the window.

'Lottie!' cried Betty and dropped the cup she was washing into the sink. 'Oh, Lottie, I'm so pleased to see you.'

'And me you, pet,' the older girl replied. 'I'll give you a hand with the washing up, then we can go into the garden for a while.' She had come just an hour after dinner time, for she knew Matron and the Master would be having their forty winks upstairs in their private rooms and so they would probably not be disturbed.

They sat on a bench under the kitchen window with their arms around each other and chatted. Or rather, Lottie told Betty about the house where she was now and the poor woman, Mrs Green.

'She's dead now, poor soul,' she said. 'But she was a nice woman. And there are three lads an' all. And Mr Green.'

'Is he nice?' asked Betty.

'He's all right,' said Lottie. Betty couldn't remember anything about the world outside the workhouse and she used to make up stories about it as though it were a sort of fairyland. Lottie hadn't the heart to disillusion her.

'When are you coming back?' she asked when Lottie said she had to go.

'I'll try to next month.'

'Promise?'

'I promise,' Lottie assured her. 'Don't cry, pet. I will, I will.'

'I reckon you're not due to three shillings a week and your board, lass. Not now you haven't got the missus to see to. Two bob is ample. After all, you've not much to do with only the three lads, an' them at school most days. I'm not paying you to sit on your arse all day,' said Alfred one Saturday afternoon after dinner. He pushed two bob over the table to her.

Lottie put the pile of plates she was holding back on the table. She stared at him, thoroughly shaken. Today she had planned to take her money and go into Durham to the second-hand market and get herself a pair of serviceable boots to replace the ones she was wearing and which were worn through and past taking to the cobblers to be re-soled. It was her afternoon off and Mr Green's too, so she was free of the lads for a couple of hours.

'I need the money, Mr Green,' she said desperately.

'Get away, what do you want money for? You get all your meals and no doubt more behind my back.'

'I need boots, Mr Green.'

'There's a pair of the wife's in the bedroom, use them,' he replied.

'I cannot, they're not my size,' said Lottie. She couldn't bear to think of wearing the dead woman's shoes. At least with any from the second-hand market she didn't know who had worn them first.

'You're getting particular aren't you? Well, I'm telling you, I'm not giving you three bob and that's the end of it.' Mr Green rose to his feet and stomped out of the room. 'Noah!' she heard him calling. 'Noah, get yourself here, I want you to put a bet on for me.'

'I'll take it, Mr Green,' said Lottie. 'I could do with a breath of fresh air.'

Alf looked at her. 'Aye go on then,' he said, as though he were being magnanimous. He had expected more of an argument from her with regard to her wages so he didn't mind letting her out for a few minutes. He handed her a note and sixpence. 'You know where the bookie's runner stands?'

'Aye, I do.'

Lottie put on her shawl and went out of the house, clutching the note and the sixpence in her hand. She walked up the street and around the corner and across the road, fighting a battle with her conscience. But she knew what she was going to do. She went past the man standing on the next corner and turned down a back street. The night-soil cart was standing there and the man was shovelling muck from the midden on to the cart before taking it out into the country to sell to the farmers. Lottie tore the note into strips and dropped them into the cart, then ran down the alley with the sixpence clutched in her hand. Before going into the house, she slipped the coin into her shoe.

'You took long enough,' said Alf when she went into the

kitchen. 'Now put my bait up and fill my flask with cold tea. Put some sugar in an' all.'

'It's my afternoon off,' she reminded him.

'Aye well, you can go after the lads get off to school. And mind, be back in time for their teas,' he warned. 'I reckon if it wasn't for me giving you a roof over your head you would be tramping the roads. That or doing hard labour in the work-house.'

Later, Lottie walked up to the marketplace. Still struggling with her conscience, she almost went back and put the bet on, for the race wasn't run until half past three. But she was lost when she saw a pair of boots, which looked almost new. They were shiny black boots with thick, sturdy soles and would last her the whole winter, keeping her feet snug and warm.

'How much is that pair of boots?' she asked the stallholder, a man of middle age.

'Two and sixpence,' he replied. 'Look at them, they're like new, could have come out of the shop yesterday, like.'

'Two and sixpence! It's too much,' Lottie exclaimed.

He looked at her consideringly. 'Go on, you can try them on if you want,' he coaxed. Customers were slow in coming that day and a sale was a sale after all.

Lottie tried them on. She laced them up and took a few steps. Oh, they were lovely, so warm and comfortable. 'I'll give you one shilling and eightpence,' she said. After all, it was a long time until next payday.

'Two shillings, and it's a deal,' he replied. 'Not a penny less.'

That left her with only sixpence and that ill-begotten, thought Lottie. It was as if she could still give Mr Green the money back. But now she had the shoes on she was loth to take them off. The horse would not win, she told herself. No one would be any the wiser, especially Mr Green. And he owed her the money and more besides.

'I'll take them,' she said and handed over the money. As she walked away, the steel studs in the heels and toes of the boots ringing on the cobbles, she felt excited and happy and guilty all at the same time. When she saw a policeman on the opposite side of the street, she blushed and hurried on. When he began to follow her she almost panicked, but how could he have found out she had taken the sixpence? What was the punishment for stealing money? Would she go to gaol or would she be hanged? They didn't transport people to Australia any more, she knew that.

The bobby walked past her and disappeared down a side street, his cape swinging. Lottie felt weak with relief. On her way home there was a sweet shop and she went in and bought tuppence worth of gobstoppers to give to the lads. Now she could not give him his money back.

'I've been waiting for you, you bloody little thief,' said Alf Green as she came in the house. He was sitting in the front room with the door open so he could catch her the minute he heard the door close behind her.

'What?'

Lottie's heart fell to her new boots and she began to shake. How did he know? She began to back off down the passage but he was too quick for her. He bounded forward and grabbed her arm and dragged her into the front room. Still holding her arm in a grip like iron, he closed the door after him. Lottie backed away but there was nowhere to go.

'H-how did you know?' Stammering, she managed to get the words out.

'The horse won. You didn't think it would win, did you? Well, it did, at twenty to one an' all. What sort of a fool do you think I am? I've a good mind to get the polis and turn you in. It would serve you damn well right an' all.'

'Please don't,' begged Lottie. 'Please don't, I beg you!'

He gazed at the small, immature figure before him: the face that was all eyes that were always peering myopically. Small as she was, it would cost him more money to get someone in her place. And she was a worker, he'd give her that.

'I've got fourpence left, look, you can have it back,' she cried and put four pennies on the table that stood in the middle of the room since his wife's bed had been taken away to the salerooms.

'I should have had ten bob,' he snarled. 'You owe me ten bob. An' you'll pay me it back an' all, I'm telling you.' He began to take off his belt, a broad, leather belt such as all the pitmen wore in the belief that it strengthened their backs. 'All right, out of the goodness of my heart, I won't turn you in to

the polis, but I'll give you the hiding of your life. I'll show
you you cannot rob Alf Green and get away with it.' He
wrapped one end of the belt around his fist and advanced on
her.

'Bend over that table,' he ordered.

# Five

Lottie climbed slowly and painfully up the stairs to the bedrooms. She was carrying the slop bucket, into which she would empty the chamber pots of the whole family before making the beds and collecting the boys' dirty clothes to put them into soak in the tin bath so as to loosen the dirt before washing day, which was tomorrow.

Mr Green and the three boys were at morning service in the Primitive Methodist Chapel up the road. Even if she hadn't had to clean and make the Sunday dinner, Lottie couldn't have gone to service. She had a black eye from where Mr Green had slapped her face as an afterthought to the beating. Lottie didn't understand why. He did not usually mark her face, though her body was covered in bruises.

Last night had been different. Mr Green had lifted her skirts before he belted her on her bare bottom. It was the first time he had done that, but then she had not stolen from him before. Lottie sighed and felt the sore spot on her thigh where the belt buckle had drawn blood. She looked down at her boots; somehow they did not seem quite so desirable as they had the day before. Oh, she had been wrong.

Alf Green sat in the third pew from the front and gazed at the lay preacher in the pulpit. Noah, Freddie and Mattie sat beside him, all scrubbed shiny clean and wearing their best clothes. They sat with their hands clasped behind their backs as their father had ordered them to sit.

'You will not show me up fidgeting,' he said and glanced at Mattie. 'Nor talking neither,' he went on. He always said this just before coming to Chapel.

He was a canting hypocrite, just like those Pharisees in the Bible, Lottie thought to herself as she moved painfully around, clearing up after the boys before starting on the dinner. The meat was roasting in the oven and filling the house with the smell of beef when she got back downstairs. She mixed the Yorkshire pudding batter and scraped and peeled vegetables, and all the time she was battling against the longing to lie down and rest her aching body. But at last she had the vegetables boiling on the hob, the beef out of the oven and an enormous Yorkshire pudding in its place. She sat down on the rocking chair and fell asleep.

It was the front door closing that woke Lottie. She jumped to her feet and groaned as pain shot through her legs and back. She leaned on the chair for support and closed her eyes.

'What the heck is going on here?' asked Alf as he came into the kitchen.

'The pudding's burning! By, it stinks!' shouted Noah. Smoke poured out of the crack where the oven door didn't quite fit against the black-leaded surround.

In the end, the family sat down to a Sunday dinner with no pudding, something the boys complained of loudly.

'Shut up, the lot of you,' said Alf quietly. He cut into his beef and stuffed a bit into his mouth. 'Get your dinner and away out to play. Lottie, sit down and eat your dinner.'

Lottie gazed at him, startled. It was the first time he had even noticed whether she ate or not. She couldn't understand why he had taken the disaster so calmly. Still, it was a relief. She wasn't hungry but she forced the food down her. She had to eat if she was to carry on. She was determined not to let him see just how much he had hurt her. She had seen what happened to the orphans in the workhouse when they allowed a thrashing to cow them utterly. Usually they ended up at the very bottom of the heap, getting blamed for everything that went wrong. Not just by the Master and Matron, either, but by some of the inmates besides.

Alf watched her covertly. She was a scrap of a lass and not a real woman yet, but when he had thrashed her last night he had gone too far, he knew that. He wasn't a bad man, he told himself. He had a right to chastise his servant, hadn't he? Wasn't it better than putting her out of the house? He was well aware that she was frightened of being sent back to the workhouse. She would be classed as an adult now and put to hard labour. Or worse, he could have had the law on her and then she would have ended up in a house of correction, or even Durham Gaol. He began to feel quite virtuous. He had acted as any master should.

'You can keep the boots,' he said.

Lottie looked up, startled. She was wearing the boots; she had thrown away her old ones. 'I can?' she asked. She tried to thank him but the apology stuck in her throat.

'I'll take the money out of your wages,' he said.

'It was only sixpence,' she mumbled.

'What was that?' He didn't wait for her to repeat it, which was just as well for she had begun to tremble and her throat had closed up so that she was incapable of saying anything more. The boys were very quiet; they stared at their father. 'You owe me ten shillings,' he snarled. 'Never mind the sixpence stake.'

'Ten shillings! I'll never pay that off. I'll have no wages at all,' said Lottie. She sat in misery.

'You'll be just like a Negro slave,' Mattie said. 'Only you'll not be in chains.' He had been learning about the iniquities of slavery in Sunday School and how the Americans had fought a war over it.

'Shut your mouth!' said his father. 'If you've finished, get away out and play and leave me in peace.'

The lads filed out, Noah pushing Mattie ahead of him. Alf rose from the table and went and sat in his chair by the fireside. He took the fire tongs and lifted a glowing coal from the fire and lit his pipe with it. He settled back in his chair and crossed his feet on the steel fender, ready for a nice quiet hour while he let his dinner digest.

Lottie moved about the kitchen, clearing the table and fetching the tin dish to wash the plates and pans and the tray, which was used to drain the dishes. A slave, that was exactly what she was, she thought dismally.

Alf watched her. She was showing signs of growing into a woman, he realized. There was a slight roundness about her behind and her waist was becoming defined. By, he had been without the comforts only a woman could give for too long. Laura had been no good to him that way since she first took badly. A man had his needs, oh aye, he did.

Last night he had not meant to whip the lass so hard, no he had not. He thought once more about it. He had lost his temper, that was it. After all, it was his own hard-earned money wasn't it? Mebbe he should not have put money on a horse, he was a chapel-going man and gambling was frowned upon by the chapel. But he didn't really gamble, no. He never joined the toss-penny schools down behind the slag heap. He wouldn't even know how to play cards. Those things led a man to perdition. But he had put sixpence on a horse because it was trained by a man from Auckland way, practically a local man. A man had to have something to take his mind off his misfortunes, hadn't he? He liked a little flutter and it didn't hurt anyone.

Last night though, he had simply been very angry with Lottie. What was she but a workhouse slut? When he had lifted her skirt it had been so that he could really hurt her by hitting her on her bare skin. There was some satisfaction in seeing the red weals the belt made on the white skin. But he had found himself aroused in a way that had had nothing to do with his temper or anger. Oh aye, she was growing into a woman and he hadn't had a woman in quite a while.

Abruptly Alf got to his feet. He needed some fresh air; he felt hot and bothered. He pushed past Lottie's slight body and grabbed his jacket from the hook behind the back door. It was his weekday jacket but it didn't matter, no one who mattered would be about at this time of the day, they would all be inside digesting their Sunday dinners.

'I'm away for a walk,' he said as he opened the door. He did not look at Lottie, who was tipping hot water from the iron kettle into the washing-up dish. She paused and looked startled, but when the door closed behind him she was glad. The uncomfortable atmosphere that had arisen in the room as she moved around, all the time aware of his eyes on her, lightened.

She grated soap into the water and added a handful of soda crystals and began to wash the dishes. Soon she had the kitchen tidied and the only sign of the dinner was the lingering smell of roast beef. Lottie went into the sitting room, the room where Laura Green had died, and sat down on a padded armchair, one of only two in the house. It was a large chair and she could tuck her feet up and pull her skirt down over them and lean her head into the slight delve made where the cushion was buttoned in the back. Within minutes she was asleep.

\*　　\*　　\*

The rest of that Sunday was uneventful. Until, that is, the three boys were in bed and asleep. Before that they had come in hungry for their tea and Lottie had made singing hinny scones and put out a pot of bramble jelly to spread on them. Mrs Bowron, from next door, had brought a jar in when she had made the jelly, for the lads had gathered the blackberries down by where the slag heap had spread out slightly into a meadow and bramble bushes had clambered over the tufty grass and bit of slag together. In spite of the poor ground, the berries were large and luscious and were a free treat the village looked forward to every year after the wild strawberries were long gone.

Noah and Freddie were laughing and chatting about the game of quoits they had played despite the disapproval of the minister who had happened to be walking past the alley at the time.

'My dad said we could,' Noah had insisted.

'I will have to have a word with your father,' the minister had replied, before going on his way.

'By, it was funny,' said Noah, with a sidelong glance at his father. But Alf wasn't even listening. He was watching Lottie and his face was quite red and strange-looking.

Lottie sat down at the table once she had served the others and poured a cup of tea for herself. Alf handed her the plate of singing hinnies and she took one, a bit surprised at his consideration. Maybe he was sorry he had hit her so hard? She turned her attention to the youngest, Mattie.

'Don't you want anything to eat?' she asked him. Mattie was sitting there with a faraway look in his eyes. He looked a little pale.

'I'm not hungry,' he said.

'If you don't want to eat, leave the table,' he father said sharply.

'I want me mam,' said Mattie.

'You can want as much as you like but she's not coming back,' snapped Alf. He was annoyed to be reminded of his dead wife.

'Come on, pet,' said Lottie. She forgot her own troubles as she saw the misery in his little face. 'Your mam's in heaven but she's watching over you. Be a brave lad now. Eat a bit of bread and butter, then I'll tell you a story when you are ready for bed.'

'Don't fill their heads with rubbish and lies mind,' said Alf sharply. 'It's Sunday, tell them a bible story.'

Lottie nodded. 'I will.'

Soon the two youngest boys were in their nightshirts, with hands and faces washed and in their beds. Lottie sat in a chair by Mattie's bedside and recounted the first bible story that came into her tired mind, the story of the boy, Samuel.

'My mam wouldn't give me up to the temple,' said Mattie. 'My mam loved me.'

'Aye, she did,' Lottie agreed. 'She still does.' His eyes were closing and she bent over him and kissed him on the cheek. Poor little lad, she thought. Oh, she remembered her own mother dying. She went out of the room, closing the door quietly behind her. From the head of the stairs she could see the light where Alf Green was in the sitting room. By, she thought, she didn't want to face him again the night. So she went up to her own small room and prepared herself for bed. It was early but goodness knows, she had to rise early too.

Lottie woke slowly; her mind felt thick and woolly. At first she hovered between waking and sleeping. She was not sure if it was a dream or real. But there was someone in bed with her and it was not Mattie. Mattie sometimes did climb into her bed when he woke during the night. He usually said nothing but huddled against her and seemed to draw comfort from her.

Lottie opened her eyes. It was not black dark in the bedroom, for the curtains were thin and there was a full moon outside. It was not a dream, she realized as panic rose in her. There was a man in her bed and he had one arm around her, holding her still, and with his other hand he was pulling up her night-gown. For a moment she was too shocked to even struggle, then suddenly she was fighting him.

'Get off me! Get off!' she shrieked but his arm was like a steel band around her thin chest.

'Shut up, shut up or I'll belt you!' the man said and it was Alf Green, of course it was. 'Don't you wake the lads, do you hear me?'

'No! No! Get off me!' she cried. She wriggled and fought but she couldn't get away from him.

'Lie still, you little brat, lie still,' he snarled. 'It will be the worse for you if you don't.' She felt his hardness against her bare skin and she screamed. Alf smacked her face hard and she knew then he would kill her if she fought him any more.

Afterwards she lay on the bed, muscles she never knew she had throbbing and painful and adding to the bruises of the night before. She sobbed quietly as he too lay quiet, panting. After a moment he spoke.

'You led me on, Lottie,' he said. 'Flaunting yourself in front of me, all day. You knew what you were up to, oh aye you did. You're a born harlot, no doubt your mother was an' all.'

He got up from the bed and pulled on his trousers, which he had dropped on the floor by the bed. 'You'd best keep quiet about this an' all. If you don't, you will be the one that folk will blame. If they believe you, that is. Nay, they won't believe you any road. Think on about that.' Alf went to the door of the room. 'Don't forget to call me for the fore shift,' he said, speaking now as if nothing had happened. 'I cannot afford to miss a shift, mind.'

After he'd gone, Lottie lay for a few moments, weeping. Was this what her life was going to be? She was despairing. She might as well throw herself off Elvet Bridge into the Wear. She would, that was just what she would do. Slowly and painfully she got out of bed and pulled on her clothes. She tied her boots around her neck, opened the door noise-lessly and crept down the stairs. Taking her shawl from behind the door she let herself out and made her way into the city, still in her bare feet.

The waters of the Wear swirled in small eddies around the solid stone stanchions of the bridge, built so may centuries ago. In the pre-dawn light, sprays of white were thrown up against the blackness of the water beneath. The bridge was deserted, as was the whole city. Shortly there would be people hurrying to work but just now, for a few moments more, there was no one except the small, slight figure of the girl standing by the parapet and gazing down into the water.

Lottie hardly felt the cold air or the even colder stones of the bridge against her bare feet. She was concentrating on the water, almost hypnotized by the sound of it. She swayed, and the boots hanging around her neck by their laces swung forward and back again, banging against her thin chest. She put her hands on the top of the parapet and felt for a foothold in the stones so she could climb up. She could barely remember her mother but suddenly she thought she saw her image in the water as the morning lightened. She found a foothold and raised herself up to the parapet.

'Oh no you don't do that, young woman!'

The voice came from behind and startled her, so that she almost fell anyway and would have done but for the two arms that went around her and dragged her down on to the safety of the roadway on the bridge. She could barely see him with her poor eyesight and in the poor light, just a hazy outline. But she knew him for a bobbie, the polis, and his seemingly enormous frame loomed over her. Lottie began to shake.

# Six

As the light grew stronger, Lottie found herself up the hill from the bridge and into Saddler Street leading to the marketplace. She passed by Malcolm's ironmonger's shop, all shuttered up still, and entered the marketplace, where a number of people were milling around on their way to work. The bobby had escorted her from the bridge and so far up the cobbled road.

'You're not going to do anything silly now, are you?' he asked, before turning back to go to the police station to sign off from his night's walking about the streets.

'I should take you in, you know. It is a criminal offence to kill yourself.'

Lottie stared up at him in misery. In the daylight he noticed the bruises on her face; why, she was nobbut a bairn, he thought and sighed.

'Did some man give you a hiding? Your da, was it? You should be a good lass you know, keep out of trouble. Mebbe you deserved it.'

Lottie shook her head but said nothing.

'Aye well,' said the bobby, 'Don't do anything daft, lass. You have your whole life ahead of you. Any road, everything looks better in the morning light.'

He turned and strode off down the hill, his boots ringing on the cobblestones. Lottie watched him go. He had been kind enough and she was grateful for that. Then she turned and went on into the centre of the marketplace. Only after just a few steps, she felt a deathly tiredness and her head began to thump painfully. She sat down at the base of the statue of Lord Londonderry, resplendent on his great horse, and leaned her head into the heel of her hand, her eyes closing.

She was still sitting on the steps of the statue when Bertha, Sister Mitchell's friend, found her. Bertha was on her way to see one of the washerwomen who worked for her in her laundry business, before going to the farm, which belonged to her future husband's family. Charlie Carr was a stickler for timekeeping and she was hurrying along when the sight of the small, huddled figure on the statue steps gave her pause.

'It's Lottie, isn't it? Lottie Lonsdale? What on earth is the matter, lass?' Bertha asked.

Lottie lifted a tear-stained face, saw Bertha and quickly tried to cover the ravages of the last few hours. She rubbed at her face with a rag she took out of her pocket, wincing as she caught the bruise on her blackened eye.

'I've . . . I fell down and bumped my face,' she said. 'I'm all right though, I am, really.'

'You don't look all right to me,' said Bertha. 'In fact you look like you've been through a war an' no mistake.' She stared at the girl, then sat down beside her on the steps, all thought of the need to get her jobs arranged so that she could get to the farm on time forgotten. She remembered Eliza Mitchell telling her Lottie was a workhouse girl and she was only too well aware of how vulnerable a girl like her, friendless and alone, could be. Hadn't she been one herself?

'What are you doing, pet? You can tell me what happened.'

Lottie responded to the friendly tone, her small attempt to cover up soon done. Besides, she did remember Bertha; they weren't truly strangers.

'Has someone attacked you?' Bertha prompted.

Lottie bit her lip. She didn't know whether to tell Bertha or not, for she was ashamed to say she had pinched the tanner from Mr Green. But in the end she had to tell someone.

'Aye,' she said and bent her head and gazed at her small hands that were clasped in her lap. They were reddened and sore, not only from their regular immersion in hot water and soda but also by the cold. And then she looked past them and saw her boots.

'It was my own fault,' she said.

'Don't be daft, it couldn't be your own fault,' Bertha declared. She forgot for a moment that she was in a tearing hurry and how angry Charlie would be if she was late going over to help his mam. She sat down on the steps beside Lottie and put an arm around the thin shoulders.

'Now then, tell me,' she said.

Lottie was desperate to confide in someone and the whole story came tumbling out, or almost the whole story. The worst of it she couldn't admit even to herself, so she blocked it off.

'Swine,' she said when Lottie was finished. 'Canting, blooming hypocrite.'

'I'm sorry,' mumbled Lottie, crushed by Bertha's verdict on her.

'Nay, lass, not you,' said Bertha. 'I'm talking about Alf Green.'

'Oh.'

Lottie felt a little better. Her body ached in parts she hadn't known she possessed and the bruises on her face and thighs throbbed. But the horrible weight inside her lifted. Bertha was talking like a friend and she hadn't any friends, not since she had left the workhouse. Yet maybe Bertha hadn't truly realized Lottie's culpability in it all.

'I should not have pinched the tanner,' she said. Then, 'You don't think I led him on, do you?'

'I do not, no. I don't blame you at all, lass. And any road, he should have given you your due. He's a skinflint and a sinner. The chapel council should be told about him.'

She sat silent for a moment and Lottie regarded her anxiously.

'They won't believe me,' she whispered and Bertha thought that was likely true.

'Howay along of me,' said Bertha suddenly. 'I'll take you to Eliza. She'll help you for sure.' She got to her feet. Charlie would have to wait and so would her washerwomen.

'Eliza? Sister Mitchell do you mean?'

'I do. Now be sharp about it, I'm late.'

Lottie had begun to feel better already, now she had a friend and somewhere to go, even if it was only for an hour or two. She began to cry again and it had nothing to do with her sore body – it was purely from relief. She did not have to go back to the workhouse, at least not yet.

'Come into the kitchen, pet,' said Eliza. 'I'll put the kettle on and you can tell me exactly what happened. Has someone attacked you? Has someone stolen your purse?' She had been in the hall when the knock came to the door or she wouldn't have heard it, it was so soft. Bertha had just brought Lottie to the door and sped on her way, for time was precious.

'Bertha brought me,' said Lottie. 'You don't mind, do you? I had nowhere else to go.'

'Course I don't,' said Eliza stoutly. The lass had a black eye; were there pickpockets at work in the city, as was rumoured? She filled the kettle and settled it on the glowing coals. By, she thought, the police should get on and catch the villains.

'What?'

Eliza was shocked out of her thoughts by what Lottie was saying.

'Mr Green did it,' Lottie said in little more than a whisper. 'I wouldn't let him do what he wanted so he hit me and put me out of the house.' She hung her head, unable to look at Eliza. When it came to it, she couldn't admit just how far Alf Green had gone, not to Sister Mitchell. She felt dirty and perhaps it had been her fault. Perhaps she had done something to make him think she wanted it. She felt confused and ashamed. So she pretended it hadn't happened.

*Mucky sod*, Eliza thought but she didn't say it. Maybe she had not understood what Lottie was saying. 'You mean he tried . . .' she stopped. The lass was but a bairn, she couldn't go on.

Lottie nodded. Her head hung even lower. 'He got into my bed,' she whispered, then quickly, 'But I got out, I did, straight away I did. Honest.'

'Mucky sod.' This time Eliza said it aloud. She wasn't quite sure what sod meant, even though she was a nurse, but it was a swear word commonly used and usually combined with mucky, hacky, dirty, filthy.

'Oh Lottie,' she said, 'let me look at you. I'll bathe your poor face, eh? I'll get clean water and put some white vinegar in it. That will make it feel better.' She handed the girl a cup of tea with sweetened condensed milk in it. 'Drink that first, it'll do you good. When did this happen?'

'Last night. I managed to get away from him. Bertha found me in the marketplace and brought me here. You don't mind do you? I mean me coming here?'

'It's all right, hinny, so it is.'

Eliza didn't know where she was going to put her but that didn't matter. She couldn't put her out, could she? She tended to the girl's bruises and made her toast and took her in to sit with her mother. Mary Anne Teesdale, Eliza's mother, was in the front room. She had had a bout of trouble with her heart that the doctors said was a result of having rheumatic fever when she was young, but was recovering nicely. At the minute she was thoroughly bored with being idle, for Eliza wouldn't let her do a thing. Hearing Lottie's problems took her mind off her own.

Mary Anne was all sympathy for Lottie and full of condemnation for Alf Green. Lottie's anxious heart began to settle down a little. She found herself telling this motherly woman all about her life in the Green household, withholding only what Alf had done to her in bed.

'The lads are all right, only Noah, that's the eldest, he's a bit of a bully. He bosses his brothers and he tried to boss me. But Mattie now, he's the little 'un, he's only seven and he misses his mam. I feel rotten at leaving Mattie. Do you think I should go back to see to Mattie, Mrs Teesdale?'

'Nay, I don't,' said Mary Anne stoutly. Her experience and intuition told her there was more to it and she could make a good guess as to what it was. 'I know it's a shame but you have to think of yourself. Any road I have an idea. Go and fetch our Eliza for me, will you?'

'Aye, I will,' Lottie replied and hurried from the room.

'I'm in a bit of a hurry, Mam,' Eliza began as she came into the front room. 'What is it?'

'Well, I'll tell you and you can think about it on your way.' She paused for a minute, then went on, 'I'm going back to Stanley, Eliza. The lads need me.'

'But you can't Mam, you'd not manage,' said Eliza patiently. 'So what's the good of talking about it?'

'I can and I will,' said Mary Anne stubbornly. 'That is . . . if Lottie here will go with me.' She turned to the girl. 'How would you like to do that, Lottie? You would have a home, and a bit of pocket money. I can't promise you more than that. And in return, you could help me with the work, what do you say?'

'Mam!'

'Mam what?' Mary Anne said, turning to her daughter. 'You haven't room for the lass, have you? It seems to me to be just the answer.'

'I will,' said Lottie, but Mary Anne and Eliza were arguing now and neither heard her.

'I'll come, please, please let me,' said Lottie louder, and this time both women stopped talking and turned to her.

'Stanley is different to Durham,' said Eliza. 'And it will be hard work, two lads at the pit and Da, and you will have to look after my mam sometimes, when she's badly.'

'I'm used to that,' said Lottie. She gazed anxiously from Eliza to Mary Anne and back again. Oh, she desperately wanted to go to live with Mary Anne, she did, aye she did. Mary Anne was like the woman she imagined her own mother would have become had she been spared. She could be happy with Mary Anne.

Eliza was not slow to see the appeal in the girl's eyes. 'I don't know,' she said. 'We'll talk about it when I come back. I have to go now.'

Of course when she came back later in the day she found it was all decided and she had no say in the matter.

'I'm not a bairn,' Mary Anne said in a firm, no-nonsense tone. 'I'm not in my dotage, neither. Lottie is coming with me and Tommy and that's an end to it.'

'By, you're definitely feeling better,' Eliza replied. 'I gather Da had no say in it either?'

'Aye, he did.'

Mary Anne nodded her head in the direction of Tommy, who was sitting by the fire with his stockinged feet up on the fender. 'Your da is the man in our house.'

Tommy grinned at Eliza. 'Aye, I'm the gaffer in our house,' he said. 'Whatever the wife says goes.'

Lottie was happier than she could ever remember being and that was even before they got to Stanley. They caught the train to Stanley, for Eliza said the weather was too cold for Mary Anne to go in the tub trap and in any case, Eliza had to catch up on her work. Not that it was warmer on the train, the third-class carriage being open to the elements, but it was quicker. And they were muffled up to the eyes in shawls and with a blanket over their knees. Tommy had walked the distance, about ten miles. As he was not working, he reckoned he had no right to spend money on the train when he could very well walk.

The day was fair: the sun was shining as they rode across the fields and past the small colliery villages where smoke curled up to the sky and the smell of the coal and coke ovens mingled with the smoke from the engine, but Lottie didn't mind that.

'Cover your mouth with your shawl, pet,' advised Mary Anne when Lottie coughed and obediently, Lottie did. Her dark eyes peered over the rim of the shawl as she gazed at the horizon of the moor or down into the valley where sheep were still out and finding some grazing despite the grass being chewed right down and the hedges being bare of leaves. But they had their thick winter coats on, she mused, and there were no little lambs. Not yet, not this high or this north. Someone had told her that, she couldn't remember who. It wouldn't have been a teacher, not at the workhouse where the main lessons were mending and cleaning.

Mary Anne watched her with a slight smile on her face. By, she thought, she had been lucky to find her really, a lass who was used to hard work and good-natured to boot. Not that there weren't many in search of work but Lottie, well Lottie had touched her heart with her pinched little face and the way she had of peering earnestly about her.

'You like to ride behind a locomotive?' Mary Anne asked in the manner of her youth when most engines were colliery locomotives.

'Oh, I do,' Lottie asserted. She had forgotten her ordeal for the minute, the train had taken her out of herself. 'This is the first time I've done it,' she confided.

'Nay, it's not!' Mary Anne was surprised for a moment, then realized that of course Lottie had had little chance of doing anything except skivvying and when she did have time to herself she wouldn't be able to afford the time or the money to ride the train.

'I've seen them, of course,' said Lottie. 'But I've not been out of Durham, except for Sherburn Hill that is.'

'Aye well, mebbe you'll like Stanley better than Sherburn,' said Mary Anne.

'Now the train's pulling in, best collect our bundles and baskets.' For Eliza had packed ham and one or two other things for them to take with them.

Tommy was waiting at the station with a borrowed trap for Mary Anne and the luggage.

'Are you not pleased to see us, Tommy?' asked Mary Anne.

'You might at least say you are, even if you don't want to give me a hug.'

'What, on the station platform?' her husband asked, looking scandalized. 'Don't be so forward, woman!'

# Seven

For Lottie, the house in West Stanley was not all that different from the house in Sherburn Hill. The work was hard and the hours long – that was the same – and there was Mrs Teesdale, an invalid just as Mrs Green had been. But the Teesdale boys were older and already working in the pit and then there was Tommy, as different from Alfred Green as it was possible to get. Yet there was a world of difference between the two households, really.

'Just call me Mary Anne, pet,' Mrs Teesdale said. 'An' nobody at all calls Tommy anything but Tommy, except for the lads.'

'By, she is a lovely woman,' Lottie told herself as she washed the dishes or cleaned after the lads, dashing the pit clothes against the wall of the coalhouse and causing the air to sparkle like the night sky as showers of coal dust fell to the ground.

Of course, some nights she got very little sleep when the lads were on different shifts and Tommy on permanent fore shift. For he had been taken on as a datal man, clearing up coal dust and small coal after the hewers and putters, and he worked the first shift of the day, starting at midnight. The putters were just young lads like Harry and a bit careless. As they pushed and heaved at the coal tubs to get them to where the pit ponies could reach – for some of the seams were too low for the beasts – they often shed coal dust and bits from top.

So it fell to Tommy and men like him to sweep up. The great dread of management and men alike was fire and if a spark from a stud in a pit boot ignited coal dust, or worse, if there was firedamp lurking, the result could be – well, it didn't bear thinking about. So Tommy went in before the hewers and sometimes left after them and all for less pay, but at least he didn't have to swing a pick for ten hours at a time as they did. Tommy got home about ten every morning except Sunday, which was his day of rest.

'By,' he said to Mary Anne one morning as he knelt before the tin bath in his pit hoggers (which were short trousers or underpants), washing the coal dust from his body, 'I never thought the time would come when my lad would be a hewer and me good for nowt but sweeping up.'

'Aye well,' Mary Anne replied, 'it's better than not working, isn't it?'

Lottie, who was standing by the table washing up after his meal, smiled. She put the last pot on the tin tray to drain and picked up the tin bowl of water to empty outside. It was time for her to disappear discreetly out of the kitchen while Tommy removed the hoggers and finished his ablutions.

She walked up the yard and emptied the dish in the gutter, then stood by the gate with the dish in her hands and looked about her. Children were playing in the back street, a narrow alley unpaved and with deep cart ruts running its length. They were playing kicky-off chock, a game that involved one boy kicking an old tin can as far as it would go and calling out a name. Any boy not in hiding by the time the second boy got the tin and brought it back to base was out. Even as she stood, a lad pushed past her and into the yard, diving behind the wall.

'Hey lad, watch it,' said Lottie, but good-naturedly. When she was little in the workhouse, she mused, they hadn't time for such games. She looked up the street to where a woman was standing on a chair and reaching up to string a washing line across from one side to another. It was Mrs Hutchins, a young woman who looked not much older than Lottie, but she already had three little bairns. *By, it must be nice to look after your own man and bairns*, she thought. *Come the day though, oh yes*. Lottie took a deep breath of the air before she turned and walked up the yard and into the house. She could get another breath of fresh air when Tommy was in bed and before Harry came in from the pit. Only by that time of the day it would smell a bit sulphurous. as the coke ovens were opened. Still, folk said that was healthy, good for the lungs.

Tommy was dressed and smoking his pipe by the fire. His braces dangled by his side and his stockinged feet were propped up on the new steel fender. Mary Anne was very proud of her fender; she had bought it with Tommy's first pay at West Stanley pit. At least she had put a deposit down on it of two shillings and was paying it off at sixpence a week.

'It'll only take twenty-one weeks, there's one week extra for the tallyman,' she had said to Lottie who, despite her lack of education, knew that it only took twenty sixpenny payments plus two shillings to add up to the eleven shillings and eleven pence the fender had cost at the Co-op store. Plus a penny for the tallyman. Sixpence was a bit excessive, Lottie reckoned.

'Howay then, Tommy, hadaway to your bed, Lottie has to get on with the work, man,' Mary Anne said now. She hadn't done much at all but she was already tired and besides, the smell from Tommy's pipe made her chest feel tight even though most of the smoke went up the chimney.

'Can I not have a pipe in peace now?' he asked and coughed long and hard. 'Now look woman, you've set me off,' he said when he could get his breath.

'Nay, it's the baccy as sets you off,' Mary Anne replied tartly.

'Aye well it clears me tubes.'

Now he was sweeping, the coal and the stone dust got into his 'tubes' even more than it had before, and Mary Anne knew it. Still she chivvied him until he stood up, knocked out his pipe on the bar of the fire and set off for bed. At the foot of the narrow staircase that went up directly out of the kitchen to the bedroom upstairs, he paused to deliver a final shot.

'One of these days, woman, I'll take off me belt and show you who's boss,' he growled.

'Aye, aye, I know,' she replied. 'Now away up the loft wi' ye.'

Albert and Harry had a chiffonier bed in the front room. When folded up it looked like a fine piece of mahogany furniture; only it was not often folded up, for the lads were on different shifts at the pit. Lottie slept on a horsehair sofa in the kitchen. It was not an ideal arrangement, Mary Anne knew that, but there was little choice. The house they had been allocated by the pit was a two-down and one-up, and the one-up had a small pane of glass in the roof to let in a little light. It was a typical miner's cottage, though some owners were building two-bedroom and even three-bedroom houses now to attract experienced pitmen to newly opened pits. Tommy was experienced but too old now.

Mary Anne pondered the situation as she sat by the fire and Lottie boiled water and carried it to the poss tub in the yard, grated soap and stood on a small stool called a cracket to agitate the clothes vigorously with a wooden poss stick. Mary Anne watched broodingly.

It was becoming increasingly hard for her to climb the stairs to the bedroom. Sometimes the pain in her chest was more than she could bear. Mrs Brown, who was something of a wise woman, made her an infusion of foxgloves but it didn't work as it had used to do. Soon she and Tommy would have to change bedrooms with the lads.

'You'll be fine, a lady of leisure when Lottie comes to work for you,' Tommy had said. And most of the time Mary Anne could make out she was better than she had been; maybe was getting over whatever it was ailed her. Sometimes, and these were getting more frequent, she could not.

She sat brooding on it when Harry turned into the gate and strolled up the yard, his bait tin swinging from his belt and his boots ringing on the stones. He had his helmet pushed back from his forehead and showing a white line above his black face and he grinned as he saw Lottie's small figure standing on tiptoe on the cracket to lean over the poss tub. Harry was sixteen now and had a little finger shortened where he had trapped it between the tub and the side of the way, but it didn't hamper him at all.

The deputy overman had bound it up for him. 'Now then, lad,' he had said bracingly, 'mind you don't get something more important trapped, you'd best keep a better look out.' Harry had even finished his shift as a putter.

'I want to be a hewer like Albert and you, Da,' he had said to Tommy.

'Like I was, you mean,' Tommy replied. 'Just watch what you're bloody well doing in future.'

That had been a few months ago and Harry had been told he could start hewing on the following Monday. So he was full of himself as he walked up the yard.

'Howay, Lottie, where's me dinner?' he cried. 'I could eat a horse, man!'

'Aye well, I cannot do everything at once,' Lottie replied, her face emerging from the depths of the poss tub. 'I'll be in in a minute and fix you a bite. It's washing day mind, I haven't had time to do much.'

Harry's face fell for a moment, but nothing was going to dim this triumphant day for long. He went into the house and found his mother bending over the heavy iron frying pan.

'Mam! What are you doing? I'll do that,' he cried, taking the pan from her hand and settling it on the bar. 'Sit down, Mam, will you?'

Mary Anne was only too happy to sit; she sank into the chair feeling as though she had been kicked in the chest.

'Lottie!' Harry shouted as he turned for the door to get the girl, but she was already on her way in, wiping her hands on her apron as she came. 'Me mam's badly,' he went on, giving her a hard stare.

'Nay, I'm all right,' Mary Anne managed to say, and indeed the pain was receding as she sat back in the chair.

'What are you doing, letting me mam lift the frying pan?' Harry demanded, giving Lottie a black look. His mood was changed completely by the sight of his mother's white face.

'I didn't, I . . .' Lottie protested, but she too was worried at how ill Mary Anne looked. 'I was coming, Mary Anne,' she said, 'you should have left it. It won't take but a minute.'

'I'll get Mrs Brown,' said Harry, taking a step towards the door, but his mother stopped him.

'No, don't do that, I'm better now,' said Mary Anne. 'Don't bother her, she'll be busy, it's washing day.'

'I don't care what day it is,' Harry declared.

'Don't, do you hear me?' Mary Anne's voice was definitely stronger, and in fact she was looking a little better.

Harry looked at her and turned back. 'Well, don't try to lift anything again,'

Mary Anne briefly considered telling him not to tell her what to do, but didn't have the energy.

Lottie looked at her and smiled. 'It's my fault, I should have had the meal ready, ' she said. 'But I just have to fry the taties and that. There's cold mutton from yesterday and I made a dish of pickle.'

Harry took off his jacket, hat and pit boots and put them in their usual corner, ready for Lottie to dash and scrape. He didn't wash his hands, for everyone knew coal dust was black but clean, and he sat down at the table, waiting.

'You'll be starving, son,' said Mary Anne. 'But Lottie won't be long now.' Oh, he was a lovely, canny lad and handsome even in his black, she thought. He shouldn't have to wait for his dinner, no indeed. They had done enough of that when the lads were on their own in Stanley. Though neighbours had been kind, and why wouldn't they be to three lads like hers? No, two, there were only two now, her bonnie lad Miley was dead and gone. A familiar fog of depression hovered but she shook it off, refusing to dwell on her loss.

Lottie put two plates of food on the table and one on a tin tray for Mary Anne to eat on her lap. Mary Anne was not hungry but she made an effort, spooning some mashed potato into her mouth. Lottie sat down at the table beside Harry.

'You watch my mother, Lottie, won't you?' Harry said in a whisper.

'I will,' Lottie replied. 'Mebbe she should have the doctor?'

Doctors were not frequent visitors to the miners' wives. The miners yes, because of the many accidents, but their wives lived their lives mostly without the benefit of medical help. The idea was new to Harry, even though when she had been staying with his sister Eliza, Mary Anne had seen the doctor often. But then, Eliza was a nursing sister, she had grown out of their ways.

'There's nowt the matter with my hearing, you know. I heard you on about a doctor and I'm telling you I will say when I need Doctor Morley.'

'Now Mam, we're only thinking of you.'

'Aye, well I'm not a bairn an' I'm not in my dotage neither,' his mother replied.

'Mebbe I should get Mrs Brown then,' asked Lottie.

'Nay man, she has enough to do, I told you. Any road, what can she do? She'll only give us some of that foxglove tea and I have plenty. No, I'm all right, I'm telling you. Now if you've finished your dinner you'd best get on with the washing. It might rain later on and you'll have missed this fine drying weather. After you've seen to Harry's bath, like.'

'You get on,' Harry advised Lottie. 'I'll fill me own bath.'

'You'll do nowt of the sort,' Mary Anne said sharply. 'It

won't take the lass but a minute. No, no lad of mine comes in after a shift in the pit and has to see to himself.'

So Lottie brought in the tin bath from its hook on the outside wall and put it before the fire and filled it from the iron kettle, and the bucket of water from the standpipe on the end of the row. There was a set-pot boiler in the corner of the yard and the water in that was heating nicely to refill the poss tub. Lottie could go out and get on with the washing, pumping the poss stick up and down and around rhythmically so that she almost hypnotized herself as she stared down at the movement of the clothes in the water.

She liked Harry, even though he had spoken harshly to her. After all, he had only been worried for his mother. Sometimes she caught him looking at her with a funny expression that made her cheeks redden. He looked away when he caught her eye though. He reminded her a bit of little Mattie, who had clung to her after his mother died. Of course he was much older than Mattie; why he would soon be a hewer making a lot of money of his own, she knew that. Hewers were the top men in the pit apart from the officials such as deputies and overmen. All the lasses would be after him, they would an' all.

Mattie, she thought, little motherless Mattie. Was he all right? If she ever went back to Durham City, to Eliza's house maybe, she would try to get to Sherburn and see for herself.

Lottie stopped possing the clothes and began lifting them out of the tub, wringing them out and tossing them into two basins ready for rinsing. This was done in the tin bath though, and Harry was using the tin bath. She blushed as she thought of Harry kneeling in front of the tin bath, sluicing the coal dust from his arms and shoulders. On one shoulder there was a blue scar where coal dust had got under the skin of a cut. There were nobbly bits on his back where he had caught it on the roof of the low seams he pushed the tubs along. All the putters had those and the ponies an' all. Sometimes she had the urge to touch Harry's marks though. How daft was that? He wouldn't want a workhouse brat like her.

Lottie had her head and shoulders deep in the poss tub, bringing out the last of the wash, when Harry's voice made her jump.

'I've brought the bath out for you,' he said. 'I'll empty it down the gulley.' He did that, then emptied a pail of clean water from the standpipe into the bath for her to rinse the clothes. Embarrassed, Lottie bent right over the poss tub to get the last cloth.

'Careful, pet,' said Harry. 'You'll get a bath yourself if you fall in there.' He caught hold of her and pulled her upright and she came up as red as a beetroot and panting.

'Your mam will be mad if she catches you doing woman's work,' she said, when she had caught her breath.

'Aye well, I had to do it when she was badly down at our Eliza's, didn't I?'

He went back into the house whistling cheerfully and for minutes after he had gone she could still feel the touch of his hands on her. And he had called her pet.

# Eight

'Our Albert's courting heavy,' said Harry. It was a Saturday, a Baff Saturday, and Harry and his father were broke, for the miners were paid once a fortnight and this wasn't Pay Saturday. They were sitting in the house having a game of dominoes for the few halfpennies left in their pockets. Tommy was hoping to take Harry's pennies to add to his own and so have enough for a pint of brown ale.

It was cosy by the fire now that the union had won the men a coal allowance and they didn't have to scavenge the pit heap for small coal nor the hedgerows for wood. Though it was March, the beginning of spring, and the nights were getting lighter, still it was cold.

'Enough to cut you in two, Mam,' Harry had said as he came in from the pit. 'I felt it coming out of the pit. It was hot down there all right.'

'Ah, man, you're that soft,' Albert had said. 'Like a lass you are.'

Harry pulled a face but didn't rise to his brother's remark. Albert was standing before the mirror in the press door combing his hair – still wet from his bath – to one side carefully before taking the comb to his moustache.

'I don't know where he's going on a night like this with nowt but a few pence in his pocket,' Tommy said grumpily. And that was when Harry dropped his bombshell.

'Courting? What do you mean?' his father asked.

'I mean he's going out with a lass,' Harry replied patiently. He picked up the wooden dominoes, holding all seven easily in his calloused hand.

'Don't cheek your da,' said Mary Anne sharply. She was sitting by the fire with knitting wool and needles, knitting pit socks, and Lottie sat on the other side darning a pair.

'Did he tell you?' asked Tommy.

'No, but it's the talk of the rows, Da. His marras were joking about it.'

Mary Anne, sitting by the fire, didn't look up but she was listening hard. Her heart began to beat painfully in her chest. If Albert was courting it meant that soon he would be getting wed and asking the manager for a house of his own and taking his pay with him. Albert brought the biggest pay into the house, he was a good hewer, oh yes he was.

There was food in the house and tea, enough for the coming week and a small amount of money for the herring man, but it was always a hard week with little to spare, especially since they had taken on Lottie. She looked across at the girl, and Lottie glanced up at her and smiled, but Mary Anne was aware that Lottie knew what she was thinking.

Tommy flung his last domino down triumphantly and rose to his feet. 'Right then, me lad, my game it is.' He picked up the few halfpennies on the table and put them in his pocket. 'I'm away for a pint, I reckon.'

'Aye, that's right, you go for a pint. Never mind leaving your lad with nowt to last the week. You go,' Mary Anne said.

'I don't mind, Mam.' Harry looked surprised. 'I'm not wanting out.'

'No an' you shouldn't be gambling neither. You nor your da, come to that. The minister wouldn't like it. Can you not have a game of dominoes without betting on it?'

'Mary Anne!' cried Tommy. 'It's not really gambling, just for ha'pennies.'

'Aye, an' toss penny is just for pennies but many a family has had to go without because of men going down behind the pit heap to play it.'

'Mary Anne,' said Lottie gently, 'you'll give yourself a pain.'

'Nay lass, not me, it's him that does that.'

'I'm away, there's no dealing with you when you're in that mood,' said Tommy. He wound his scarf around his neck and pulled on his cap. 'I'll not be late,' he said, his hand on the sneck as he pulled the back door to after him.

'Aye go on, you'll take no notice of me,' said Mary Anne bitterly, but Tommy didn't hear her. He was striding down the back street, jumping the puddles in the dirt road and feeling as good as he did when coming to bank after a shift. Released, that is.

'Mam, it didn't matter to me,' said Harry. He glanced across at Lottie, who had her head bent over a sock with a wooden egg inside it. Carefully she threaded the needle across a hole and pulled the wool through and peered rather short-sightedly at her work. Her cheeks were a becoming shade of rose as though she were blushing, or was it just the heat from the fire? He couldn't tell.

'Do you think it's serious?' Mary Anne asked, changing the subject.

'What?'

'Our Albert and this lass,' said Mary Anne.

'I don't know. He tells me nowt,' Harry replied. 'Do you fancy a game of dominoes, Lottie?'

'Indeed she does not!' snapped Mary Anne. 'Who is it, any road?'

'Who is what? Lottie, howay, have a game.'

'I don't know how,' said Lottie shyly. She had finished her darning and now she rolled up the sock with its twin and put the wooden egg in the sewing basket by her side.

'I'll show you,' said Harry, then to his mother, 'It won't hurt if we're not gambling, will it?'

'Aw, go on then,' Mary Anne replied. 'The lass, who is the lass?'

'You mean the lass our Albert is going out with? Why, it's Dora Parkin. Her da's the horseman at the Co-operative Society. Howay then Lottie, let's play.'

'Just one game,' said Mary Anne. 'I'm wanting me bed.'

The two young people didn't question that. Both knew there was no way Mary Anne would leave one of her sons on their own with Lottie at this time of the night. During the day it had to happen sometimes, but that was different. There would be no carrying on in her house, no there would not. Mary Anne did not say it aloud but she might as well have done. Not that she thought Lottie was that type of lass but human nature being what it was, well . . .

The lay preacher taking the service the following Sunday was Master at the Wesleyan School. He was a middle-aged man who came from Durham City; he had come from a family converted to Methodism early in the century. His grandfather had been a hard-drinking, bad-tempered man who had rolled into a camp meeting more by accident than on purpose and offered to fight the preacher to show him how wrong he was. In his cups, Josiah Bateman was the sort of man who enjoyed a punch-up. He rarely made it down the pit on Mondays as a result of his riotous behaviour over the weekend. But Josiah left that meeting sober and having seen the Light, something his long-suffering wife thanked God for every day.

Josiah Bateman the third was a very different sort of a man, for the family had risen steadily, being sober and industrious. He had attended the Methodist College and was an upstanding member of the burgeoning community built around West Stanley mine. He was in his late twenties and sported luxuriant sideburns a shade darker than his light brown hair.

'I have decided, along with the committee of course, to start an intermediate class for adult literacy,' he said.

Lottie had been searching in her pocket for her penny, for the offering always came after the notices, but she stayed her hand and gazed up at Mr Bateman. She was not sure what intermediate might mean, but was it any good for her?

'I know that most of you can read a little and sign your names even, but I want to be able to introduce you – or those of you who are, let's say, disadvantaged in this way – to the world of literature. Anyone who wishes can come along at eight on Wednesday evening. To the schoolroom, that is. Er, for those who can afford it the cost will be one penny per week, the money to go to the Relief of Widows and Orphans Fund.'

Lottie stared at him as the plate was passed around by the stewards. He used a lot of words she was not sure of the meaning of, but she thought she had got the gist of what he was saying. This was her chance to learn to read a proper book.

'Can lasses come as well as lads? ' she asked him as he shook her hand at the door. 'I mean to the classes?'

'Why, you will be very welcome,' Mr Bateman beamed at her. 'Can you read at all?'

'A bit,' said Lottie and blushed. She was ashamed of her lack of reading; in these modern times nearly everyone was learning to read. Why there was a National School in nearly every community.

'Wednesday, eight o'clock, do not be late,' he said and turned to the next person waiting to leave the chapel.

'Can I have Wednesday night off?' Lottie asked Mary Anne when she got back to Burns Row. 'Only there's a class at the schoolroom and it's about books.'

Mary Anne rarely went to chapel these days. The minister visited her instead.

'You can, pet. Only, I cannot pay you any more. You know how things are.'

'No, no, I'll manage, I will. I'm grateful for what you've done for me any road.'

'We suit each other, Lottie. You're one of the family now,' said Mary Anne warmly.

Wednesday evening came around and Lottie made her way to the schoolroom in good time for the class. In fact, she was too early in her eagerness and had to wait by the chapel door for the steward to come and open up. When he did, she sat down on a form at the back, where she hoped Mr Bateman would not take too much notice of her. If he asked her to read anything aloud she would die of embarrassment, she was certain of that. She kept her head down. The forms were filling up and there was a buzz of conversation around her.

'Do you mind if I sit here, Lottie?'

Harry's voice close to her ear made Lottie look up in surprise. His shift at the pit had finished barely half an hour ago. He must have run home, had his meal and his bath and then out to the chapel in that time. Automatically, Lottie shifted up on the form to make room for him.

'I didn't know you were coming,' she said. 'I didn't know you were interested in liter . . . er, books.'

'Well, I am,' said Harry. His hair, still wet from his bath, glinted in the light from the hanging lamps above.

'But you went to school, you can read,' said Lottie.

He shook his head. 'Not too well. I went down the pit when I was seven, so after that I didn't have much schooling except for Sunday School.'

A hush descended on the schoolroom as Josiah Bateman climbed the few steps to the platform. He had a sheaf of papers and books under his arm and he spent some minutes arranging them on the lectern. The class watched him in silence, for there was not a person there who wasn't a little in awe of him, despite his kindliness.

Lottie even forgot her shyness with Harry as she listened raptly to Josiah Bateman's opening talk. She couldn't see him too well as she was at the back of the class and he was on the platform, but she could hear him perfectly and by, he had a lovely voice, a voice that made you interested in what he was saying. He spoke for almost half an hour on the advantages of being able to read fluently enough that you did not have to spell out the longer words; something not very common in the rows.

'This is an age of opportunity,' he said, his voice so fired with enthusiasm that he carried everyone in the schoolroom along on its tide. 'We must seize every chance for improvement. I will read a short piece from the work by Mr Charles Dickens, *Oliver Twist*. I believe everyone in the room will want to know what happened next, even if it means deciphering it for oneself.'

Lottie was enthralled to the extent that she even forgot who it was sitting by her side. Harry, though he was interested himself, could not help himself glancing sideways at her face, tilted so that she could peer at the platform and the man at the lectern reading so expressively from a large, leather-bound book.

Lottie was struck by the similarities between Oliver and herself. He was a workhouse lad; she was a workhouse lass. She burned with trepidation when he asked for more food, for she knew too well that was unheard of. He had been put out to work in the community and so had she. No one had considered the welfare of the young boy Oliver; he had had no one to turn to and neither had she had anyone to protect her from Alfred Green.

The evening was almost over. Mr Bateman was closing the book and Lottie desperately wanted to know what happened next. But she was no nearer to improving her reading, she realized. He had given out no tips on reading – none at all – he had simply read out the tale of the workhouse lad.

'I'll walk you home, Lottie,' said Harry. 'Did you enjoy it now?'

'I did, oh aye, I did,' she replied fervently. There was a buzz of conversation as people began rising to their feet and putting on mantels and coats. They stilled as Josiah Bateman called from the platform.

'If you want to know what happened next in Mr Dickens's story, I have booklets with the next chapter at the door. They are free but when you have finished with them I want them back to pass on to others.'

Outside, the spring evening was turning cold. Frost sparkled from the ruts in the dirt road and the moon had a ring of white around it. Lottie pulled her shawl closer around her shoulders and folded her arms beneath it. The booklet, issued by the Institute for Adult Literacy, was clutched in her hand. She could hardly wait to get home so she could look at it.

The two people walked with a careful distance of about a foot between them. Even so, she was as aware of him as if they were actually touching. Harry was a canny lad, she thought; a canny lad and a bonnie one an' all. But there was plenty of time for lads. She had little time to herself but she was determined she was going to improve on her reading so she could read a whole book like *Oliver Twist*. Up until now she had not realized that all she needed was practise: the more she tried to read the more she would be able to. At least that was what Mr Bateman had said. Oh, he was a lovely man, Mr Bateman. A man like her father might have been if he hadn't died. Well, he could have been like Mr Bateman, couldn't he?

'Well, was it a good night?' asked Mary Anne as they came into the warmth of the kitchen and Lottie shed her shawl, hanging it behind the back door.

'Aye, it was,' Harry replied. 'The teacher read us a story by that Mr Dickens.'

'But did you learn anything?'

'Well, not really.' Harry rubbed his hands together and walked around the tin bath, still standing on the floor before the fire with dirty water and floating coal dust in it. He held his hands out to the fire to warm them. 'It's a bit parky out there,' he observed.

'I'll empty the bath and then make us cups of cocoa,' said Lottie. She was brought down to earth by the fact that there were still jobs to be done before she could lie down on her makeshift bed on the sofa and dream of being able to write stories like Mr Charles Dickens. Or even of being able to write at all, anything.

'I will do it, I should have done it afore but I was in a

hurry,' said Harry. So once again his mother was scandalized by the sight of him doing what should have been done by a woman: emptying the bath and taking the water outside and the bath too, hanging it on the nail on the outside wall while Lottie spooned cocoa into mugs and poured in hot water. A dollop of condensed milk and the drink was ready.

'What about you, lass, I can see you liked it by your face,' said Mary Anne as they sipped their cocoa.

'I did, oh yes, I did,' Lottie said fervently. She thought of the booklet waiting for her. She would try to decipher it by the light of the fire as she waited for the time to come around when she had to wake Tommy for his fore shift.

# Nine

## 1876

'I want you to be my girl properly,' said Harry. He carried on walking, not even looking in Lottie's direction, but his face was suffused with red.

Lottie stopped walking and stared at him, biting her lip. 'I don't want to be anyone's girl, Harry,' she said. 'Not really. We are friends, aren't we? That's enough. We have plenty of time.'

Harry finally looked at her properly. 'I'm eighteen coming up, Lottie. Albert was courting when he was eighteen. Why shouldn't we?'

'And look at them, Harry,' said Lottie. 'Albert and Dora aren't happy, are they? And there's war on between the families, what with Dora having a bairn and them not wed yet. I don't want to be courting seriously, Harry. I don't want to have a bairn yet and I don't want to get wed neither. Not for ages, years and years.'

'All lasses want to get wed,' said Harry. 'What else can they do? Go and be someone else's skivvy?'

Lottie began to walk on rapidly. 'Like me, you mean?' she called back to him over her shoulder.

'Aw, Lottie you know I didn't mean it like that,' said Harry, hurrying after her. 'You're not a skivvy, You're . . .you're . . .'

'A skivvy,' said Lottie.

'No, nay. You're one of the family,' Harry protested.

Lottie relented and stopped walking. She turned to face him. 'No, I know you didn't mean it.' She looked down at the book in her hand. It had been lent to her by Josiah Bateman. *Jane Eyre*, it was called – the story of an orphan girl.

'I know you like this sort of story, Lottie,' he had said to her. 'And Charlotte Bronte was an excellent writer, though a trifle sensational.' He bit his lip. Perhaps he should be encouraging her to read Charles Kingsley instead.

Harry was slightly jealous of Mr Bateman's influence on Lottie. He didn't like the way she gazed up at the older man with such rapt attention. He didn't like it that Mr Bateman had taken Lottie in to Durham to be fitted with spectacles either. But he didn't mind the happiness he saw on her face when she came back wearing them. Lottie had always had good near sight and could read now and do close work, stitching and mending. She could sew as fine a patch as his mother if not better. But she had not been able to recognize anyone from only a few feet away before she got glasses.

She had come home from the oculist in Silver Street in Durham wearing the spectacles and exclaimed about everything she saw, not least the dust on the brown boards of the kitchen ceiling. She exclaimed over the sheep and lambs she saw on the hillside behind the village; she exclaimed at the beauty of the colours of the gases she saw rising from the coke ovens when they were at work.

'Think about it, Lottie,' Harry said now.

'Think about what?'

They were turning into Burns Row. The sun had sunk behind the houses and there was a slight haze in the air as the colliery chimney belched out smoke.

'Lottie!'

Lottie, who had been thinking of the pleasures to come, when all the family were in bed or at the pit and she could sit before the fire with a stub of candle and read from her book, heard the outrage in his voice and brought her mind back to the present and what Harry had been talking about.

'I will,' she said, then stopped before turning in at the back gate. 'It would worry your mam. You know how bad she is these days. Albert will be moving out, it's not right they should be living in separate houses, not when they have little Bertie. If we moved out, Tommy and Mary Anne would be left on their own.'

'I didn't say we should get wed,' said Harry. He kicked at the wall by the gate with the steel cap of his pit boot. 'I'm only eighteen yet. But I'm earning good money hewing. We could get wed when I'm twenty-one, but I'm just saying we could be courting now. Be my lass, Lottie.'

'Aw, Harry,' said Lottie, and hurried into the house before he could say any more.

'Mind, you're a bit past your time, aren't you?' demanded Albert as they went in. 'I said I'd meet Dora at nine o'clock, she's going to be mad.'

'I told him to go,' said Mary Anne tiredly. 'Lord's sake, I can be on my own for a few minutes. Any road, Tommy will be up soon.'

'Mary Anne, I'm that sorry,' said Lottie. 'I didn't realize it was so late.' She put her book down on the table and took off her shawl. 'We got talking.'

'Talking, were you?' Albert was already on his feet and pulling on his jacket. 'Well, that's all right then.'

'Albert . . .' Harry started to say, but stopped as he saw his mother's face. Mary Anne's eyes were ringed with a dark brown discolouration and her face and neck were puffy, as were her hands and feet. Her heart was failing, had been failing for a long time, but now the process seemed to be getting faster every day. She could no longer lie down in bed but had to be propped up to breathe. They were afraid to leave her on her own in the house.

'You should be in bed, Mam,' he went on. 'Howay, I'll carry you through and Lottie will undress you.'

'I was trying to let Tommy sleep as long as he could,' Mary Anne said, fighting for breath.

'Aye well, it's time now.'

Lottie looked in the oven to check on the bacon and potato panacklty. It was bubbling away fine, so she pushed the iron kettle from the bar on to the fire. Before long she and Harry had Tommy up and, dressed in his pit clothes, eating his supper, and Mary Anne safely tucked up in bed in the front room.

Albert was away to see his lass and bairn. The minister had been giving them a bad time, saying they should get married. Dora had been in tears about it last time he'd seen her.

'Mam's badly, Da,' said Harry. 'Real badly. What are we going to do?'

Tommy shook his head. 'We've had the doctor and he did nowt. I thought he might have done. Bloody witch doctor, that's what he is. I mean, there's still smallpox about for all their talk of being able to stop it with this newfangled vaccination.' Tommy shoved a forkful of bacon into his mouth.

'Da, that's got nowt to do with Mam and her heart. The dropsy's getting worse, you must see that.'

Tommy pushed his plate away and sat down by the fire to lace up his pit boots. Harry and Lottie watched him, waiting for his response.

'Da?'

Tommy straightened up. He pulled on his cap and tied his muffler around his neck. Then he spoke.

'I tell you what I'm going to do. I'm away to Durham the morn and I'm going to fetch our Eliza back wi' me. She'll have to help out for the now.'

'But . . . but what about your bed? You cannot walk all day and go down the pit on a night, man!'

'It wouldn't be the first time,' said Tommy stolidly. He picked up his stick, which was standing in the corner by the fire, and walked over to the door. 'Good night to ye,' he said and pulled the sneck to behind him.

'Harry,' Lottie began but Harry cut her short.

'I'll go meself,' he said. 'I'll set off now. It's nobbut a few miles, I've walked further down the pit. I'm not wasting money on the train.'

Lottie sighed. 'At least get some supper into you first, Harry,' she said. She did not argue with him. It was true that he was in better shape to walk to Durham than his father and he would get some sleep before walking back in the early morning, in time for the back shift.

The doctor and medicine and a few extras to tempt Mary Anne's appetite had taken all the spare money they had. Illness could be very dear, Lottie thought dismally as Harry's pit boots rang on the stones as he walked down the yard to set off for Durham City. And at the pace Harry could walk, he could do the six or seven miles in an hour or very little more. But would Eliza be able to come? She was married to Peter Collier, the union man, and something almost unheard of, she still worked as a nurse in the pit villages around Durham.

The other thing was that Eliza had written to say she was having a bairn in a few months' time. A call from the postman was a rare event in the miners' houses, and especially in 35 Burns Row, but now Harry and Lottie were such good readers, they could read a letter to Mary Anne and Tommy.

Lottie cleared the supper things and hung Albert's pit clothes

by the fire to air, ready for him going on fore shift. She filled
his bait tin with bread and bramble jam made from the fruit
she had picked last autumn and made sure his metal water
bottle was full. Then she checked on Mary Anne, who was
propped up by pillows in the double bed in the corner of the
front room, dozing fitfully. There was little coal in the bucket
by the room fireplace so she took a shovelful from the fire-
back in the kitchen and banked up the fire with that. At last
she was free to read her book for an hour or so before Albert
came in.

The book had dropped on to her knee and she was dozing
herself when she woke with a start. She was stiff and aching
from sleeping in the chair and she put her hands to her back
and stretched luxuriously. It was the sound of Albert's pit
boots coming down the yard that had woken her; a moment
later he opened the door and came in.

'I'm late,' he said, and indeed the pit hooter was sounding
down the rows, calling in the men on shift.

'I'll go in to bed,' said Lottie. She had taken to sleeping
on a shakey-down in the front room when Tommy wasn't
there. It allowed the lads some privacy to change in the warm
kitchen. She lay for a while after Albert went out, running
down the yard and up the row, catching up with the rest of
the men converging on the pithead. She could hear the tramp
of their feet on the stones and then there was quiet. Not total
quiet: Mary Anne's breathing was laboured and rasping and
she kept muttering unintelligibly in her sleep.

The firelight flickered and played on the walls of the room,
recently lime-washed on the orders of the mining agent, for
there was cholera about in the county; mainly around
Sunderland way it was true but it could sweep through the
pit villages, with their midden heaps and lack of piped clean
water.

Lottie watched the flickering light, seeing strange shapes in
the shadows and weaving stories about them; fantastical stories,
for she couldn't get back to sleep. She lay and thought about
Harry. Oh, he was a canny lad, he was. She was very fond of
him. Most of the girls her age had already paired off with a
lad. They were 'walking out', or some even courting, which
in West Stanley was the equivalent of being engaged to be
married. Even more, in spite of the minister's disapproval. But

what was a young couple to do? The wage a young hewer brought into the home was often vital when fathers were disabled in the pit or even just too old to hew. And the lasses now, they so often had to take on the running of the home when mothers were worn down and ill.

In the flickering firelight, Mary Anne moved restlessly as she laboured to breathe and Lottie got up to check on her. But Mary Anne settled down again and Lottie got back on to her shakey-down.

Aye, Harry was a nice lad and she didn't want to cause him any grief. But he was a stay-at-home lad; all the books he got from the literacy class were enough for him. He had no wish to travel further than Durham and then only when there was something momentous on, like the opening of the Miners' Hall in North Road. That was taking place in June and was all the talk in West Stanley.

Lottie turned on to her back and stared at the ceiling. She would settle down with Harry, she acknowledged to herself, but not yet. She was going to write, she was indeed. Only she had to be able to support herself. Just now, she did not really get a wage from Tommy and Mary Anne, for they simply didn't have the money, but she had her keep. The boys gave her tuppence each for what she did for them, but that was the only actual cash she had.

She did not feel herself hard done by. It was nice living as part of a family. If only she could get on and do what she most wanted to do, she thought. She had a pile of exercise books, bought for a penny a time over the weeks from Mr Bateman, who bought them by the gross for a ha'penny each at Andrews and Co. in Durham City. The profits from this enterprise went towards the educating of the poorest children in the place, for even at the new National Schools the children were expected to pay threepence a week to learn reading and writing and adding up.

She had started to write stories in the books and she was almost ready to show them to Mr Bateman, but so far she had not been able to summon up the nerve to do so. And that way of thinking was not going to make her rich and famous, no it was not, she knew that. Lottie sighed and closed her eyes. Only supposing Mr Bateman told her she was wasting her time? Sleep overcame her.

Lottie woke to the sound of the back door opening and closing. Weak daylight was filtering through the curtain and Mary Anne was very quiet in the bed. Lottie scrambled to her feet and pulled on her old stuff dress, drawing the waist in by pulling the tapes threaded through and tying them at the back.

'Are you decent, Lottie?'

It was Harry's voice; he must be back from Durham already. The room was cold, the fire out. She combed her hair back from her face with her fingers and turned to the bed, at the same time calling out to Harry.

'You can come in Harry.'

Dear God, Mary Anne was very quiet and very still. She reached a hand out and touched the older woman's forehead. It was cold. Frantically she pulled the patchwork quilt up over Mary Anne's chest and shoulders.

'Fetch a shovelful of fire from the kitchen grate, Harry. Hurry!'

'What is it? What's wrong?' Harry was behind her. He peered over her shoulder. 'Pull back the curtain, Lottie,' he cried and she ran to the window and let in more of the dawn light.

Mary Anne was gone, passed away during the night, during the short time that Lottie had slept, and she felt like a murderer.

'I thought she was just cold, Harry. I thought she was asleep. It's my fault, Harry, I should have been awake.'

'Yes, you should have been,' said Harry harshly. 'It's no good bringing in fire from the kitchen now, is it? She's gone.' He kept his eyes on his mother's face for a few more moments, then turned away.

'I'll go for me da and our Albert,' he said. He did not look at Lottie as he went out. 'I reckon you were likely scribbling in that bloody book of yours,' he said. His face was white and strained, but he did not weep. He was a man and a hewer and they did not weep.

Lottie did not blame him for what he said. She blamed herself. This was the second time this had happened when she was supposed to be looking after someone. She was no good, selfish, she told herself. Mechanically, she began to tidy the bed, pulling the quilt even closer around the still figure.

*     *     *

'I've worked out what should be done,' said Eliza. She had come over from Durham in her little tub trap. The trap was standing in the back street now, for the funeral was over and the family gathered in the kitchen. The minister had gone, along with all the neighbours who had been there for the funeral tea of ham and pease pudding and stotty cake; followed by funeral cake, a sort of light fruit cake.

Tommy, sitting by the fire and smoking his clay pipe, did not look up or take any interest in what was said.

'Me da's in a world of his own,' Albert had commented to Harry and Dora.

Harry nodded, but in truth he too was taking little notice of what was being said.

'Lottie cannot stay here, not on her own in a house with three men.'

Lottie felt as though her heart had dropped into her boots. They were going to tell her to go. Well, she deserved it, for she had neglected Mary Anne when she was dying. She stared at her hands, red and chapped from so much immersion in soda water, and yet marked with a couple of blue scars where coal dust had got into the chaps when she dashed the pit clothes on the outside wall.

'I reckon it's time Albert and Dora were wed,' Eliza went on. Everyone of the family looked up, apart from Tommy, who took the pipe from his mouth and spit coaly phlegm into the heart of the fire, where it hissed for a few seconds.

'We cannot! Not so soon after Mam died,' said Albert, and Dora began to tremble and clenched her hands together to stop it.

'Well, you needn't have a do,' said Eliza. 'A nice quiet wedding in the chapel with just the minister and the family. You would be all right with that, wouldn't you, Dora?'

Dora gave her a quick glance and nodded.

'Well then, I'm sure the agent will agree to Albert taking over this house. Only Tommy and Harry will have to stay.'

Nothing was said about where *she* was to go, thought Lottie and immediately felt even more guilty for thinking of herself again. She rose to her feet.

'I'll take a breath of fresh air,' Lottie murmured and went out. No one said anything and she thought they hadn't even noticed her but Eliza had watched her progress up the yard and saw her pause at the gate. She looked across to her husband, Peter Collier, the union man, and he nodded.

'Lottie can come back to Durham with me,' she said.

'You're right bossy, our Eliza,' said Albert.

'Can you think of anything else to do?' demanded Eliza.

He shook his head. In fact, he was well pleased with the plan.

# Ten

Though Lottie had some bad memories of Durham, she loved the narrow streets of the ancient city, especially the busy shopping streets leading out of the marketplace. She looked forward to going for the 'messages' to Lockey's, the tea dealer and family grocer, whose shop was at 14 Market Place and where exotic foods could be bought. Luxury items such as imperial plums in bottles and crystallized fruits and ginger and many different cheeses such as Cotherstone and Wensleydale and even Stilton.

Not that Lottie did much shopping at Lockey's, as everyday shopping was done at the Durham Co-operative Society, which everyone was beginning to call The Store. Lottie took the order in weekly and it was delivered by the Store horse and cart the following day. But Eliza, being six months into her pregnancy, took some strange fancies, and Peter did his best to indulge her even if it was only a quarter pound of Cotherstone cheese from way up Teesdale.

Peter did not earn a great wage and of course Eliza could not work while she was expecting, that would have been a scandal. As far as possible, women stayed in seclusion when in a certain condition, at least in a town such as Durham. It was not a pit village. But he was a union man and in regular work now the union was legitimate and becoming stronger. So Lottie had instructions to buy a jar of imperial plums this day at the beginning of June. For tomorrow, 3 June, the new Miners' Hall was to open officially and the family were coming in to witness it and Eliza wanted a special tea.

Plum pie and custard was very special, and there were cold cuts of pork from the Store and tomatoes even, Spanish tomatoes that is, for even the forced tomatoes from Peter's coal-heated greenhouse in the back garden were far from ready as yet. Though there were lettuces, also brought on in the greenhouse.

Lottie thought back over the few weeks she had been living in Durham as she walked along Saddler Street towards the marketplace. Everything had changed in her life. She hadn't seen Harry since she had been here and she missed him, as well as Mr Bateman and the literacy class.

'You must join one here, there must be one,' Eliza had said. She had noticed Lottie's exercise books and asked about them. Eliza was a woman who had forced her way up in the world; she had trained as a nurse against all odds and she had loads of self-confidence, for hadn't she had Mary Anne for a mam and Tommy for a da? Whereas Lottie was shy of pushing herself forward. But she would, she told herself, sometimes she could, she would have to if she wanted to realize her ambitions.

Pausing before the window of Andrews and Co., the stationers in Saddler Street, Lottie read the advertisements in the newspaper stuck to the glass. By, it was good to be able to do that, she told herself. She should stand up and do things for herself, she must have a good mind or she wouldn't have got so far, would she?

And Mr Bateman said she had a good mind and he should know, he was so clever himself.

### GOVERNMENT EMIGRATION TO
### NEW SOUTH WALES
#### Reduced Rates

Now, she knew where that was for hadn't Mr Bateman told them about Captain James Cook, who had been born just over the Tees and had mapped out New South Wales? It was in a place called Australia, Mr Bateman had said. Maybe one day she would even travel to New South Wales, when she sold a book. Not that she had any idea how much she would get for writing a book, but surely it would be enough.

One evening, Mr Bateman had put on a slide show and there were pictures of the people who were native to New South Wales. They were as black as any man up from the pit and wore hardly any clothes, which Mr Bateman had said was because it was so hot. One day she might go there. She could do anything she put her mind to, even travelling the world. Lottie sighed. So long as she wasn't too timid about it, she told herself.

There was an advertisement for Dr Gray concerning vaccination for smallpox. 'Smallpox is raging,' it stated. 'Vaccination is the only way of preventing its spread.'

Lottie shivered. By, she didn't want smallpox. Even if it didn't kill you, it left a person badly scarred. She decided she would ask Eliza about vaccination, how much would it cost.

'I'd best get on,' she murmured to herself and turned away. She had taken no more than a couple of steps when she heard her name called.

'Lottie! Lottie Lonsdale!'

It was a lad, a pit lad of about ten years old. He was in pit clothes and his face and hands were black. She didn't recognize him as he ran up to her and he grinned and his white teeth gleamed whiter against the coal dust.

'Noah?' She asked hesitantly.

'Nay, I'm Matthew. Can you not bring me to mind?'

'Mattie! By, how you've grown,' said Lottie. 'You're working down the pit now?'

'I am,' said Mattie proudly. 'I'm on fore shift. I just came into Durham on a message for me da.'

A gentleman walking by with a lady took hold of her arm and pulled her to one side so that neither of them came within a foot of the black boy, which was the term used by the townspeople for the pit lads.

'They shouldn't be allowed on the streets with decent people,' the woman said loudly. 'It's no wonder there are such awful diseases about.'

Lottie glared at her and her escort but they were hurrying away now. Frightened of contamination, no doubt. Mattie saw she was angry.

'Take no notice, I don't,' said Mattie. 'I should not have come in before I had me wash but Da was in a hurry.'

He must have been, thought Lottie. What was he thinking of, sending a lad on an errand when he'd been working down the pit all night? Counting in her head, she decided that Mattie could be no more than ten years old.

'You went away and you never came back to see us,' said Mattie suddenly. 'Why?'

Lottie felt so guilty she didn't know what to say. She stared at the young boy. He was tall for his age but pinched-looking and now she noticed how tired he looked beneath the grime. And thin: why, he hadn't a picking on him.

'You were all right, though, weren't you, Mattie? I mean, your da would get someone else to take my place, didn't he?'

'Aye. But Betty's not like you, Lottie. She's a workhouse lass like you but she's different.'

'Betty? What's her other name? I might know her.'

'Bates, and she knows you. Why did you go away and not come back, Lottie?'

'I had to, Mattie. I'm sorry. I'll keep in touch now though, Mattie, I'll write to you. I can read and write now. I couldn't before, not properly.'

'Promise?'

'I promise. I have to go now, I have messages to do and so have you,' she reminded him.

She watched as he sped along Sadler Street to the bookie's. Alf Green was still gambling then, she thought. He should have been in a comfortable position now, an overman at Sherburn Hill Colliery. His youngest lad should not have had to go down the pit so young. He could still have been at school, for Mattie was a bright boy.

As she went on her way to Lockey's Provisions shop she felt a small, nagging worry about Betty Bates, living and working in the same house as Alf Green. She would have to keep in touch with Mattie, ask him how Betty was. She might even go to see her. When Alf Green was safely at work, of course.

'They're back,' said Eliza, coming into the kitchen of the house in Gilesgate which she and Peter had moved into when they married. 'Push the kettles on to the fire, Lottie, please.'

Eliza had been sitting by the front window waiting for the men of the family to return from North Road, where the Miners' Hall had been officially opened that very day, Saturday 3 June 1876. All the family were aware of the importance of the occasion. The Durham Miners' Association had been meeting in the Market Hotel, but now they had their very own hall in North Road. Even little Bertie sat quietly on his mother Dora's knee and stared solemnly around at the assembled family.

'Here, let me help you with those, Lottie,' said Eliza's son Tot. He walked quickly over to the range to where Lottie was lifting heavy iron kettles. 'They're too heavy for you.'

Lottie stood up straight from bending over the bar and gave him a startled glance, as did his mother and Dora. Males did not, as a rule, help with domestic chores; they rarely even noticed them.

'I can manage,' said Lottie. 'I'm used to it.'

'Nonsense, Lottie, I'll do it,' said Tot, and made a show of placing the kettles on the glowing coals. 'There you are.'

Oh, he spoke lovely, thought Lottie. He was like a proper gentleman and he was *so* good-looking, with his dark wavy hair and the dimple on his chin.

'You're blushing,' said Dora.

'Nay, it's just the heat of the fire,' Lottie protested, but her cheeks flamed even more. Tot smiled at her and she began to feel strange, a bit light-headed. She hurried away to the front room where a large mahogany table was set with the best linen tablecloth and Sunderland chinaware. She began to rearrange the plates of ham, pease pudding and tomatoes and the dishes of plum pie and egg custard.

In the kitchen, Eliza and Dora smiled at each other in understanding. Eliza walked over to her son, her gait slightly awkward due to her late pregnancy.

'Leave the lass alone,' she said softly. 'Unless you mean something by it.'

Harry scowled; he had watched the little byplay and felt a sudden onrush of jealousy. As soon as he had *Master* Thomas Mitchell-Howe on his own he would put him straight, he told himself savagely. Lottie was his lass and always had been.

'What did I do?' Tot was the picture of innocence.

'You know well enough,' said his mother. 'Behave yourself or you'll be on your way back to school with a flea in your ear.'

'I haven't to be back until Monday!' said Tot, looking less of a young gallant and more of a schoolboy. He was sixteen, but suddenly he seemed much younger. Yet he had seemed so much a man of the world to Lottie a few moments earlier.

'Well, mind what I say,' warned Eliza, then the matter was

forgotten as the men came into the house talking of the grand new hall. Some settled on the chairs in the front room, but a few of the miners were happier on their hunkers in the yard with their backs against the wall and their pipes in their hands. It would be soon enough to be indoors when the tea was ready.

'Mind, who would have thought it?' asked Tommy of no one in particular as he drew long and hard on the stem of his clay pipe.

'What? Who would have thought what?' asked Albert, a trifle impatiently.

'I mean, the union with a grand hall in North Road and the Owners' Association having to meet with our lads.'

'Aw, Da, they had to do that in '72 when we got rid of the yearly bond. And the Miners' Hall was paid for fair and square by the lads themselves. We have some power now, man.'

There was much nodding of heads and a chorus of 'Ayes.'

Too much power, thought Tot. At least that was what the general opinion was at school among both masters and boys. Then, as the talk among the pitmen turned to the state of the coalface and how wet some seams were 'inbye' and all the other parts of their work that pitmen found so fascinating to talk about, he wandered away from them, gravitating naturally towards where the women were finishing laying the table, moving between kitchen and front room. Dora had brought little Bertie out to his father, for the baby would not be laid down to sleep on an unfamiliar bed.

'Albert, hold the bairn,' she said and the men stopped talking shop and grinned at the young father.

'Who's the gaffer in your house then, Albert?' a couple of them asked jokingly.

'The bairn,' said Albert ruefully, but he took Bertie willingly enough.

'It's always the same,' Tommy observed. 'If there's a babby in the place, it gets all the attention.' And so it did.

'By you're a big lad to still be at school, Tot,' said Albert as they sat around the remains of the feast. Tommy was feeling in his waistcoat pocket for his tobacco pouch but he looked across at his eldest son.

'Education is a marvellous thing,' he said. 'I only wish we'd had the chance of schooling when we were bairns.' He smiled at his daughter's son, Tot, who was a bit red in the face.

Tot was a weekly boarder at a school in Barnard Castle. He had an inheritance from his father's family, who were business people in Northumberland, and this paid for his education.

'I'm going to be a soldier,' he said now. 'I need a good education to get in.'

'You do?' said Albert, looking surprised. 'There now, I thought all you had to do was hold out your hand and take the Queen's shilling.'

'Leave the lad alone,' said Tommy. 'You're nowt but jealous.'

'Nay, I'm not . . .' Albert began but Peter Collier, Eliza's man, cut in. 'We'll talk about something else, eh? On an important day like today we have a lot to celebrate, haven't we? The union is going to go from strength to strength, I'm telling you. The owners have to listen to us now. Why, Mr Crawford says . . .'

Tot wandered out into the kitchen, uninterested in what the General Secretary of the DMA had to say. He was interested in Lottie, his mother's maid of all work.

'Are you wanting something, Tot?'

His mother was sitting at the head of the kitchen table with the women around it, Lottie included, for there was not space for them to be comfortable at the table with the men in the front room.

Lottie was telling them how she had met Mattie Green on the street outside Andrews the day before but she stopped as Tot came in.

'Not really. I'm just fed up with mining talk. If it's not how wet a seam is or the relative merits of a Stephenson and a Davy lamp it's about getting one over on the owners. Don't they know the owners give them their bread and butter?'

There was a sudden shocked silence. Dora found her voice first. 'Is that what they learn you at that fancy school in Barney then?' she asked. She had Bertie back from his father and he was sleeping in her arms supported by her shawl, while she ate and drank with her free hand.

'You don't think they earn their bread with their own sweat then, do you not?' asked his mother. 'If you don't, then mebbe it's time you left that school and went down the pit yourself.'

Though she spoke quietly enough she was seething with anger and there were red flags blazing on her cheeks.

Tot looked at her as though she had suddenly lost her senses. 'I'll not do that,' he said positively. 'No indeed, I will not.'

'Well then?'

Tot considered his position; he was far from being slow.

'Well, I know the men work hard. They have to but it's the owners and management who do all the planning, risk their money.'

'While the men risk serious injury or their very lives,' said Eliza. She was remembering some of the men she had nursed over the years.

'Sometimes . . .' Tot had been going to say that often it was the men's own carelessness but he bit back the words. Though that was often said in the newspapers when an accident happened.

'There's no such thing as an accident, there is always a cause,' Mr Dunne, his form master would declare.

'Well?' prompted Eliza.

'It takes both sides,' mumbled Tot. 'I'm just going for a walk.' He passed Lottie, not even looking at her, and went out of the back door and up the yard. His feelings were very mixed up indeed.

# Eleven

'I do hope Tot is not going to make a fool of himself over Lottie,' Eliza said to her husband as they sat down in the front room on opposite sides of the fireplace. It was ten o'clock in the evening and the room was darkening and becoming cooler, so Peter raked a few coals down on to the fire from the shelf at the back and it flickered into flame. He did not reply to Eliza immediately but sat back in his chair and gazed at her thoughtfully.

Eliza was looking tired; soon they would go upstairs to bed, but they were both enjoying these few minutes on their own after the bustle of the day.

'He's nothing but a lad, Eliza, but he's got his head screwed on aright,' he said at last. 'It'll be years yet before he gets serious about a lass. Don't make trouble till it comes. Any road, he'd do a lot worse than Lottie.'

'She's not the girl for him,' Eliza insisted.

'You mean she's not good enough?'

'No . . . She's a lovely lass, I know she is, but . . .'

'A workhouse lass?'

'We don't know who her parents are,' said Eliza lamely and blushed as Peter stared at her. 'Well, he'd be happier with someone else. He might meet someone who can talk to him . . .'

'Oh Eliza, I don't know what you're thinking of. They are both far too young to know what they want yet. Tot has his way to make in life and with the advantages he has, he should go far. And Lottie, well, I didn't think you of all people would hold her poor beginning against her.'

'I don't, no, I don't. Of course not.'

Yet in spite of her protestations, Eliza felt confused. She liked Lottie; she was fond of her even. Hadn't she been good to the girl? Only she had such ambitions for her son. And the little one in her belly too. She put a hand over her waist as she felt the baby move vigorously.

Peter stood up and came over to help her out of her chair. 'Bed for you,' he said as he helped her to stand. 'It's has been a busy day. A tremendous day.'

It was a busy night as well – there was to be very little sleep for anyone, as Eliza's baby came into the world. Lottie was roused at midnight by Peter knocking at her bedroom door.

'Get up, Lottie, please. I want you to see to Eliza while I go for the midwife,' he called.

Lottie jumped up and pulled on her clothes and ran down from her attic bedroom to the first floor. She could hear Eliza moaning softly, though she was not crying out. The baby was early, Lottie knew that; it was not due for another month. But babies came when they thought they would, she knew that too from her years helping out in the workhouse, where premature babies were common. They often died, which was something else she had experience of and she felt a pang of anxiety. Maybe today's celebrations had been too much for Eliza.

'Get the rags from the bottom drawer of the tall chest, Lottie, there's a good girl,' Eliza whispered breathlessly before stiffening and moaning again, a long drawn-out moan. Afterwards she whispered again, 'You shouldn't be doing this, a young lass like you,' but she grasped Lottie's hand tightly as she came back to the bed with the pad of rags Eliza had prepared to lie on during the birth.

Lottie watched her face anxiously as she laid down the pad and helped Eliza on to it. By, she looked badly, she did, her face drawn and white and great dark circles under her eyes. Where was the midwife? Eliza needed the midwife now, she did. The pains were on her, and they were closer by the minute and at last she had lost her self-control and was screaming with each pain.

'Mam? Mam? Are you all right? Mam, is it the baby?' It was Tot, knocking at the bedroom door.

'Send him away,' said Eliza. 'He shouldn't be here. Oh, it's not right, it's not decent.'

'Do not worry about that,' Lottie said soothingly as she left her side and went to the door, opening it only a crack. 'It's the baby, Tot. Go down to the door and see if your step-father's coming with the midwife.'

'But . . .'

'Now, do it now!' said Lottie urgently as there came another cry from the bed. She closed the door and ran back to Eliza.

'He's coming, I can tell. Lottie you'll have to help me.'

'I will, I will,' said Lottie. 'It will be fine, you'll see.' But she was filled with dread. There must be something wrong, it was all happening too fast. As she pulled back the sheet to look, she saw the baby's head, a fuzz of dark, wet hair and then a little face, red as beetroot and with the eyes screwed tight with rage. She was just in time to catch and support the head as the rest of the body slithered out.

'It's a girl, Eliza, a little lass,' she said and Eliza lay back on her pillows, panting. Just at that minute she felt she didn't care if it was a brass jug, she was so glad the baby was out. She felt faint and she had a small ache in her chest from the great efforts she had made to birth her.

When Peter returned it was with a woman from the next street. She was an untrained midwife as so many of them were, unlike Eliza who was a Nightingale nurse. They had been expecting the midwife from the county hospital.

'She was out on a difficult case, Dr Gray too,' explained Peter. 'I did my best.' He had his head poked around the bedroom door, for it didn't do at all for him to actually be in the room.

'Wait downstairs,' ordered Mrs Young, the woman he had brought, pushing him out and closing the door. She came to the bed, rolling up her sleeves and putting on her apron, which she had carried rolled up under her arm.

'We want nowt with men in here,' she went on. 'Now let's have a look at you.' She was the picture of efficiency and determined to show she was as good a nurse as Eliza, for all the other woman's book knowledge and hospital training.

Eliza was feeling less breathless and even euphoric that the ordeal was over in the main. 'Mrs Young,' she said. 'There's hot water and soap over on the washstand there. You'll want to wash your hands. But as you see, the baby is born and she is fine. You'll be wanting to check her over?'

Mrs Young bridled. 'Of course,' she said. 'Though my hands are quite clean, as you can see. I would not have come if I'd realized the bairn was already out. You did not book me, did you? I came out of the kindness of my heart.'

'Of course.' Peter had insisted she book Dr Gray from the hospital.

'It is a long time since Tot was born, Eliza,' he had said.

'And I'm not as young as I was,' Eliza had replied. She was only too well aware of the dangers, for she met them every day in her work. Well, now it was too late for Dr Gray to come and the baby was fine anyway and so was she, though exhausted.

In fact, Eliza was too exhausted to say more to Mrs Young and too happy to get annoyed with anyone. She had her baby, a bonnie little lass with dark hair, lying against her forehead, which had paled from the bright red it had been and now was nicely pink. Lottie had wrapped the baby in a winceyette sheet and now Mrs Young unwrapped her and checked her over.

'Aye, a bonnie bairn,' she said, quite forgetting she was intending to be as cold and lofty as she thought Nightingale nurses were. 'Mebbe you got the dates wrong, she's plump as a nine-month babby.'

'You could be right,' smiled Eliza. Her eyelids drooped, she was almost asleep.

'Aye well,' said Mrs Young. 'We'll see you comfortable now.'

The nurse was untrained but she was capable, thought Eliza as she drifted off to sleep after being 'seen to', as Mrs Young called it. It seemed like a week since yesterday and the family party.

The midwife soon had the baby asleep too, in the wooden rocker cradle made by Peter. It had high sides and a wooden hood to protect the baby from draughts and was low to the ground so that a foot on a rocker was enough to rock it gently. Lottie tiptoed about putting the room to rights.

'You can fetch her da now, Lottie,' said Mrs Young. 'But he must be quiet about it, not to disturb mother or bairn.'

Peter and Tot were waiting at the foot of the stairs for the summons and when they entered the bedroom Eliza opened her eyes and smiled at Peter.

'You did well, lass,' he whispered. Tot stood just inside the door. He was white and shaken by the events of the night; he could not forget the cries of his mother as she brought his sister into the world.

'Never mind Tot, he thinks he's something special because he goes to that fancy school in Barnard Castle,' said Harry. He and Lottie were sitting on the banks of the Wear down by the race-course in Durham. It was Sunday, a week and a day since the birth of Anne Elizabeth Collier. Harry had come, supposedly to inspect his new niece, but in reality to see Lottie. He had had an uneasy week thinking about Lottie being in the same house as Tot, even though it was only at weekends.

Lottie watched as a punt glided by on the opposite side of the river, a girl with a parasol sitting at one end while a student in a blazer and boater hat manipulated the pole with long, graceful movements. He was showing off his tall, lithe figure to the girl, of course. She heard her trill with laughter as they passed.

There was a man on a bicycle coming along the towpath, calling through his loudhailer at a crew rowing rhythmically along the middle of the river. 'In!' then 'Out!' he bellowed as the water rippled by the hull.

'You're not listening to me, Lottie,' Harry said in exasperation. He had walked the miles to Durham that morning and Lottie had shown no signs of being extra glad to see him. He felt ill-used and jealous.

'What?' asked Lottie.

'I thought you were my lass,' said Harry.

Lottie jumped to her feet. 'I'm nobody's lass but my own,' she said lightly. 'Howay now, I must get back to make the tea. And you an' all, you're on fore shift aren't you?' She set off along the towpath, then cut up into Old Elvet.

'Lottie, wait. I want you to tell me there's nowt between you and Tot.'

'There isn't,' she replied. 'He's going to be somebody though, maybe even get elected for parliament. He's told me.'

'He talks a load of tripe, he does,' said Harry angrily.

'Well, we'll see. Any road, I'm not going with anybody, I've told you. I'm going to make something of myself. I'm going to be a writer.'

'You're talking soft an' all,' said Harry, which was just about the worst thing he could have said if he wanted to influence

Lottie. She bridled, and set off over Elvet Bridge, at a faster
pace than the scullers below. Harry followed, as frustrated as
ever.

Later, when all the work was done, Eliza and her baby settled
for the night and Peter working on union papers in the sitting
room – something about a sliding scale arrangement, whatever that was – Lottie sat by the open window of her attic
bedroom, looking out over the city.

Here she was, almost seventeen and she still had not made
any progress towards her goal in life. Oh, she had written a
few short stories and had even sent them off to publishers but
they had been returned with notes such as, 'Too fanciful, unbe-
lievable,' or, 'Not true to life.'

But she had a copy of *The Durham Post* before her on the
rickety little table she had placed by the window and she had
read it through and through. Josiah Bateman had sent it to
her and on an inside page he had marked a notice advertising
a competition they were having for a short story. The prize
was ten pounds and a free place on a writing course to be
held in the Town Hall, and the tutor was an English graduate
of the university.

'You can do it, Miss Lonsdale,' the note that had come with
the paper read. 'You have the ability. Just write about something you know and keep it simple and true to life.'

Oh, she would do it, she would. She had bought decent
foolscap paper from Andrews' shop in Saddler Street and when
she had the story written in her exercise book she would copy
it out carefully using the foolscap and send it in to *The Durham
Post*. Only it had to be in by Tuesday and she had not even
begun it, and it was already Sunday night.

The moon shone through the attic window and illuminated
the empty page of her exercise book. She didn't even know
what she was going to write about. Surely her life, the people
she knew about, were far too ordinary for a paper that was
read by educated folk, university folk, the 'others' who lived
in the city but separately, apart from the miners and other
workers?

'Keep it simple,' Josiah Bateman had written. 'And about
what you know.' Well, she would, but what could she write
about? The workhouse? That would be altogether too much

like a copy of Charles Dickens and a presumption. She could write about her life with Alf Green, she thought. But no, she couldn't, she could not.

The moon was sliding behind a cloud; now she had to light the precious bit of candle she had saved. She would do it. She came to a decision suddenly. She dipped her pen in the inkwell and began to write. She wrote until the candle flickered and died and she could barely see the page she was writing on, let alone what she was writing. But she had finished her story.

The following night, Lottie copied her story on the good foolscap paper and printed at the top, 'The Bonnie Pit Laddie', by L. Lonsdale. She wrapped it in brown paper salvaged from the parcel of groceries delivered by the Co-operative store van, and wrote the address of *The Durham Post* on the outside.

'Is it all right if I go for the messages first thing this morning?' she asked Eliza. Eliza was at last allowed out of bed and was sitting by the fire in the front room, rocking the cradle gently with one foot. She was feeling much better herself, but of course was not allowed out amongst other people, for she had not as yet been 'churched', something that was ritually necessary after a birth before a new mother could mix. The plan was to have the baby baptized the following Sunday in Elvet Chapel and the mother 'churched' at the same time.

'Go on then,' Eliza replied. 'Will you fetch me a bottle of gripe water for Anne Elizabeth? I fear I should not have eaten cabbage yesterday, the bairn's suffering for it. It must have affected my milk.'

'I will.'

Lottie took her basket and list of messages and sped up the stairs to put her story in the bottom of the basket, for she had not told anyone what she was doing. She let herself out and sped along to North Road and the offices of *The Durham Post* and slipped her story through the letterbox. There, she thought, feeling slightly light-headed. She had been in time.

# Twelve

'There's a letter for you, Lottie,' said Peter one morning a few weeks later. He smiled at her as he brought in the post from the front doormat. 'It looks very official, a brown envelope. I thought it must be union business, I nearly opened it.'

Lottie suddenly felt a great fluttering in the region of her stomach. She took the envelope and stared at it. It was addressed to an L. Lonsdale, Esquire.

'Whoever it's from thinks you are a man, Lottie.' Peter studied her small, trim figure and the heart-shaped face framed by soft, brown hair. The spectacles perched on the end of her nose seemed to suit her somehow, he thought. In any case, they made her dark eyes appear even larger than they actually were. It was the first time he had really noticed what she looked like since he had met her, and there was no doubt in his mind that she was growing into a very nice-looking woman.

'Aren't you going to open it, Lottie?' asked Eliza.

Lottie looked up from her scrutiny of the letter, her face rosy. 'No, I'll read it later,' she said. 'After breakfast.' She pushed the letter into her apron pocket, which only served to make the Colliers glance at each other with raised eyebrows. Lottie was not usually the secretive type, thought Eliza.

Lottie had been secretive about the competition though. If the editor of *The Durham Post* had written to say she was no good and would she not bother him again, something she thought a real possibility, she could not bear anyone else knowing of her humiliation. Maybe she should stick to skivvying, she thought. She stared at her plate of porridge. It was good porridge, with real milk from the dairy and even a sprinkling of sugar, and normally she enjoyed it. The food in this house was the best she had ever eaten. But all she could think of was the letter in her pocket.

Peter finished his own breakfast and rose to go to the Miners' Hall in North Road. His mind was already running on the work waiting for him there. He kissed Eliza and the baby and nodded to Lottie. The letter was none of his business anyway.

Eliza had not forgotten it though. 'Go on, go up and read your letter in private,' she said. 'I'll side the table. I'll manage fine on my own for a while.' Indeed, Eliza was looking well and full of energy. Little Anne was a good baby and little trouble. Already she slept through the night, and without her nursing to occupy her mind and body and with Tot away at school, Eliza had begun to work alongside Lottie.

Back in the attic bedroom, Lottie sat down at her little table by the window and opened her letter. There was but one sheet of paper, headed with a stamped *The Durham Post*, and her heart began to beat wildly as she drew it out.

> *Dear Mr Lonsdale,* (it read)
> *First of all, I am sorry to have to tell you that your story did not win the competition.*

Lottie's heart plummeted; for a moment she could not see to read the rest of the letter. Her hand fell to her lap. She was not good enough; she would never be able to make her living writing as she had hoped and dreamed.

Gradually her sight cleared. She was used to disappointments, for hadn't she had them all her life? Her hand trembled only slightly as she lifted the letter and began to read the rest.

> *However, there is no doubt that you have a singular talent, and with nurturing and hard work you should do well. In fact, we intend to print a selection of the entrants to our competition and, with your permission, will include 'The Bonnie Pit Laddie'.*

> *I gather that you must be a very young man and we are looking for someone of your calibre to train in our business.*
>
> *If you are interested at all in this position, perhaps you would call in at the office this Friday coming at ten o'clock in the morning.*
>   *Your obedient servant,*
>   *Jeremiah Scott (Editor)*

Lottie stared at the letter, reading it over and over. A position on the newspaper? Where she could write for a living? Oh yes, she was interested, she was indeed. Only wait, the editor thought she was a man. He would not want a woman, especially not a seventeen-year-old, uneducated woman. It was no good her hoping he would.

She stared out of the window at the rooftops of Durham spread below her on the falling ground. It was a fine day: the sky was blue and wisps of smoke curled up from some of the chimneys, making a light haze. In the distance she could see the castle and cathedral even higher and seeming almost like fairy-tale buildings through the haze.

By, she thought wistfully, her life would be like a fairy tale if she were actually taken on by the editor of *The Durham Post*, oh yes it would. But she was not going to bank on it; she couldn't bear the disappointment if she did.

'Lottie? Are you coming down?'

It was Eliza calling her. Lottie collected her thoughts. She could not sit up here all day, for there was work to do, the messages to fetch. She pushed the letter deep in her apron pocket and went down to the kitchen to wash the breakfast dishes.

Eliza was breast-feeding the baby, with her shawl drawn modestly over her opened bodice. It was just possible to see the top of little Anne's head and nothing else, but she was sucking noisily and occasionally giving a tiny grunt.

'I reckon I must have got my dates wrong,' said Eliza, laughing. 'She's far too strong to be much premature.'

'Aye,' Lottie replied vaguely; she was still dreaming even as she plunged her hands up to the elbows into the soapy water and began to scrub at the porridge bowls.

'Mind,' said Eliza mildly, 'you look away with the fairies.

That must have been an interesting letter you had.' She looked across at Lottie enquiringly, but Lottie said nothing. Eliza lifted Anne from her breast and held her over one arm while she rubbed her back. Anne burped and a small trickle of milk ran down from the side of her mouth, which Eliza wiped away with a cloth, before transferring her to the other breast. 'Well?'

Lottie looked over her shoulder, her hands still in the ironstone sink. 'The letter?' she asked. 'Aye it was.'

'Aw, howay Lottie, surely you can tell me, I'm your friend.'

Lottie took her hands from the sink and dried them on the bottom of her apron. Then she took the letter from the apron pocket.

'You can read it if you like, Eliza.' She handed it over.

'Are you sure? I don't want to pry.' But Eliza was obviously dying to read it. Even as she spoke, she was opening out the sheet of paper.

'Lottie!' she cried. 'By, isn't that grand? You've got a story in *The Post*! How much do you think they'll pay you?'

'I don't know,' said Lottie. In truth she hadn't even thought of the money she might earn.

'And a job! You know, Lottie you're a really clever lass, you deserve something better than scrubbing and polishing for a living.'

'What about you?'

'Nay, we'll be fine. I'm not going back to work, not while Anne is little. I can stay at home. I wouldn't dream of holding you back, anyway. Don't worry about us. I can always get another girl if I do go back to nursing.'

Also it would mean that Lottie would not be in the house all the time when Tot came home, thought Eliza, but fleetingly. Peter had made her feel slightly guilty for worrying about Tot and Lottie.

'But it'll likely come to nothing,' said Lottie as she picked up the porridge pan and began to scrub at the bits of porridge stuck on the sides like glue. 'The editor thinks I'm a man. He likely wouldn't want me.'

'Well, you'll never know until you try, will you?' said Eliza as she fastened herself up and put the baby against her shoulder to raise any wind.

\*   \*   \*

The offices of *The Durham Post* were situated about a fifteen minute walk from Peter and Eliza's house, but Lottie set off a good half hour before ten o'clock, which was when she was supposed to be there. She had hardly slept all night, for her thoughts were a mixture of excitement and dread. One minute she was full of confidence, and the next she sure the editor would turn her down when he realized she was a woman, and a servant at that.

It was a quarter to ten when she arrived outside the door. She stared at the wooden plaque bearing the name of the news-paper and, in smaller letters beneath,

*Jeremiah Scott (prop. and editor).*

Mr Scott owned the paper then. He was probably like one of those old gentlemen she saw sometimes, walking in the city wearing a top hat and with a gold watch chain across their waistcoats.

Lottie turned and walked up the street, glancing at the front of the DMA building. There was a notice about Mr Macdonald MP, something about a public meeting. She paused to read it and as she was doing so, the door opened and Peter Collier came out.

'Now then, Lottie,' he said. 'I saw you through the window. Away to see Mr Scott, are you?'

'I am, yes,' said Lottie.

'Go on then, it's no good being nervous. I'm sure you'll be fine, Scott is a nice fellow, you'll see.'

'He doesn't know I'm a lass, though,' said Lottie.

'Ah. Well, he soon will. That is if you ever go in to see him. Go on, he won't bite. Any road, he likes your story doesn't he? Would you like me to walk along with you? I can.'

'No, I'll be all right.' Lottie smiled at him and turned to walk back along the street.

'Good luck!' he called. With him watching her, she walked back to the door of the newspaper office and went in.

There was a man standing behind a counter looking over his spectacles at her. He was aged about fifty and had bushy side whiskers, contrasting with thin hair on top of his head, and he was holding a sheet of foolscap in his hand.

'Yes, young lady?'

His observing eyes swept over her, taking in her best

cotton shirtwaister and black serge skirt. The skirt had previously belonged to Eliza before she had put on weight and had been much too long for Lottie, so she had altered it. She wore a little bonnet of black straw with a silk carnation on one side, tied under her chin with satin ribbons. She and Eliza had spent most of Thursday evening renovating the bonnet and Lottie had felt quite pleased with the result, but now she was not so sure as she saw the gentleman's expression as he gazed at it. Still, she lifted her chin and gazed back at him.

'I have come to see Mr Scott, Mr Jeremiah Scott,' she said and her voice faded into a small squeak on the second 'Scott'.

'Who?'

The question was something of an impatient bark. Lottie repeated it, a little too loudly this time.

'Mr Scott is busy. He has an appointment at ten.'

So it was not him, she thought. 'I have an appointment with him at ten,' she said.

The gentleman stared at her. 'Your name?' he asked.

'Miss Lonsdale. Miss Lot . . . Miss Charlotte Lonsdale,' she replied and came closer to the counter. She saw that the paper in his hand was her story, 'The Bonnie Pit Laddie'.

The gentleman still stared at her. Then he went to a door set in the wall to one side of the counter and opened it.

'Jackson!' he called and a moment later a young boy came hurrying through.

'Yes, Mr Scott?' he asked.

'Take the young lady up to see Mr Jeremiah.'

The boy opened a door in the counter and let Lottie through, with a murmured, 'This way, Miss.'

Lottie was thoroughly confused by this time. According to the boy, this was Mr Scott. Her brain didn't seem to be working properly; it was a minute or two before she realized there must be two Mr Scotts. This one stood looking after her over the top of his spectacles as she went through. She glimpsed a very amused expression on his face as he went to the opposite wall and pulled a strange tube from a hole and spoke into it, then laughed. And she felt a spark of annoyance. He had better not be laughing at her.

She followed the boy up two flights of stairs to the top of the building. On the way they passed the open door of a large room with big printing presses clanking away in it and a couple of men with eye shades tending them. As they ascended the last flight, the sound of the presses faded away and the noise became not much more than a background murmur. When Jackson knocked and opened a door for her to enter, it was almost gone.

The room was large and airy and the windows looked out over the city to the hills and fells beyond. In the middle of the room was a large oak desk and behind it sat a man dressed in a tweed suit and floppy bow tie. He rose as she entered but did not smile.

'*Miss* Lonsdale,' he said. 'Come in and sit down.' He stood as she crossed the room, her boots sinking into a brown, figured carpet, and sat down at a chair pulled up on the opposite side of the desk.

'You are a girl, Miss Lonsdale,' he stated accusingly. 'I thought you were a lad.'

'I did not say I was a man, Mr Scott,' said Lottie. By now she had lost some of her shyness. Any road, she told herself, he was just going to tell her to go back to her kitchen. A heavy disappointment began to settle somewhere over her stomach.

'That is true,' he admitted as he sat down. He picked up a printed paper and glanced down at it. Lottie watched the top of his head. His hair was a bright tawny colour and he wore it short and combed back, but without any dressing so that the front lock fell forward and he brushed it back with his hand impatiently. His hand had ink stains along the first two fingers but the nails were square and cut short and straight across. She wondered how old he was. Not so old as Peter Collier but older than Tot or Harry. Late twenties, maybe. He looked up suddenly and she blushed to be caught studying him.

'Miss Lonsdale, as I said in my letter, I do think that you have a special talent. I confess I was surprised when my father said you were a girl.' He stopped and smiled at her, and his smile was friendly enough for the feeling over her stomach to begin to evaporate like mist in the sun.

'Tell me about yourself,' he commanded.

'Well, I was brought up in the workhouse . . .' she began, determined to tell him all. She watched his expression but it did not change. His dark blue eyes showed only interest.

'Go on,' he said.

By, he was a nice man, a lovely man, she thought, and gave him the story of her short life, holding back only the bit about Alf Green.

# Thirteen

'Well?'

Eliza was dusting the fretwork decoration on the sideboard in the front room when Lottie came home. She was using a cockerel's tail feather to get right into the holes between the carved mahogany. In the corner, baby Anne was asleep in her wooden cradle. Eliza gazed at Lottie, framed in the room doorway. Lottie's face was pink and her eyes behind the glass of her spectacles shone.

'I am an apprentice at *The Durham Post*,' she said.

'An apprentice journalist? Oh, LOTTIE!' Eliza went to her and hugged her. 'By, I'm over the moon, I am. I knew you could do it.'

'Well,' Lottie admitted. 'Not really an apprentice journalist. Just a dogsbody at first. Mr Jeremiah said I had to learn how the business worked. I'm on a month's trial and then, if I'm good enough, I will sign the indenture papers.'

Eliza checked on the baby. 'Let's go and make a cup of tea. You can tell me all about it then. We don't want to wake Anne.'

Lottie fairly danced after her along the passage to the kitchen. She took off her bonnet and laid it carefully on the press, then pushed the kettle on to the fire from the bar. It began to sing at once. She went about making the tea in a dream as Eliza brought out fresh milk and put the sugar basin on the table. Normally they would just have used condensed milk, which was already sweetened, for an extra cup of tea such as this, but today was a celebration.

'Now then, tell me,' Eliza commanded, when they were settled in chairs on opposite sides of the fireplace. 'Exactly what happened, mind, what was said and everything.' So Lottie started from the beginning and the dusting and sweeping and nappies soaking in a bucket waiting to be washed were forgotten as she recounted the events of the morning.

'I thought the editor's name was Scott,' said Eliza. 'Why did you call him Mr Jeremiah?'

'It is father and son,' Lottie replied. 'Mr Jeremiah is the editor; I think the older Mr Scott must be retired or something . . . oh, I don't know. They were both surprised when they saw me, but do you know, Mr Jeremiah doesn't care that I'm a woman, he's very modern. Oh he's a lovely man, Eliza, a right bonnie lad.'

Eliza was amused. 'He is, is he? Well mind you don't go losing your heart to him.'

Lottie was shocked. 'Nay, man!' she exclaimed. 'It's not like that. I mean he's not a gentleman to look down on a workhouse lass. He wasn't bothered at all when I told him about that. He did ask about my schooling and I had to tell him Mr Bateman taught me at the adult classes at the chapel in West Stanley. And he knew Mr Bateman, wasn't that funny?'

'Mmm,' said Eliza.

'I have to start next week, Monday morning sharp at eight o'clock.' Lottie glanced across at Eliza, biting her lip. 'I mean, I won't go if you want me here, Eliza. I won't just let you down. I told Mr Scott that.'

'No, I think you should go,' said Eliza. 'I'll manage fine.'

'Well, I mean, I have to live up by North Road,' Lottie went on. 'Newspaper workers have to be available, that's what Mr Scott said. But I'll get a half-day on a Saturday and I'll come to see how you are managing. They put the paper to bed on a Friday.'

Oh, she had learned the jargon already, thought Eliza. Fortunately Lottie didn't see the amused expression return to Eliza's face.

'I saw Peter on North Road,' Lottie was saying. 'Do you know, he was looking out for me? He wished me luck. I gave his name as a referee, do you think he'll mind? Mr Bateman's an' all, I'd best write to him and tell him.'

'Peter won't mind and neither will Mr Bateman. They'll be delighted that you're getting on.'

There were sounds from the front room; the baby was waking. Lottie got to her feet and, 'I'll fetch her for you,' she said. 'And I'll clean the house from top to bottom so you won't have much to do next week.'

'Get along with you,' said Eliza. 'The place is like a new

pin already. Bring Anne and then go on up to the attic and write your letter.'

'You haven't mentioned money,' Eliza said as Lottie put the baby into her arms. 'Will you be able to manage?'

'I will, I think. Mr Jeremiah said the paper will pay the lodging and give me a shilling a week at the beginning. Then we'll see, I suppose.'

'One shilling! Lottie you won't be able to manage.'

'I will. Because I'll get paid for my stories an' all. And Mr Jeremiah says I'll get seven and six for 'The Bonnie Pit Laddie'. It will come out next week. Seven shillings and sixpence! It will last for weeks, won't it? Then I'll write another story.'

Eliza was dubious but she did not want to say anything to take away from the girl's happiness and good fortune. She sat in her nursing chair, suckling the baby and gazing into the embers of the fire as Lottie ran upstairs, humming to herself. *Goodness knows*, she thought, *the girl was due some good fortune.*

On Sunday afternoon, when Lottie was all ready to move lodgings to a small close off North Road named Amy Yard and Eliza and Peter were out walking with the baby in a sort of basket on wheels, which they called a perambulator, Lottie decided to visit Mattie in Sherburn Colliery. It was a fair walk to the pit village but she cut along a path through the fields and managed the walk in well under an hour.

She went with mixed feelings. Apprehension in case she met with Alf Green, though he was usually out on a Sunday afternoon, preaching at some country chapel in the circuit. But she had to see Mattie and make sure he was all right.

The meeting with Mattie in Durham City kept coming back to her memory, and despite her excitement at her newly opened-out future, she had to see him again.

It was something she had been meaning to do ever since she had returned to Durham, even before she had seen Mattie in the city. She had to make sure he was all right, and besides, she wanted to know about Betty Bates. She was anxious about the girl she had looked after in the work-house. She felt guilty that she had not looked for her since. In fact, she felt guilty about both of them.

Why was Mattie working already? His father was a colliery overman, he surely could afford to keep the boys on at school, then apprentice them to a trade. Mattie was bright; he could even be a mining surveyor or if not, at least he could be a colliery joiner or other tradesman.

Lottie's heart beat faster as she approached Sherburn Colliery. The mining rows lay before her and in front of them the field where the boys played. Originally it had been part of a large meadow but half of it was taken up by the spoil heap from the mine. The rest was still grassed and used only by a few galloways: pit ponies that were old or injured. Today there were none, just a group of boys kicking an old leather football about.

With a sigh of relief she saw that Mattie and his older brother, Freddie, were among them but not their elder brother, Noah. Noah was too much natured like his father and had delighted in tormenting Lottie. Did he torment Betty? she wondered.

Oh, she should have been in touch before now, she should have.

These thoughts ran through Lottie's head as she went to the edge of the field and called Mattie over. He looked across at her, kicked the ball to his brother and walked over.

'Wot cheor, Lottie,' he greeted her, in the local idiom. He was dressed in a clean shirt and trousers that came just below the knee, with a cap on his head and pit boots on his feet that looked enormous on the ends of his thin legs. But there were coaly rings around his eyes where he hadn't quite got the coal dust off, and also in his ears.

'What have you come back for?' Freddie had come up behind Mattie and his face was very unfriendly.

'I came to see you both,' said Lottie.

'Took your time, didn't you? But then, what do you care for us?'

'I do care. I've been away. Well, West Stanley, any road.'

Freddie grunted then turned away, back to his game, muttering something about West Stanley not being a million miles away. Lottie decided to leave it and turned to Mattie.

'Are you all right, Mattie? I mean . . . are you happy? Do you like working in the pit?'

'I'm fine,' said Mattie, but he looked down at the ground

as he spoke and pushed a stone about with the end of his boot.

Freddie was watching them, Lottie suddenly realized, and he was close enough to hear what they were saying. Mattie was not going to say much. She stepped closer to the boy.

'Are you? Do you wish you had stayed on at school? You could have learned a trade.'

'Nay.'

She wasn't getting anywhere, she realized. 'Will you walk a bit with me? Tell me how Betty is?'

'You can go and see her yourself. Me da's away to Thornley.'

'Still, will you go with me? I'm a bit nervous.' She was appealing to the man in him – shamelessly, she knew. He nodded.

'I'm away home,' he called to his brother. But Freddie had lost interest, he was dribbling the ball up the field with a crowd of lads after him. He kicked it between two imaginary goalposts defined by a couple of coats laid on the ground where the post would be, then turned, flushed with success.

'Hey, Mattie!' he called but Mattie and Lottie were gone, over the dirt road speckled with coal dust and behind the first row of houses. He hesitated for a moment, then carried on with the game.

Betty was in the kitchen of the house where Lottie had been a maid of all work when she first left the workhouse. She was quite a few years younger than Lottie, about fifteen, but she was already as tall. Her hair was a mousy blonde and she was red-cheeked with blue eyes, and quite plump. When she saw Lottie she took a step forward, then folded her arms across her pinafore and stopped.

'Lottie,' she said, then looked away and her cheeks reddened even further. The reason was obvious: Betty was well-advanced in pregnancy.

Lottie tried hard not to look as concerned as she felt. She went to the girl and put her arms around her and hugged her.

'Oh, Betty,' she said. 'I should have come sooner.'

'Why?' asked Betty harshly. 'You're not me mam or me sister. I'm nowt to you, nowt at all.'

'Oh, but you are, Betty,' Lottie protested. 'I thought about you a lot. I missed you, I did.'

'No, you did not,' said Betty. 'If you had you would have come to see me.'

Lottie had no real excuse. She had been away in West Stanley, but she could have walked to Durham, it wasn't so far. She could have tried to find Betty when she left the workhouse, but she had not. She felt hopelessly guilty and there were no excuses for her, she realized.

'I'm sorry, Betty,' she whispered.

'Do not be sorry for me,' Betty replied. 'I'm all right. Me and Alf are going to get wed. He promised me.'

'Oh Betty, you're not old enough to get wed!'

'Aye, I am,' Betty asserted. 'Alf says I am.'

'Betty, can I have a scone?' Mattie, who had been lingering in the doorway of the kitchen, asked. There was a tray of scones, just out of the oven, on the fender.

'Go on then,' said Betty. 'Then go on out and play, lad.'

'Will I see you before you go back?' Mattie asked Lottie as he took a scone and covered it liberally with blackberry jam from the jar standing open on the table.

Lottie promised him he would.

When he had gone, the two girls sat down on the settle.

'I'm having a bairn,' said Betty, blurting it out suddenly.

Lottie nodded. 'I can see that,' she replied. 'It's Alf Green's, is it?'

Betty nodded. 'Why aye, it is. So we're going to be wed. I told you.'

'Do you love him, Betty?'

'I do that.' But Betty looked uncertain, as though she wasn't quite sure what love meant.

'I suppose he's away at Thornley Chapel,' Lottie said bitterly. 'He's a bloody hypocrite.'

'Nay, he's not at chapel,' declared Betty. 'He's stopped going to chapel. No, he's away to the card school at Thornley. Last week he won three pounds! He reckons he'll spend it on the bairn when it's born.'

'If he doesn't lose it this week,' said Lottie.

'He won't, he said he'd leave it here,' said Betty, but she looked even more uncertain.

'Did they throw him out of the chapel because of the bairn?' asked Lottie.

'No, we're going to be wed, I told you. No, it's because

someone saw him at the pitch and toss, a snitcher, that's what. You know how they don't like the gambling. But Alf makes money at the gambling, he does, I told you. Why should he give it up? It hurts nobody, does it?'

'Well . . .' Lottie began, thinking of all the lives she had heard of being ruined by even such a small game as pitch and toss penny. But she could see it was no good saying that to Betty. The lass was simply trying to make the best of her situation. She changed her tack.

'How old were you when Alf got into your bed?' she asked.

'Old enough,' Betty mumbled, her cheeks turning to beetroot. 'Any road, it's none of your business. He loves me, he says he does.'

'You're barely fifteen now,' said Lottie. 'You're still a bairn.'

'I'm not! I'm a woman now, doesn't this show I am?'

Betty put a hand on the bump under her pinny. Her voice trembled and she looked close to tears. Lottie decided she was doing no good, no good at all. It would only hurt the lass if she told her about Alf and what he'd done to *her*, Lottie.

This sort of thing happened so often to girls from the workhouse. They were sent out as skivvies to whoever wanted them and no real checks were made on them and how they were being treated. She herself had been so lucky to get away, and lucky that Bertha had found her and taken her to the Collier family. She could have ended up on the streets, or at worst, in the River Wear.

'Mebbe Alf Green will marry you,' she said. 'Mebbe you will be fine.'

'Aye he will,' Betty replied. 'He will, I'm telling you. You needn't worry about me. You never did before, did you?'

Guilt descended once again on Lottie's shoulders. She should have looked the girl up and made sure she was all right. But so should the Parish Officers, she thought after she said goodbye and promised to come back again.

'Send Mattie to let me know if you need me,' she said to Betty as she went out. 'Promise me you will. He'll be able to leave a note at *The Durham Post*.'

*Surely Mr Jeremiah wouldn't mind that?* she thought, as she walked along the row. No, he would not, he was such a lovely man.

She turned the corner and back to the playing field but the

lads had gone on, probably to the quoits alley, for she could hear excited voices from there. As she walked back over the fields, she wondered if Mr Jeremiah would be interested in the story of Betty and the other workhouse girls like her. He might well be, she decided.

# Fourteen

'The Bonnie Pit Laddie' was on the third page of *The Durham Post* on the following Saturday and beneath it there was a short biography of the writer, the paper's newest apprentice.

'You done good,' said Jackson. 'Mind, I'm glad I don't have to go down the pit when I read that. How do you know about what it's like?'

'I have friends in the pit,' sad Lottie. She smiled at the boy. He was the same height as she was, about five feet, but still only fourteen. Jackson was his baptismal name; his full name was Jackson Hadaway. Quite a lot of boys were christened with their mother's maiden name.

Lottie had been working at the paper for five and a half days and it felt as if she had been there for weeks. She spent most of her time in the office or running errands, doing much the same work as Jackson. It had been a great thrill for her the day before when she had seen her story actually in print for the first time and her name above it. And now the paper was on the streets being sold in the marketplace, on Elvet Bridge, Silver Street, everywhere. She was in heaven, she felt. *Oh, please don't let me wake up and find it was all a dream.*

Maybe the readers would hate her story of the lad who went down the pit at six and sat on a cracket by a doorway, opening the leather curtain to allow the corves to pass through and closing it afterwards so that if there was a pocket of firedamp and it took hold there would not be a clear passage for the resultant fire. A lad who begged candle stumps from the miners going off shift for when his own ran out and he was frightened of the black dark. Of course, in the modern times of the 1870s, they had Stephenson safety lamps, not candles, but it hadn't been so long ago when there were no safety lamps.

'Lottie!'

The shout came from the front office, the one open to the public. She left Jackson to finish mashing the tea and hurried through. Mr Scott, Mr Jeremiah's father, was there behind the counter, while in front of it was an august-looking gentleman with a copy of the newly published *Post* in his hand.

'Yes, Mr Scott?'

'This gentleman is Dr Welles. He is from the university. Dr Welles, this is the author of the story you have come here to discuss.'

If Lottie had not been in considerable awe of the learned doctor she would have laughed at his astonished expression. As it was, she blushed, held out her hand and withdrew it quickly when it became obvious that he was ignoring it. He appeared speechless, but he soon recovered. Dismissing Lottie with a cool glance, he turned back to Mr Scott.

'What do you mean by this, Sir?' he demanded. 'Are you telling me a wild tale?' He shook the paper he was holding in Mr Scott's face. 'It says in your paper, sir, that this disgraceful story was written by Mr L. Lonsdale. Now you say it was by this chit of a woman. I will not be played with! I . . .'

'This is Miss Lottie Lonsdale,' interposed Mr Scott. 'Now, as I gather you have a complaint, I will call my son, the editor. It is he you should speak to. Meanwhile I suggest you treat our staff with proper respect.'

He walked over to the speaking tube on the wall and turned the handle. In the distance there was the sound of a jangling bell.

'Jeremiah?' he said after a moment. 'There is someone here to see you, a Dr Welles from the university.' He listened with his ear to end of the tube for a moment, then put it back on its hook and returned to the counter.

'If you would be so kind, Dr Welles,' he said formally. 'Miss Lonsdale will show you up to the editor's office.'

The learned doctor coughed loudly, glared at Mr Scott and followed Lottie up the stairs, past the open door of the room where the now silent printing presses were housed and on up to the top of the building to Mr Jeremiah's office. She knocked and opened the door in response to his 'Enter!' and ushered Dr Welles in, before going back out and closing the door behind her.

Outside in the passage, Jackson popped out of the room next door, where he had been hovering, and winked at her.

'Ould sod,' he said amiably.

'I thought doctors were supposed to be kind folk,' said Lottie. 'I wouldn't like him looking after me if I was badly.'

Jackson laughed. 'He's not that kind of doctor, Lottie,' he explained. 'Nay, he's a Doctor of Divinity when he's at the university.' He had only found out the difference himself a few weeks before, when Mr Jeremiah had explained it to him, but he enjoyed showing off his superior knowledge to Lottie.

Lottie could hear the murmur of voices from inside the office. Now and again she could make out a word as the voices got louder, so she walked along to the head of the stairs, for she did not want Mr Jeremiah to think she was listening at the door. She was there for only a minute or two when the door opened and Mr Jeremiah and the visitor came out, Mr Jeremiah calling for Jackson.

'Show the reverend doctor, out, Jackson,' he said to the boy, then, 'Lottie, come in here a moment please.' He held the door open for Lottie as he bid the doctor good day.

'You will hear more of this,' warned Dr Welles and marched off after Jackson, his moustaches quivering.

'I will look forward to it, Sir,' the newspaperman replied. He followed Lottie into his office and closed the door, then walked around his desk and sat down.

Lottie trembled as she stood before him, rather as she had trembled as she stood before Matron's desk in the workhouse after some minor misdemeanour. Dr Welles was a reader of *The Post* and he hadn't liked her story and maybe other readers wouldn't like her work and she would be forced to leave the paper. All her dreams would come to nothing.

'I'm sorry, Sir,' she said, not looking up.

'Why? What for, exactly?' asked Mr Jeremiah. He sat back and gazed at Lottie. 'Dr Welles? It's true he thinks we should not have printed a story about a little pit lad. He thinks the pit folk should not be featured in *The Durham Post*, that the good people of the town should not have to read such things over their toast and marmalade. But that is his opinion and I suppose he is entitled to it.'

*What will I do if I have to leave?* The dark thought ran through Lottie's head and there was an edging of panic to it.

She dared not look at Mr Jeremiah. It was a minute before she realized what he was saying now.

'However, I did not call you in to discuss Dr Welles. I wanted to say that I think you have done well this last week. How do you find the work?'

'I-I like it, Sir,' she stammered. Mostly it had entailed helping Jackson fetch and carry for the two older reporters, George Petty and Edward Dixon, though Edward was more of an illustrator than a reporter. Lottie was fascinated by the way Edward could sketch a few lines on to a blank page and there, to the life, would be the person he was sketching. Once or twice she had gone out with the two of them on a story and though she was only there to watch and learn she had been filled with the excitement of it. Her thoughts returned to the present as Mr Jeremiah spoke again.

'Good. And how do you like living at Mrs Price's house?'

'I like it there, Sir.'

It was different living in the house around the corner to anything Lottie had experienced before. Mrs Price and her daughter, who helped her with the meals and housework, called her Miss Lonsdale, for one thing. It sounded very strange to her ears. The food was plentiful and wholesome and she enjoyed it. Only she would have to get used to one thing. After dinner she was expected to retire to her own small room on the first floor, and consequently she spent more time in her own company than she had ever done in her life and sometimes she felt lonely. But she filled the time by starting another short story.

'Call me Mr Jeremiah,' the editor was saying. 'Everyone else does.'

'Yes, Sir, Mr Jeremiah.'

'Are you writing another short story?'

Lottie nodded. 'Aye, I am,' she said, becoming animated at the thought of her new story and lapsing into the vernacular. 'It's about the workhouse. Is that all right, Mr Jeremiah?'

Jeremiah smiled and his eyes twinkled and crinkled up at the corners. His mouth was open to show his teeth and they were white and even with none missing, which was unusual for a man of his age, thought Lottie. He must be almost thirty years old. Most men she knew had few teeth and the ones they had were rotten or discoloured. She had a funny feeling in her insides when she looked at him. She glanced away in case he noticed.

'When you have finished it I would like you to bring it for me to read. But I wanted to see you about something else. I want you to learn how to use a writing machine.'

'A writing machine?'

'That's right. I have one on order and when it arrives you will be spending some time learning how to use it. Now, I think you should have the rest of the day off. Saturdays are quiet days, as we have put the paper to bed on Friday. Be back here at eight o'clock sharp on Monday. Now run along, Lottie.'

Lottie felt elated and at the same time apprehensive as she put on her cape and bonnet. She had heard of writing machines, of course she had, but she had not actually seen one. Was it difficult to learn to use one? She walked around the corner to her lodging and let herself in, before going straight upstairs to her room.

Half an hour later Lottie set off walking towards Gilesgate to visit Eliza. It was a sunny day but with a chill breeze, but still she was glad to be out in the fresh air and sunshine. As she walked along, her mind was on the plot of her story. It was a tale of the Miners' Gala, when miners from all over the county converged on the city and then frightened the city folk by their very presence among them. Hundreds and thousands of them, marching through the streets and following their brass bands down to the field by the river, where they had a meeting. Men such as Dr Welles; she pictured him in her mind's eye, looking outraged (by, Edward Dixon would be able to make a grand cartoon of him, he would).

Lottie was taken up with the idea. She pictured the young putters taking hold of the man and throwing him up in the air over and over again and finally tossing him in the Wear. It was a grand thought and just what a lot of the nobs were afraid of.

She sighed as she turned into the street in Gilesgate where Eliza and Peter lived. It wouldn't happen, it couldn't. It would be like that time in Manchester she had read about, only at Peterloo, as the meeting came to be named, the militia had been called out and there had been people hurt, even killed, and bairns an' all. Lottie shivered. Dear God, she thought, do not let it happen here.

'Good morning!' she called as she let herself in the unlocked door of her friend's house. Eliza came through from the kitchen with the baby Anne on her hip and a beaming smile on her face.

'Lottie!' she cried. 'I wasn't expecting to see you until tomorrow.' The smile was replaced by an anxious expression for a moment. 'You haven't lost your place, have you?'

'No, I have not!' Lottie replied. 'In fact Mr Jeremiah says he's very pleased with me. No, I have the afternoon off, that's all. We put the paper to bed on a Friday and so there's not much to do on Saturdays. Oh, Eliza, Mr Jeremiah's grand to work for.'

Eliza laughed. 'Howay through to the kitchen and we can have a talk over a cup of tea.'

Lottie followed her along the passage and as they entered the kitchen the back door opened and Tot came in.

'Mother . . .' he began, then stopped when he saw Lottie. His whole demeanour changed. Where before he had been slouching forward and looking uninterested, suddenly he was almost swaggering and his dark blue eyes, so like his mother's, were twinkling in a broad smile.

'How nice to see you, Lottie,' he said and she went pink. She put up a hand and pushed her metal-rimmed spectacles up her nose. Oh, how she wished she did not have to wear them, she did indeed. Lads were not attracted to lasses who wore spectacles, she knew that. Not that she had cared before, being too intent on getting an education and succeeding as a writer, and she still was. But Tot must be just playing with her, looking at her like he did. He wasn't serious.

'Hello,' she said softly. She had a copy of *The Durham Post* in her hand and she held it out to Eliza. 'My story is in it,' she said simply.

'Aye, you said it would be,' Eliza replied. 'Come on then, sit down and we'll have a read of it. I'll just mash the tea first.'

'I'll read it out loud, if I may,' said Tot.

Tot spoke nicely, as the masters had taught him at his school, but still with a trace of local accent. As he read about the miners and their families walking through the boarded-up streets of Durham she was reminded of the time, still talked about in the north-east, when George Stephenson put his plans for a national railway system before the House of Commons and how the members had laughed at his thick accent and derided him for not being a gentleman. Perhaps the masters were right in getting the lads to modify their local accents if they wanted to get on in the outside world. Tot finished the tale of the small boy in the pit who was frightened of the dark and handed the paper back to Lottie with a smile.

'It is interesting, Lottie,' he said and she felt a small quiver of disappointment.

'You didn't like it,' she said.

'Yes, I did,' he protested. 'Only, why do you not write about something everyone is interested in? Most people don't want to know about grubby little pit lads.'

'Thomas!'

Eliza was angry and shocked that he should say or even think such a thing.

She frowned at him.

'Well, it's true,' he said, but he flushed a little with embarrassment as he remembered his mother's brothers were miners.

'If that's what that school teaches you I will bring you away,' Eliza said grimly.

'He is right though,' said Lottie and Eliza stared at her. 'I mean,' the girl went on, 'that is what Dr Welles said this morning. He came into the office and complained to Mr Jeremiah. Mind, Mr Jeremiah gave him short shrift.'

'I should think so an' all,' Eliza declared, then turned back to Tot. 'You should remember that you might have been a pit laddie yourself; you have mining blood in your veins.'

'My father was a carpenter. That's different.' He paused for a moment before going on. 'I'm sorry though, if I sounded proud. I was just saying how I think some people will see it. Just like Dr Welles.'

He smiled at Lottie and his dark blue eyes appeared to deepen. The fluttery feeling rose in her again. By, she thought, she was a fool. She needed to take a hold of herself.

Tot, watching her face, saw the pink rising in her cheeks and the way her brown eyes, already enlarged by the spectacles, brightened. He was not a bad boy but the other boys influenced him to some extent at his school. They seemed to think servant girls were fair game. His feelings were mixed, however. After all, Lottie was his mother's friend, and in any case, no longer a servant girl.

Lottie, for her part, was young and curiously naïve, considering her encounters with Alf Green. She was halfway to falling in love with him, but still determined to put her writing career first.

'Let's take a walk, Lottie,' he said suddenly, then looked at Eliza. 'That would be all right, wouldn't it, Mother? The fresh air will give us an appetite for tea.'

'Oh, but . . .' Lottie said.

'That would be grand,' Eliza declared, brushing aside Lottie's protest. 'Go on, it will do you good after that stuffy office.'

As Lottie went back into the hall to pick up her shawl and bonnet, Eliza whispered to Tot, 'You behave yourself, mind.'

Tot's expression of outraged innocence was a sight to see.

They walked along, heading generally towards the Wear, then along the banks as far as the footpath allowed, keeping a small gap between them until the path became narrow and the way uneven. Tot took hold of her arm just above the elbow and guided her along so as to avoid the roots of the trees leaning over above them. She was very conscious of his fingers through the thin stuff of her sleeve. No one had ever treated her like this – as though she were a lady – and she felt confused.

'Let's sit down and rest for a minute or two,' he said, leaning even closer towards her so that their faces were very close together. And this was Tot, Eliza's son whom she had known for years, she thought. No, she couldn't do this, she could not indeed.

'I have to go,' she said. 'I have to get on.'

'Just for a minute?' he coaxed 'Tell me about your work at the newspaper.'

But she had pulled away from him and was hurrying along the path to where steps led up to the bridge over the Wear. Suddenly something had reminded her of Alf Green.

# Fifteen

'Did you enjoy your walk?' Eliza asked as Lottie walked into the kitchen, still wearing her bonnet and shawl. 'Where's Tot?'

'He's coming. Only I had to get on. I must go back and do some work.'

'Not without your tea, surely? I've made egg and bacon pie – your favourite!'

'Mrs Price gives us supper. She might be annoyed if I said I'd already eaten. I should have told her, you see.'

'A cup of tea and a scone won't hurt. Howay, take your bonnet off,' Eliza insisted.

Lottie divested herself of her outdoor things and hung them up in the hall, thinking she could not offend Eliza. She was still in the hall when the door opened and Bertha Carr came in, bright-eyed and rosy-cheeked and in an all-enveloping cloak.

Lottie's pulse, which had begun racing inexplicably, settled down. For a moment she had thought it was Tot and she wasn't quite ready to meet him again, not yet.

'Now then, Lottie,' said Bertha by way of greeting. She too took off her outdoor things and Lottie saw she was quite advanced in pregnancy.

Lottie murmured a greeting and smiled at the girl who had rescued her when she had run away from Alf Green and didn't have anywhere to go. There was another bond between them: they were both workhouse children.

'Eliza has been baking,' she said, just above a whisper and Bertha smiled in understanding. Eliza's pastry could be as tough and flat as cardboard or as light and fluffy as Bertha's. It all depended on how long her mind wandered as she stood by the table with her hands in the mixture. This time Eliza's pastry was a success. It smelled wonderful and tasted even better.

'This is a nice surprise,' she said to Bertha, while sliding a generous slice of pie on to her plate. 'That Mrs Carr let you out, I mean.'

Bertha's mother-in-law and Charlie himself thought a woman in an 'interesting condition' should hide away from the outside world until the baby was born.

Bertha nodded. 'Aye, I know. But they are out visiting themselves. They've gone to see her brother, who is ailing. I slipped out while I had the chance. I'll be back before they are: the brother lives up the dale, between Stanhope and Rookhope. I reckon they won't be back for hours and hours.'

Lottie's thoughts began to slip away as she thought of a plot for a new story, one where a young mother comes into labour when she is on her own, and her neighbours did not even know she was expecting a baby. She could weave an exciting tale around that, she reckoned.

'You have to have some fresh air and exercise,' said Eliza judiciously. This was the new thinking in midwifery circles.

'I'll walk back with you, Lottie. When you're ready,' Tot's voice whispered in her ear. Lottie jumped and spilt her tea into her saucer. She had not even heard him come in and it flustered her.

'No,' she said, quite loudly, so that the two women glanced at her in surprise.

'I would rather go on my own. I have things to do.'

She stood up. 'I'd best be away,' she said abruptly and fled.

'Lottie,' Tot began, prepared to argue and insist, but it was too late, she had gone. He smiled a secret smile.

The two women looked at each other in understanding. 'I reckon Lottie has a soft spot for your lad and he knows it,' Bertha said quietly, leaning over and speaking in Eliza's ear.

'Aye well, she'll get over it,' Eliza replied. 'He has his way to make in the world; he wants nowt with lasses for a few years yet.'

'Are you talking about me?' asked Tot. He was busy cutting himself a large slice of pie, before sitting down and sinking his teeth into it.

'Never you mind,' his mother answered. 'Eat your tea and go on upstairs and finish your weekend task.'

Tot grimaced. He was allowed to come home each Saturday

at midday until Sunday evening suppertime, but he had to write an essay or complete a maths problem before his return.

Lottie wandered across the city, down the hill and up the next one, on her way to her lodgings in Amy Yard. As she walked, she thought about Tot. By, he was a bonnie lad, he was indeed. But he knew it too, even if he was cloistered away in that school in Barnard Castle. Soon he would be out of it and off to university, and it was a good thing too. For no good would come of them going together. His mother would definitely not like it and Eliza had been good to her. Tot had his future to think of and couldn't be tied down. She too couldn't allow herself to get sweet on a lad, for she had her dreams of being a writer to follow.

Lottie sighed heavily as she turned into North Road. A cold wind was blowing and she pulled her shawl closer around herself. It would soon be autumn. Oh indeed, she could think of plenty of reasons why she and Tot should keep away from each other. She had to forget about Tot and concentrate on her work and she would. The future beckoned and Tot could not be a part of it.

The house in Amy's Yard was quiet except for the murmur of voices from behind the door of Mrs Price's parlour, which was not quite shut. The lodgers were eating their supper. Lottie went into the room, apologizing for being late, and ate some cold beef and pickles followed by rice pudding and stewed prunes.

Afterwards she ran up the stairs to her room and took off her outdoor things, before settling down at the table by the window and opening her exercise book. She stared out over the rolling fields and woods, not even seeing the colours darken and the mists rise as the sun went down. She was plotting her story. She picked up a pencil and began to write, stopping only to light her stub of a candle with a lucifer. By the time the stub was finished, so was the story and Mrs Price was banging the gong in the hall, calling her lodgers down to a cup of tea before bed.

'I've brought in my new short story, Mr Jeremiah,' said Lottie, as she stood before the editor's desk.

'You worked over the weekend then.' Jeremiah Scott sat

back in his chair and gazed at his newest recruit. 'I'm not sure if you should have been working on a Sunday,' he went on, but his look was far from disapproving and his blue eyes twinkled.

'Oh no, I finished it on Saturday evening,' Lottie hurried to explain.

Jeremiah laughed. 'I'm not a strict believer in Sabbath observance, don't worry. But I don't want you turning up to start a new week already tired.'

'No Sir, I'm not. Tired, I mean.'

'Good. Leave the manuscript with me then. I'll look at it when I have time.'

Feeling a bit deflated, Lottie left the office. Of course, she told herself, it was the start of a new week and Mr Jeremiah had work to do and downstairs George Petty, the reporter, was waiting.

'Come on, young Lottie, you and I are off to the magistrates' court to see who is up before the beak. The boss says I have to take you with me, so you just watch me and keep quiet, m'dear, mebbe you'll learn something.'

'I've changed my mind, George.' Mr Jeremiah said, appearing on the stairs behind Lottie. 'I think I'll take Lottie to the magistrates' court and show her how to go on. You don't mind hanging around the office doing a few odd jobs, do you?'

George looked slightly startled but agreed to the change in plan and Lottie found herself following Mr Jeremiah out of the office.

Jeremiah stuffed his pencil behind his ear and his notebook in the pocket of his all-enveloping raincoat, which he wore all the time when outside in the open air unless the temperature soared to the eighties, which didn't happen very often in Durham. He marched off towards Elvet, where the prison and magistrates' court were situated. Lottie trotted behind him, tying the ribbons of her bonnet as she went.

First in the dock were two men who had assaulted a policeman while they were being removed from The Bottle Makers' Arms at Seaham Harbour. They were seamen from one of the collier boats, which plied its trade between Seaham and London. Lottie watched them as they stood in the dock. It was easy to see they were seamen, with their weather-beaten complexions and rough jerseys. They got short shrift from the magistrates, who fined them twenty shillings and costs or the option of seven days hard labour.

Lottie had her notebook and was trying to take down all the facts as Mr Jeremiah was doing, scribbling away in Pitman's shorthand and covering the pages with a speed Lottie could only envy. She would master it, she would, she told herself. Only it was very hard.

The next up was an old woman caught begging on the platform of Elvet railway station.

'We cannot have decent people accosted and pestered for money as they go about their business,' said the magistrate presiding. He was the owner of a local dye works, a Mr Ferens, master of the East Durham hunt. He eyed the woman in the dock with disfavour. She was perhaps sixty years old, though she looked older, with straggly grey hair and a lined face. She was toothless and kept sucking her gums from anxiety.

'No Sir, Your Honour,' she mumbled. 'I will not do it again, only I hadn't eaten for days, I was desperate hungry, Your Honour. I was badly – I couldn't work.'

'Nevertheless, you must not beg on the streets,' said the magistrate. He consulted the two others on the Bench for a moment. 'You must apply to the Poor Law Guardians for a place in their institution. Do not appear before the Bench again.'

'I won't go into the workhouse, Sir,' the old woman said, lifting her chin defiantly.

'Be very careful what you say or you will find yourself in the gaol,' said Mr Ferens. 'Consider yourself lucky not to be fined ten shillings.'

The old woman was led away and Lottie was left indignant at her treatment, with pity for the woman and something approaching hatred for the magistrate. There he sat, looking self-satisfied, and she would dearly love to hit him in his fat belly with her fist. Or tweak his nose or stand up in the reporters' box and give him a piece of her mind. She could see it in her mind's eye, her telling him what she thought of him and everyone in court cheering, even the lawyers and the bobbies, and Mr Ferens would be mortified, oh aye, he would.

'Lottie! Will you listen to me?' Suddenly Mr Jeremiah's voice penetrated her consciousness. 'Don't sit there dreaming. I want you to write a report about Mrs Betts.'

'Mrs Betts?' Lottie was mystified.

'That old woman vagrant. Lottie, do pay attention.'

'Was that her name? I did pay attention. I thought the poor thing should have been listened to with a bit of sympathy, not threatened with gaol.'

'Did you now? Well, I'm telling you, you will never make a reporter unless you get the facts and report them even-handedly. Now listen to what's going on girl! You didn't even have her name, for goodness sake!'

'I will, I'm sorry. I got all the rest, Sir, I did truly.'

'Hmm.' He glanced at her notebook: there were a few lines scrawled there. 'Well make sure you get all the facts this time.'

Another defendant was being led into the dock, this time a burly young miner in a crumpled pair of trousers and red braces over a white, collarless shirt.

The clerk to the court read out the charge. 'Albert Dick. Drunk and disorderly, Your Honour.'

Mr Ferens was frowning down at a paper on his desk. 'It says here you were rolling about in the road at five o'clock on Sunday morning singing an obscene song and disturbing the peace.' He stared at the prisoner. 'Sunday morning,' he repeated. 'The Sabbath day!'

'Eeh, no your Honour, I was singing Cushy Butterfield. It's not obscene, nay, it is not,' the prisoner said earnestly. 'I'll sing it for you if you like. "She's a braw lass and a bonnie lass and she . . ."'

His voice was loud but quite tuneful and the reporters grinned at each other. The magistrate was not amused.

'Be quiet!' he shouted and the miner obediently stopped singing. In the end, he was sentenced to seven days in custody. Lottie licked her pencil and scribbled in her note-book, 'Albert Dick, miner. Seven days. Drunk and dis-orderly.'

'Are you sure you got the facts?' Jeremiah asked. He had been watching Lottie's vivid little face as different expressions chased themselves over it. Behind the glasses her eyes were shining warmly.

'I did,' Lottie replied and handed over her notebook. Oh, but she had a lot more in her head than on the page, thought Lottie. She could write a story about the people in the magistrates' court, she could indeed. Or a few short stories.

'You'll have to learn shorthand,' said Jeremiah.

'I will. As soon as I can afford Mr Pitman's book.'

'I'll lend you mine,' Jeremiah offered. 'It's a bit dog-eared but still readable.'

'Oh, thank you, Mr Jeremiah.' Lottie was delighted. She smiled at him mistily before putting taking off her spectacles and wiping them, then putting them back on her nose. The problem with them was that she needed them to see the people in the court but she had to take them off to read and write.

She was a bonnie little lass, Jeremiah told himself. A neat little figure she had an' all.

'Howay then, I'm a bit peckish. We'll get a penny dip at the butchers over the bridge on the way back. I haven't time for a proper dinner.'

'But . . .'

'I'm buying,' he said, anticipating her objections. Anyone could see the lass had next to nothing.

They sat on the steps of the statue of Lord Londonderry on his horse in the marketplace to eat their dips. The place where Lottie had sat years ago when she ran away from Alf Green, she reflected. By, she'd done the right thing there, she had indeed.

By, Mr Jeremiah was a lovely man, she thought. He was trying to put her at her ease, she knew that. Why else would a great man like a newspaper editor sit on the steps of a statue and eat a sandwich for anyone to see?

'In the usual way of things, any work you do while being employed by *The Post* belongs to the newspaper, Lottie,' said Jeremiah. 'I thought you understood that.'

Lottie stared at him, then at her manuscript on the desk before him. Oh, she was simple-minded, she should have known, she should have read the terms of her indenture. How would she manage?

Jeremiah studied her face as conflicting emotions came and went on it. She was so open; he could see all she was thinking. He looked across at his father, who was standing by the window of his office looking out across the city streets to the wooded hills beyond.

'Father?' he said and Mr Scott senior turned back to face

the room. He knew what his son was asking, though not a word was spoken. They both knew Lottie was talented; they also knew she had only what she could earn. When she finished her apprenticeship, albeit in seven years time, they would want her to write for them, even if only on an occasional basis. He cleared his throat.

'I think we can afford to pay Lottie something for the work she has done out of hours,' he said and Jeremiah nodded.

Lottie was overwhelmed with relief. 'I'd be so grateful, Mr Jeremiah, I would,' she said. 'I'll do my best for you, truly.'

'Indeed you will or you'll find yourself in more trouble than you can imagine,' Jeremiah replied drily. 'Now be off with you. George will be writing up the court notes and you will watch and help where necessary.'

'Yes, Sir,' said Lottie and turned for the door.

'I will let you know what my father and I decide about payment for your stories. If we decide they are good enough to publish, that is. Oh, and the writing machine – the type-writer it is called – will be delivered today. You will be required to stay back to familiarize yourself with it.'

'Yes, Sir,' Lottie repeated and went out. By, he was a lovely man, a grand man, Mr Jeremiah, she thought again. He was a good master, straight-talking, but kind and understanding. And when she looked into his eyes it made her feel funny: warm but strange. Aye, a lovely man indeed. Lottie ran down the stairs to the reporters' room, where George and Edward Dixon worked when they were indoors. Edward was out on a call with his camera. His photographs were beginning to be used in the paper but his camera was bulky and unwieldy and useless indoors without flares.

She was looking forward to trying the writing machine. Oh, she was so lucky to be working here on *The Post* instead of doing someone else's washing or brushing a stair carpet down. The future beckoned brightly. Lottie hadn't given a thought to Tot Mitchell-Howe all morning. She could manage fine on her own without a sweetheart.

As for Mr Jeremiah, it did not occur to her to consider him in such a light. But he did have nice eyes. When he looked at her she felt warm all over.

'Lottie? About time an' all,' said George. 'I would have had these notes all finished if I'd been on my own but the boss says I have to go through them with you, so come on in and we'll begin. Where have you been, any road?'

'I had to see Mr Jeremiah,' she replied as she sat down on a stool by his side. As she went over the events of the morning with him, comparing her notes with Mr Jeremiah's, she had to admit that she had a lot to learn; she had omitted so much. But when she had mastered Mr Pitman's shorthand she would do better. She would start that very evening, if she could keep his copy of Mr Pitman's book. Right after she had mastered the writing machine.

# Sixteen

## 1885

Lottie pulled the last page of her article from the type-writer and put it together with half a dozen others on the left of her desk. There, that was her 'Home Notes' for this week for *The Durham Post*. She rubbed her forehead to ease the incipient headache she could feel hovering above her eyes and put on her spectacles, or glasses as they were often called now.

She stood and stretched her arms above her head, then rubbed the back of her neck before moving to the window and staring out at the driving rain. In the garden, the roses were being dashed about by the wind and snails were crawling along the path. Above the hedge, she could see the trees waving their branches, and a woman was hurrying along the path beneath them, her hand holding her hat on and her skirt swirling out behind her, wet and bedraggled.

It was June and so far it did not promise to be a good summer. Lottie had hoped to take a walk in the park before having a sandwich and cup of tea and then settling down for the afternoon to work on her current novel. She might still do that, raining or not.

As she walked along the path edging North Road, wrapped in an oilskin over her jacket and with her umbrella rolled, for the wind was far too gusty to risk putting it up, she went over her morning's work in her mind. There were several small para-graphs and items concerning subjects that were of interest to women, the latest fashions appearing in the shops being the most important. The narrower skirts appearing in the window of H and J Ferens, and the cotton jackets in Johnston and Coxon in Silver Street had taken up a few lines in this latest article. But really, she found this sort of thing of little interest.

What she did find interesting, she reflected as she climbed the hill into Wharton Park, were the human interest stories she found all around her in the busy little city, and these she used as the basis for her short stories. Jeremiah Scott published them in *The Durham Post* and she made a fair living from them and her articles. Oh, Jeremiah had been good to her. And when he had married a girl from the Surtees family, a gentlewoman, she had felt pangs of jealousy even though she knew she herself came from too humble a background altogether to even think he might consider her in that way. She was a colleague; maybe not even that, but an underling. Still, she had dreamed.

Her feelings had been all mixed up, she told herself. She had been silly. She wanted nothing to do with marrying anyone; she had her career to think of. Hadn't she already got one novel accepted by Bloom Bros, a publishing company in York?

*The Clouds Stood Still* was the story of a girl, a middle-class girl, fighting to be allowed to study to become a lawyer at university. An idealistic girl who dreamed of fighting in the courts for the rights of the oppressed. She won through in the end against all odds, but of course it was a fairy story. It just couldn't happen. She would not have got into university, she would not even have been taken on as an apprentice by any law firm and she most certainly would have been laughed out of court if she did. Yet Mr Bloom, when Lottie had gone to see him in York, had liked her novel, and she had been filled with elation. It was scheduled to be published in November and she could hardly wait. If only it had decent reviews! If only it were reviewed at all, she told herself as she began the descent down the other side of the hill.

'Lottie? Lottie Lonsdale! Goodness, I haven't seen you for such a long time, how are you?'

Lottie had been oblivious of the people walking past her, she was so deep in her own thoughts. She looked up as a man stopped in front of her, blocking her path. It was indeed a long time since she had seen him, for he had been away in Oxford, pursuing a degree; afterwards staying on with a rich friend, according to Eliza. He had grown into a man, a man as handsome as he had been as a boy. It was Eliza's son,

Thomas, or Tot, as he had called himself. Lottie stared up at him, speechless for a moment. For he was good-looking indeed, with a shock of dark hair and violet eyes with long lashes any girl would die for. He stood there, looking down on her and smiling, and her heartbeat quickened. She blushed like a sixteen-year-old might.

'Grand. I am well,' she managed to stutter and his smile widened.

'Mother said you were a lady reporter. You've done so well, Lottie!'

'Thank you, Tot,' she said demurely. The rain had stopped and the sun was coming out. She opened her oilskin jacket and let it hang open, for suddenly she felt too warm.

'I call myself Thomas now. Tot was a babyish name.' he said. 'Are you going somewhere? If you have the time, I thought we could sit on a bench and talk a while.'

'I was just in need of fresh air and exercise,' said Lottie. 'I worked all morning on my article for the paper. I intended going back to work on my new novel but I can spare some time. After all, it is ages since I saw you, though I do hear about you from your mother. She is so proud of you, Tot – I mean Thomas.'

'Well then, that's fine. We'll walk, shall we?' Thomas offered her his arm and they continued along the path, but the first bench they came to was far too wet to sit on and so were the others. In the end they continued on into the city and Thomas bought bottles of dandelion and burdock from a street vendor and penny dips from a butcher in Silver Street, as they had years ago when she was the housemaid and he still a schoolboy.

They laughed together as they at last found a bench that had dried out in the sun, down by the river with the castle towering above them. And Lottie lost some of her shyness and was charmed by him just as she had been when a young girl. After they had eaten, they dipped their handkerchiefs in the river by the weir to wipe their fingers and had to hold on to each other as they did so, for the Wear was swollen with peaty water coming down from the dale after the heavy rainfall of the last few days. Today droplets from the water coming over the weir were sparkling in sun, in tune with Lottie's happy feelings.

Eventually they walked on along the riverside and now as she placed her fingers on his arm, she was very conscious of his other hand covering them. Still, as they drew nearer to Elvet Bridge, she knew the afternoon with him was drawing to a close. Oh, but it had been grand, it had indeed. She gazed at the river for a few moments. She had told him something about her career and he had seemed truly interested and congratulated her on her book. Yet she knew he was more interested in her than her work and with anyone else this would have annoyed her, yet with him it did not matter, she was glad. She was captivated completely and utterly and Thomas was all she could think about. Oh, she knew it was too quick but she couldn't help herself.

They had been holding hands on the riverbank, but when they came to the bridge they moved apart slightly and she put the gloved tips of her fingers on his arm and yet she was supremely conscious of the warm flesh through the material of his coat and the cotton of her gloves. They wandered up into the marketplace and on to North Road. It was a fair distance to walk and the day was quite advanced as they passed by Wharton Park, but all too soon they arrived at the small house, which Lottie had rented after her success with her articles and which gave her the solitude she needed for her work.

'May I come in?' Thomas asked her. Lottie had been in a slight panic that he would leave her at the door and she would not see him again for months. After all, she did not know if he felt as she did herself. She knew nothing of his life, really. She hadn't even seen him for years. She did not see so much of Eliza and Peter nowadays. They were all so busy with their own lives: Peter with the union, which was growing from strength to strength, and Eliza with her work as a district nurse. Was Thomas just being polite, walking his mother's former servant home? She looked up at him for a moment without speaking. Did he think she was fast, letting him hold her hand?

'I have a fair walk home,' he coaxed. 'A cup of tea would be very welcome. If you're worried about what the neighbours might say, well, I *am* an old friend, am I not?' The lace was twitching in the front room window next door; Lottie saw it with the corner of her eye. It wasn't important, let the neighbours gossip, she didn't care.

'Of course. Come in,' she said and led the way.

'Show me where you work,' said Thomas, as she placed the kettle on the gas ring, which stood to one side of the fireplace on a metal tripod where one day she meant to install one of the new gas cookers. 'I want to know everything about you.' The room was upstairs and at the front of the house so that she could see out over the city and hills beyond. *Why not?* she thought. It wasn't her bedroom, for she slept in the front room downstairs. Once again she led the way.

Standing by her desk, she looked down at the old typewriter she had bought second-hand from Mr Scott when it was replaced by a newer model. There was a small pile of foolscap to one side and her shorthand notebook. Nervously, she fiddled with them, setting them square to each other.

Thomas came up behind her and put his arms around her and she stiffened for a moment, then relaxed against him. Whether he felt as she did or did not, it didn't seem to matter now, he wanted her and she wanted him.

Lottie was naive and innocent – despite Alf Green – when Thomas Mitchell-Howe took her, there on the couch that stood in her workroom, and afterwards she felt a sense of fulfilment; that this was what life was all about. But most of all, she was filled with joy and happiness. Surely he must feel the same? She gazed up into his face and was convinced she saw her own feelings reflected in his eyes as he smiled down at her. It was as though the wound that Alf Green had inflicted on her was healed.

Thomas was happy too. Lottie was such a sweet, attractive little thing and he had wanted her for so long, ever since he was a schoolboy. He thought of other girls he had known: the sisters of his friends for the most part, or the servant girls who lived and worked at the university in Oxford. His friends' sisters were not averse to a little flirting but they were strictly chaperoned and certainly not for anything more. The servants were fair game so long as he was discreet. After all, they were in the university but not of it.

Earlier in the morning, Thomas had asked his mother, Eliza, how Lottie was getting along. He still had sweet memories of her from when he and she had dallied by the Wear when they were young. He had been fond of her and now he realized he still was.

'How is your old maid, Lottie getting along? I suppose she is married now with half a dozen children?' he had asked Eliza.

'Indeed no,' his mother replied, frowning slightly at his description of Lottie as 'her old maid'. 'Lottie is my friend, rather than a servant, Thomas, and she is an independent woman. She has her own house and writes a column for *The Durham Post*. And she is a fully-fledged novelist, with a book coming out later in the year, I believe.'

'Her own house?'

'Yes, she has. It is over by North End, past Wharton Park.'

'Wharton Park? Isn't that the one where the Miners' Gala is held? I remember it.'

Thomas remembered going there as a boy with his mother and stepfather, and it had been a great time with colliery bands playing and roundabouts and games for the children. Of course, the speeches from the platform had been tedious but the boys had enjoyed themselves anyway.

He folded his paper and got to his feet. 'I think I'll take a walk, Mother,' he said.

'In this rain?'

'I feel like some exercise. A walk will do me good.'

'Well, don't stay out too long and catch a cold. I have enough to do with Anne.'

Eliza watched him as he opened the front door and stepped out. Oh, he was a lovely lad, she thought proudly, as she so often did. She worried that he was bored back home here in Durham. There was no denying the place was quieter than Oxford or London, where some of his friends lived. Just at the moment he had little to do but wait to take up the position with Brownlow, Brownlow and Snape, Barristers at Law, whose chambers were in Newcastle-upon-Tyne. But that would only be a couple of months, thank goodness; he would join them in September.

Still, Thomas was a grand lad, he was indeed. There had been a time when she had thought he would rebel and insist on following his father's trade and become a carpenter. He certainly had his father's hands, square, strong and capable-looking.

That time he had run away from home and tried to join his father's family in Northumberland was still the stuff of nightmares to her. Now, though, he seemed to have forgotten his dreams of being a carpenter. He was a gentleman; a proper gentleman as his forefathers had been before gambling took hold of them.

As Eliza ran upstairs in response to a call from Anne, who was in bed with a feverish cold, she still felt that old fear at the back of her mind. Please God, she prayed, don't let Thomas get the gambling fever as his father had done. Such misery it had caused the family! But he would not, she told herself. He had as much of her in him as he had of his father. He would be careful and not be taken in by the promise of a big win, he would not.

She attended to the little girl, making her a warm drink of blackcurrant tea sweetened with honey and hushed her off to sleep afterwards, but all the time she couldn't get her anxious thoughts away from Thomas. She lay on the bed with Anne still cuddled in her arms and uncharacteristically fell asleep herself, only to be plagued by nightmares in which Thomas was inextricably intertwined with Jack, his father. They were standing on the top of a cliff and then they were both falling towards the sea below. Thomas was crying for her and she struggled to reach him before waking to find herself clutching at little Anne. It was Anne who was calling,

'Too tight, Mammy, too tight!'

Eliza soothed her and tiptoed out of the room, feeling groggy and with a headache. She was worrying about nothing, she told herself. Thomas was not a gambler, indeed he was not. He was a lawyer and as such had a brilliant future ahead of him with Brownlow, Brownlow and Snape. He would have enough to occupy his mind without gambling.

Thomas, sitting on the couch with his arm around Lottie in the little house in North End, was quiet, happy to sit there all evening, it seemed. Lottie, looking up at him, tried to guess his feelings. Did he despise her now for giving in so easily to him? He looked down at her with a depth of feeling in his eyes and smiled and she was reassured. But she was coming down to earth, aware of the world as it was. They could not stay as they were, hidden from disapproving eyes forever, and besides she had work to do. And there was Eliza. It would hurt Eliza, who had been so good to her. Even though they were such good friends, Lottie knew Eliza wanted someone better than a workhouse skivvy for her son. And that, she reminded herself, was exactly what she was.

She sat up straight, away from the feel of his arm around her shoulders, his body against hers, then got to her feet and straightened her dress.

'Where are you going?' asked Thomas. 'Come back here.' He held out his arms and smiled, his dark eyes crinkling at the corners and bewitching her. She made herself resist.

'I must work and you must go. Your mother will wonder where you are,' she said softly.

Thomas dropped his arm and sighed. It was true. They could not go against all the rules and social mores of the small town society. Reluctantly, he too stood up and started to take her in his arms again but she backed away.

'Thomas, please. You can come back tomorrow. You must get back – look, it is almost dark outside. It might be dangerous crossing the park. I've heard there are footpads there after dark.'

He laughed. 'You are worried about me? You are so sweet, Lottie. But don't worry, I will be fine, I can look after myself.' He leaned forward and kissed her with his hands behind his back, being careful not to touch her otherwise. 'I'm going. See, I'll always do as you say. I'll see you tomorrow. Don't come downstairs, I'll let myself out.'

He ran down the stairs and she could hear the sound of his footsteps fading as he went down the street towards the city.

Lottie stood where she was for a few moments, her arms crossed over her breasts, which were aching and slightly sore from his attentions. She was a wanton and abandoned woman, she thought dreamily, and she should be thoroughly ashamed of herself. But strangely, she was not. Eliza would not stand in their way, surely? Not when they truly loved each other. In any case, she was not a skivvy from the workhouse now.

She was a writer, a fully-fledged author and she was going to be famous one day soon.

Lottie attacked her work with renewed enthusiasm. She couldn't wait until all of her dreams came true.

# Seventeen

'Thomas, where have you been? I have been asking every- where for you,' Eliza said as he entered the house.

'I went for a walk. I told you I was going for a walk,' Thomas replied. He flushed slightly. Did she somehow know? No, of course, she could not. Unless some busybody had seen him go into Lottie's house and told her. He felt like a guilty schoolboy. 'Where did you think I was?' he asked, his voice sounding belligerent even to his own ears, while Eliza looked sharply at him.

'I don't know. Only . . .'

'As it happens, I met Lottie. That's a coincidence, isn't it? I mean we were just talking of her earlier on.'

'Yes. Well, there was a message for you, from Brownlow, Brownlow and Snape. They want you up there as soon as may be.'

Thoughts of Lottie were driven from Thomas's head. 'They do?'

'I said so, didn't I? They have found you rooms and you are to take the train – tonight if possible, tomorrow at the latest. I have packed you a bag.'

'How do you know? Did you open my post?' Thomas frowned. His mother seemed to think she had a perfect right to interfere in his life, he thought angrily. Everything in this house was everyone's business. Well, he was no longer a child. He had been on his own for the last few years and had grown used to being a private sort of person. Soon he would be totally independent financially: a lawyer and a celebrated one too. He had high ambitions.

'I did not,' said Eliza. 'Only there was a telegram for you. Of course I opened a telegram, it could have been bad news.' In her experience, telegrams were usually bad news and told of a death in the family or at least an accident.

'A telegram? They must want me in a hurry.'

Thomas felt a thrill of satisfaction. He was needed for the first time that he could remember and the feeling was very pleasant. 'I'll go up tomorrow. Do you know the time of the first train? Or do you think I should take the night train?'

'I found out for you. There is a train at ten thirty tonight. But I think you should wait for the morning. There is one . . .'

Thomas interrupted her. 'No, I'll take the night train. Then I can be at chambers early in the morning.' He studied the yellow wire form as though trying to wring more information from it. 'It doesn't say why they want me early, does it? I wonder about that.'

'Well, there's not much room on those forms, is there? And every word counts. It is a penny a word, you know.'

'Yes, of course I know. I am accustomed to wires. They are used often in Oxford and London for everyday communications and not just emergencies.'

'Mm,' Eliza replied, knowing she should feel suitably humbled but in fact smiling secretly to herself. All her plans for Thomas, for her little Tot, were coming to fruition. She cut sandwiches for him for the train and put in a bottle of cold tea, well sweetened. He liked that.

'You'll let me know how you are getting on?' she asked, as he came downstairs, washed and changed and looking very dashing indeed in his caped overcoat. Even though it was summer, he would need it for a night journey going north to Newcastle.

'I'll write,' he promised and pecked her on the cheek. 'Goodbye, Mother.' He picked up his bag and opened the door, then turned back. 'Give my best to my stepfather, won't you?' He paused, then went on, 'and Lottie too, if you see her.'

'Lottie?' Eliza was a little surprised, but after all, Thomas and Lottie had been friends in years gone by.

'If you see her,' Thomas repeated. 'I told you, I met her while I was out walking.' He went off down to the end of the street where he could probably pick up a cab to take him to the station. Eliza watched him from the doorstep. By, she thought, he was a grand lad, she was proud as punch of him. Not a lad, though, she reminded herself as she went in and closed the door behind her. He was a man, a gentleman. He would not disgrace his name as his father had. Still, she should not think ill of the dead. Except for the gambling, which had infected him like a fever, Jack Mitchell-Howe had not been a bad man, just his own worst enemy.

Thomas had not forgotten about Lottie altogether in his eagerness to get started properly on his new career. As he mounted the train in Durham and took his seat, he told himself he would write to her at the first opportunity. She would understand. He did consider sending her a wire so that she did not wait for him the next morning. But after all, Lottie had a simple, provincial soul and a wire would probably alarm her unnecessarily.

Lottie waited happily for Thomas to come back on the following day. She slept well and rose early. The dawn chorus from the woods was in full swing. Though more muted than earlier in the year, it was still tuneful and raised Lottie's spirits even further. She decided to begin work on her novel immediately, for she had time to make up from the day before and she did not want to fall behind. The pile of typescript by her side had grown at a respectable, steady rate when she at last sat back and stretched her arms above her head. She had a small crick in her neck and she rubbed at it with one hand and yawned hugely.

Thomas would be here soon. She would make up a picnic and afterwards they would walk in Wharton Park. She would buy crumpets from the baker down the road and they could toast them when they came home afterwards, for by that time it would be evening. Lottie shivered with anticipation. She ran downstairs and into the small kitchen. There was only a heel of bread in the pottery storage jar so she went out to the baker's, hurrying so as to be home before he came.

'Where's the fire?' a neighbour called, laughing as she ran back down the street, her basket with the fresh-baked loaf and bag of crumpets swinging. She laughed with him and waved.

Thomas was not waiting on her doorstep as she had imagined he might be. She went in and through to the kitchen and cut sandwiches and wrapped them in a clean cloth and added a bottle of dandelion and burdock and two cups, placing everything in the basket and adding a cloth to cover it all.

By twelve o'clock she was ready and waiting. She stood in the window looking out on to the street and waved to passers by, who waved at her, but there was no sign of Thomas. At one o'clock she ate a sandwich to settle her stomach. When a neighbour went by for the second time and looked curiously at her, she retreated from the window. The sun shone down on the street outside and by three o'clock a beam was finding its way into the room as it began its descent in the sky. Lottie watched the dust motes dancing in the light as the beam fell on a patch of carpet. She really ought to close the curtain a little or the carpet would fade. Then she decided to lose herself in her story.

As the bells rang out for five o'clock, Lottie picked up the few sheets she had typed, read them through, tore them in two and went over to the fire, where she put them on the fading coals and watched as they slowly charred, then burst into flames. They were rubbish. An editor would score them out with a pencil. In fact, the whole book was rubbish. No publisher would consider it.

What she needed was some fresh air to clear her mind; that was it. Lottie went downstairs and pulled an old shawl around her shoulders. She didn't bother with a hat. Bonnets were going out of fashion anyway. And those new hats, which perched over one eye, were neither use nor ornament. She was only going to the park after all – a hat was not necessary.

Half an hour later or thereabouts, Lottie found herself at the top of Eliza's street. She had not meant to call on Eliza, she told herself, it had just happened. But as she was so near . . . If someone mentioned they had seen her to her friend, Eliza would wonder why she, Lottie, had not called when she was only a few steps away. And most likely Thomas was out somewhere. If he was in, she would simply face him coolly and pretend yesterday had not happened. She was still dithering when she heard Peter's voice close behind her.

'Lottie? How nice to see you! Are you coming for your tea at our house?'

'Oh, Peter, you made me jump. I-I was just out walking and I found myself here. I was thinking of something else. No, I'm not expected . . .'

'Well, for goodness sake, there'll be enough for an extra one, I'm sure.' He held out his arm. 'Howay, then, I'm inviting you.'

'Well, what option do I have?' Lottie laughed and put her
hand on his arm and they marched down the street.

'I've brought a visitor for tea and she's fair clemmed, I'm
warning you, Eliza,' Peter called out as he banged the door
to behind them.

Eliza came through from the kitchen, wiping her hands on
her apron.

'Lottie!' she exclaimed. 'I was just thinking about you.
Come on through and we can talk while I finish off the meal.'

'I don't want to put on you,' Lottie murmured. 'If you
haven't enough I don't mind.'

'Nonsense, we can always squeeze in one more. Any road,
Thomas isn't here so we have enough and to spare.'

'Thomas isn't here?'

Eliza was leading the way into the kitchen and so didn't
see the look of disappointment on Lottie's face.

'No. He had to go to Newcastle last night. There was a
wire for him from Brownlow. That's the barrister who has
taken him on. It came yesterday morning but Thomas was out
for a walk. He didn't get in until late and so had to go practically straight out again for the night train. They needed him
to start straight away.'

Eliza laid an extra place at the kitchen table. This house
had a dining room but it was rarely in use except at Christmas.
The kitchen was the hub of the house, as it had been in her
mother's house.

Peter came in from the backyard and washed his hands
under the cold water tap. 'I'm hoping to get a slabstone sink
installed,' he told Lottie. 'With a proper drain to the outside.
They are the latest thing. The committee are considering it.'
The house was owned by the union and rented out at a conces-
sionary rate to Peter as an official. Lottie listened but the
words did not register. For a moment she thought she was
going to faint. She sat down at the table quickly and murmured
something in reply. As Eliza and Peter talked on, she sat
quietly, though her thoughts were in turmoil. She jumped when
she realized that Eliza was addressing her.

'Lottie? Are you all right?'

'Aye, yes, I am,' she said and picked up her knife and fork
and attacked the plate of Irish stew before her. Thomas hadn't
even said goodbye. Had he thought she was a loose woman

for letting him have his way with her? Maybe he had. If he hadn't time to come himself he could have sent a lad with a message or even a telegram. He would have done if she meant anything to him, she thought miserably. She chewed stolidly on a piece of meat, then swallowed and took a drink of water.

'Lovely stew,' she said. She could feel the lump stuck halfway down to her stomach. 'I didn't know Thomas was going so soon,' she went on, unable to keep off the subject of her lover.

'Oh no, he wasn't,' Eliza replied. 'No, they needed him, I told you. I don't know why. No doubt he will tell us when he writes.' She looked keenly at Lottie's flushed face and remembered her old fears that there might be an attachment between her son and the girl. But no, how could there be? They had been practically children the last time they spent any time together.

'Thomas said he met you yesterday,' she remarked casually.

'Yes. In Wharton Park it was. I had been working all morning and I was out for some fresh air.' Lottie bent her head and ate a forkful of carrot. That went down easier.

Little more was said. When the meal was over Lottie helped Eliza with the dishes. Peter had to get back to the office for a meeting and Eliza was busy seeing to little Anne's bedtime.

'I must get back, I don't want to be caught in the dark,' said Lottie. 'Thank you for the meal, it was grand.'

Eliza watched her walk rapidly up the street, a small figure with her shawl over her head, for an evening breeze was blowing from the north-east. Then she went in and closed the door.

It was just as well Thomas was working away in Newcastle, she told herself, for she was beginning to realize that Lottie did have feelings for him. It was not, she told herself, that she thought her friend was not good enough for her son. But he had his way to make in his profession, hadn't he? Perhaps in a few years' time when both Lottie and Thomas were established and she could say, 'my daughter-in-law, the authoress', or 'my son, the barrister'. But many things could change in a year or two. He might meet someone else, for instance.

Lottie went back to her little house, where it was not until she was safely behind the closed door that she felt able to relax. She sat down in the tiny kitchen without bothering to light the lamp, for there was a little light coming in through the window from the moonlight. It was cold, for the fire had died away to grey ash, but she didn't feel it. She had shed a few tears behind her shawl on her long walk back but now she merely felt numb. After a while, she went into the front room, which she had made her bedroom, preferring to use the upstairs room as a workroom, and poured water from the jug into the basin on her washstand and splashed it on her face and arms. Then she went to bed.

She had to forget Thomas, she told herself. What would he want with a brat from the workhouse? He would marry a posh girl from Newcastle with a family and dowry and good-looking an' all. From now on she would throw herself into her work. Lottie expected that she would have a sleepless night, but she was worn out with the emotions of the last two days and she fell deeply asleep.

Thomas was thinking fondly of Lottie as the night train clanked its way slowly up the line to Newcastle. It stopped at all the little stations in between and seemed to him to take an interminable time to get to the point where it crossed Stephenson's railway bridge over the Tyne and puffed to a halt in Newcastle Central Station.

He was fond of her, oh yes he was. But did he love her? He wasn't sure. She was a sweet little thing and clever too, the way she had educated herself against all odds, and she had talent: hadn't she had a book accepted for publishing? That was an achievement, was it not?

He would write to her soon, he thought as he climbed down from the train and walked along the platform and out of the imposing stone entrance designed by John Dobson, as most of this area of Newcastle was. First though, he had to find his lodgings, and tidy himself up ready to present himself at the chambers of Brownlow, Brownlow and Snape as soon as he could manage it.

As it happened, Thomas was caught up in the excitement and novelty of his work in the big city. He had been a pupil in chambers in London and so was familiar with the work, but somehow everything was slightly different in this northern place. He also found himself invited to the homes of his colleagues – the elder ones that is – and to social events with the younger ones. Yet he intended to write to her, he thought one evening, as he struggled with his bow tie before the mirror in his rooms. Except that tomorrow he had been invited to the races by Robert Pyle, a pupil in chambers. So the letter would have to wait.

# Eighteen

Lottie walked along to the pillar box at the end of her road and stood before it for a moment, looking down at the card she had written to Eliza and Peter. In it, she apologized for not going to see them for a few weeks.

'I've been so busy,' she had written. 'What with my column for *The Post* and my novel, which I hope to have finished by November, when *The Clouds Stood Still* is published. Still, I hope to come to see you next weekend, if that is all right by you.'

She had considered asking after Thomas but somehow couldn't think of the right words. Any way, Thomas would have got in touch with her if he were at all interested. That day had been a lie; he had simply wanted her. She was just another lass who had been taken down by a lad – didn't it happen all the time? Lottie slipped the postcard into the pillar box and turned to walk home. As she walked, the tune of an old song ran through her head, over and over; she couldn't get rid of it.

*Oh, don't deceive me, oh, never leave me,*
*How could you use a poor maiden so?*

Well, she would not go begging to Thomas, she would not indeed. Lottie lifted her head, marched up to her door and let herself in, and soon she was hard at work at her desk. She did not need a man. Hadn't she managed without one up until now? Let ignorant people look on her as a poor spinster unable to get a man. She thought of the loathsome Alf Green, who had taken her down when she was nobbut a little lass. No one else was going to get the chance.

As the days went by, Lottie did succeed in putting Thomas Mitchell-Howe out of her mind. She was immersed in her work. She rose early in the morning and wrote for two hours before breakfast; then, after a rushed cup of tea and a slice of toast, went on until mid-afternoon. The pile of typescript grew into a respectable heap on her desk. She tended to work straight on to the typewriter, doing only a few notes by hand first, for her training at *The Durham Post* had stood her in good stead.

She was working steadily away at about ten o'clock one morning when she was interrupted by a knocking at the street door. Pausing for a moment, she cocked her head. No one knocked on her door, since she had made it plain to her neighbours that she hated to be disturbed. Lottie had started typing again before the knock was repeated. Annoyed, she made her way downstairs and unlocked the door, and there on the doorstep stood Eliza.

'Good morning, Lottie,' Eliza said pleasantly. 'Can I come in?'

Without waiting for a reply, she stepped over the threshold, past Lottie and directly into the kitchen-cum-living room.

'Of course you can,' murmured Lottie. She glanced out into the street before closing the door. Dolly, the old pony who pulled Eliza's trap as she visited her patients, was chewing contentedly on the contents of a nosebag. Eliza was intending to stay a while then.

'It's nice to see you, Eliza,' said Lottie, as she followed her friend into the kitchen. 'I'll put the kettle on, we'll have a cup of tea.'

'Only if you have the time,' Eliza replied. 'I know you must be busy. It's such a long time since you came to see me.'

Lottie blushed. 'I'm sorry,' she said. 'I know it's true. But I have been busy.'

'Too busy for your old friends, eh?'

'I was planning to come this next weekend,' Lottie murmured. She made up the fire and settled the kettle on top of it, then got out cups and saucers.

'You don't look very well, Lottie. Is something the matter?' Eliza gazed at the younger girl. Lottie was pale, and behind her spectacles her eyes were dull and there were dark rings around them. 'Your eyes look sore,' she went on. 'You must be straining them, Lottie. You should be careful. You know your eyes are weak.'

'No, I'm fine, really,' Lottie protested. 'Maybe I've just sat too long at the typewriter, that's all.'

'No you're not,' Eliza declared. 'Are your menses all right?'

'I-I don't know . . .' Lottie faltered. She had not even thought about her monthly periods. Maybe they were late, now that she did, but she had often been irregular.

'I bet you're not eating properly,' said Eliza. 'Don't be daft, Lottie, you cannot neglect yourself like this. Sit down and have your tea. I've brought some of my own gingerbread, that'll do you good. You're thin as a lathe, lass.'

Lottie obediently drank her tea and ate a piece of Yorkshire parkin. 'How is the family?' she asked. 'Peter and little Anne?' She paused before adding, 'Have you heard from Thomas? How is he getting on?'

'Oh, I don't hear much from him, he's so busy, you know. Just like you, when I think of it.' Eliza favoured Lottie with a direct stare. 'You have to make time for your friends, Lottie. Otherwise you'll find yourself without any.'

Suddenly Lottie felt sick. Mumbling something, she fled out into the yard and vomited into the drain that ran down the centre. Panting, she slowly stood up straight and wiped her mouth with her handkerchief.

'Now then, Lottie, howay in and sit yourself down. I think you have some explaining to do.'

Eliza was standing in the doorway. Lottie hesitated for a moment and then walked towards her, feeling a bit dizzy.

'I must have eaten something that disagreed with me,' she said.

'I don't think so, Lottie my girl,' Eliza replied.

They went into the kitchen and Lottie sank down on a chair. Her friend followed and sat down opposite her.

'Who was it?' Eliza asked. 'By, there's always some swine willing to take a lass down, there is an' all.'

'I don't know what you mean,' said Lottie.

'Come on, you're not the young lass brought to me by Bertha all those years ago. You know very well what I mean. How long since you had a period?'

Lottie stared at Eliza as she realized what her friend was implying. She had been completely gormless if it was true. How long was it since her last monthly? She counted up in her head, making a mistake and starting again. Eliza watched her as the knowledge dawned on her that it was more than a month, more than two months. The remaining colour left her face.

'I'm never regular,' she faltered.

'How long?'

'Ten weeks, I think.'

It had been a couple of weeks before Thomas. Thinking of it, Lottie felt a different kind of sickness. She stared at the floor, avoiding Eliza's gaze.

'Now then, Lottie, tell me who it was. He'll have to wed you, whoever it is. Do you love him? If you do and he loves you, then you can get wed as soon as maybe. Mind, I didn't know you were courting even, is that why you haven't been to see us much?

'We cannot get wed. I'll bring the baby up on my own.'

'On your own? Nay pet, you cannot make a bastard of it, you cannot. It's not the bairn's fault. No, he'll have to face up to it, whoever he is. You can get wed and make the best of it. Or . . . He's not married already is he? Don't say that, please!'

Lottie shook her head. 'He's not married. Only he doesn't live here any more.'

'Well, we must find him. Now, do you know where he is?'

'I don't know.'

Eliza was running out of patience. She rose to her feet and adjusted her nurse's bonnet. 'Now look here, Charlotte Lonsdale. I'm telling you now, you'll have to find him. He's been where he shouldn't have been and he'll have to pay the consequences. Is he chapel? If he is, the minister will make him do what's right.' She pulled on her gloves and fastened the buttons at the wrists. Eliza was angry. Angry with Lottie for getting herself into this situation and angry at her apparent stubbornness.

'I have to go now, I still have half my rounds to do, but I want you to come home with me tonight while we thrash this out. It's all right, Peter is away at a meeting, something about the National Union of Mineworkers. We'll have the house to ourselves after little Anne is in bed. Now, be ready. I'll be back for you about six o'clock.'

'I have to work,' said Lottie.

'Be ready.'

After Eliza had gone – sweeping out of the door, removing Dolly's nosebag and climbing into the trap, then clicking her tongue at the Galloway and sending her trotting off along the street and all in a minute or two – Lottie sat down again, her mind in a whirl.

'I am expecting a bairn,' she said aloud but she found it hard to believe. What would she do? She panicked for a moment but then, as her chaotic thoughts quietened, she began to make plans. She was luckier than most in that she had a profession now and it was work she could carry on with, even with a baby to look after. Surely Jeremiah wouldn't turn her off because of her disgrace, would he? And if her books, the one going into print at this very moment and the one she was writing, made any money, she would manage a lot better than some poor lasses, turned off by their employers for their sins.

It was all 'ifs' though. What if her books flopped, and Jeremiah did refuse to take any more 'Home Notes' from her? In some agitation, Lottie got to her feet and began tidying the place: scrubbing the kitchen table, black-leading the range and polishing the brass fender and handles of the fire irons.

That took all of half an hour, for they had already been cleaned the day before. Changing tack, she washed and changed into her best dress and pretty jacket, which was fitted at the waist and flared out slightly over a small bustle at the back. She tidied her hair and put on a little hat with flowers on the brim and which tilted over one eye. Then she picked up her reticule, checked that she had clean handkerchiefs and her purse with enough money for a train to Newcastle and left the house.

'Lottie! How lovely to see you. What are you doing in the big city? But come in, come in do,' said Thomas. He happened to be in the ornate entrance hall of Brownlow, Brownlow and Snape, in Potter's Yard, a small close where most of the old houses were taken up with law firms' chambers. He was wearing a black suit with a frock coat and a shirt with a high collar and necktie, which made him look very important and came up to the base of his ears. He was carrying a sheaf of important-looking papers under his arm. Oh yes, thought Lottie, important was the word for him, and she was intimidated slightly. Nevertheless, she walked into the hall and smiled bravely up at him.

'I came to see you,' she said and he smiled.

'Come into my room. I will order tea.'

The room he led her into was not large, but the window

was tall and swathed in red velvet. Outside, the light was beginning to fade, for it was six o'clock in the evening and the end of September. The train from Durham was faster than it had used to be but still took almost two hours. She had found the chambers by the simple expedient of taking a cab.

All the way up from Durham, Lottie had been rehearsing in her mind what she was going to say to him. She would wait until there was no one else there, she had thought, picturing it in her mind. She would not embarrass him before his workmates, no she would not. Colleagues, not workmates, she reminded herself. She would put the situation to him calmly and reasonably. She pictured him sitting at a high wooden desk such as that used by Bob Cratchett in *A Christmas Carol*. A desk in a room with grimy windows letting in little light. Well, the windows let in little light but that was because there was little to let in, it being evening. But there was a good oil lamp on the desk and an opulent leather sofa by the wall.

'You're lucky to catch me here, everyone else has gone home,' said Thomas. 'I'm so pleased to see you, Lottie, come and sit down and I'll order tea. Do you know, I was thinking of writing to you tonight to explain why I had to leave so suddenly.'

'I'm expecting a babby,' said Lottie. She hadn't meant it to come out like that, it just did. Thomas halted with his hand half-lifted to pull the bell. Lottie, fearing her legs might give way at any moment, sank into the soft velvet cushions of the sofa.

'What did you say?'

'A babby, a bairn. I've fallen wrong.'

'Who was it, Lottie? I'll find him and make him marry you, I swear I will!'

Lottie shrank inside. How could he ask her who was the father? The look on her face gave him pause.

'Is it mine? It cannot be, we were only together the once!' Thomas stared at her in disbelief.

'It only takes the once,' said Lottie, as though explaining to a child.

'Yes. Only – does my mother know? Did she say you had to tell me?'

'She doesn't know. Well, she knows I'm expecting but she doesn't know about you.'

Thomas suddenly no longer felt like an up-and-coming

lawyer in the big city showing off to a pretty girl. His mam would kill him, and his stepfather wouldn't be very happy either. They were a chapel family and they would expect him to do what was right by a lass in Lottie's situation. The veneer he had acquired in his posh school and university was melting away. He was a lad from Durham; the mining communities of Durham at that.

'I'm not a whore,' said Lottie. She was beginning to get angry; he had been silent too long. She rose to her feet and walked to the door. 'I'll find a place to stay the night and catch the train home come the morn. I just thought you should know, it was only right. But don't you worry about me, I'm not destitute. I can look after myself and a bairn.'

She swept out of the room, her head held high, though her spectacles were becoming misty so that she could hardly see. Thomas stared after her, before jumping into action and hurrying after her.

'Lottie! Lottie! Come on back here, I didn't mean . . .'

Lottie walked on around the corner into Northumberland Street. She had no idea where to find lodgings, but she could always go back to the station and there would be a train home eventually. Thomas caught up with her and grabbed her upper arm.

'Lottie, I didn't mean anything; it was just a shock, that's all. Come on, I'll stand by you, I will, I promise.'

Lottie stopped walking and turned to him. She took off her glasses and peered up into his face under the light of a street lamp. His eyes looked practically navy blue, she thought distractedly.

'Well?'

Thomas swallowed hard, his mind racing. 'Come back to my lodging,' he said, then seeing her expression, 'No, I don't mean my rooms. The landlady will look after you, give you a room for the night. She is a friend of mine. Come on, Lottie. You cannot be wandering about Newcastle at this time of night. We can talk about this, what we are going to do.'

What we are going to do, thought Lottie. Was he going to marry her? Did she want him to marry her? If she was honest, she did.

# Nineteen

Thomas hired a chase and they travelled to Gretna Green to be married.

'This is a dream,' she whispered to herself. 'It isn't happening. I'll wake up in a minute.' Only it was happening and it was no dream. But how had it happened?' She sat up in bed on the morning after her marriage (a hurried affair conducted by a Presbyterian minister who had just finished marrying a couple from Kent and had two other couples waiting after Lottie and Thomas). She gazed at the thin gold band on the third finger of her left hand, bought at the shop next door to the church, for they had decided against a wedding over the anvil at the blacksmith's shop.

'We are Christians after all,' Thomas had said.

She looked down at his head on the pillow next to hers. He was still fast asleep after his exertions of the night before. His hair was dark against the white of the pillowslip and dark lashes fanned his cheek. Oh, he was a bonnie lad, even with his deep, blue eyes closed, he was an' all. He was her husband though, and she had planned that she would not get wed until she had made a name for herself as an author. She would not be dependent on a man, she had always told herself, and here she was caught in the same silly trap that caught all silly young lasses.

Carefully, Lottie turned back the bedclothes and got out of bed. It was a fairly small room and the bed was but a step away from the window. She stood looking out on a yard not dissimilar to the backyards in a colliery village or even her own in Durham. It had been hard getting a room at all; Gretna Green was full of people, mostly young couples. The sky was overcast and rain splattered the windowpanes.

Lottie shivered. Maybe she had done the wrong thing, after all. She could have gone away from Durham, had the baby on her own. Writing was a craft that could be followed anywhere. She could have pretended to be a widow. That might have worked decades ago, but now that all births had to be registered by law her baby would be branded a bastard.

Lottie put a hand over her belly; she had to protect her baby. She knew that in her mind, though not yet in her emotions. Apart from the physical symptoms, she would not be aware that there was anything different. Should she feel different? The questions ran endlessly though her thoughts. Behind her, Thomas turned over in bed.

Why had he married her, any road? He was way above her station now, a professional man. He did not need a lass from the workhouse dragging him down.

He had risen without her noticing and her doubts melted away as she felt his arms go around her waist as he pulled her body against his, and it was warm and exciting against hers.

'Come on back to bed,' he said in her ear and nibbled at the ear lobe.

She forgot everything but him.

'Please don't be angry with us,' wrote Lottie in the note she had sent to Eliza just before leaving Newcastle. 'We love each other; I think we always have done.'

They stayed in Scotland for one night only, a Saturday, and travelled home to Durham on the train. After all, Thomas had to attend court on Monday morning. And Brownlow, Brownlow and Snape knew nothing of his sudden entry into matrimony. The journey took hours and they had to change at Carlisle and Newcastle but Lottie didn't care. She was only sorry when at last they alighted on to the platform at Durham. The time had come to face Eliza. Would she still be her friend as well as her mother-in-law?

'A fine way to go on,' said an unsmiling Eliza in greeting. 'It's a scandal all right. I'm disappointed in you both.'

Nevertheless, she came forward to meet them as they entered the house and kissed Lottie on the cheek, before turning to Thomas.

'You should have told us, you really should have,' she said, looking hurt.

'Did you think I would stop you?' She paused and gazed at them both. 'You are truly wed, aren't you?'

'We are. I'm sorry, Mam,' he replied, his cheeks reddening like those of a schoolboy caught in some minor misdemeanour. 'I mean for doing it this way.'

'Aye well, it's not the first time you've run off, is it?' Eliza said tartly, but her expression was softening.

Lottie realized she was referring to the time when he was ten years old and had run off to his father's family in Alnwick. She relaxed a little; it was going to be all right. Though Eliza had not yet spoken to her directly.

It was not until Thomas had returned to Newcastle on the eight o'clock train that the two women talked. Thomas had wanted to see Lottie safely home in North End first, but there was simply not enough time.

'Lottie will sleep here, she can go home tomorrow,' Eliza decreed.

'Will you be all right?' Thomas asked, as he kissed Lottie goodbye.

It was as if getting wed was already eating away at her independence, she thought, but still, she nodded. 'Why wouldn't I be?' she replied.

'I'll come back for you at the weekend.'

She watched the cab disappear into the distance before coming back into the house and facing Eliza.

'Now, lady, you kept very quiet about this,' said Eliza as Lottie returned to the kitchen. 'How far are you gone?'

'I don't know, mebbe eight weeks?'

'It's eight weeks since Thomas went to Newcastle.'

'I know. We only did it the once, Eliza.'

Eliza looked sceptical. 'Dr Gray always said it didn't happen the first time.'

'Eliza, I'm telling the truth. Thomas is the only man I've been with and that nobbut the once!' The image of Alf Green rose to plague her. She lowered her gaze.

Eliza gazed hard at Lottie then sighed. The younger woman's face was white and strained as she insisted on her truthfulness.

'Aye well, what's done cannot be undone. Sit down and we'll have a cup of cocoa before we go to bed. By, but I didn't want my Tot to be saddled with a wife and bairn so early in his career.'

'I can keep myself and the baby,' Lottie declared, showing some spirit.

'Don't be soft! An' make my lad something less than a man?' Eliza retorted.

They sank into silence. Lottie drank her cocoa as quickly as she could though it was piping hot, before going up to the little room that had been Thomas's and preparing for bed. She drew the curtains back before climbing into bed and lying on her back, staring out at the scudding clouds above the city.

'Are you asleep?

Lottie looked back at the doorway where Eliza stood, a candlestick in her hand, the candle flickering and casting eerie shadows on the ceiling. She walked in and stood beside the bed.

'I'm sorry if I was harsh, Lottie,' she said in a low tone. 'I was disappointed, that was it. We'll say no more about it, eh?' She leaned down and kissed Lottie on the cheek. 'I know what it is to love a man.' After all, she mused as she went to her own room, better a daughter-in-law she knew and liked than some la-di-da society madam from Newcastle.

'You're married? Well! I am surprised,' said Jeremiah when she went into the offices of *The Durham Post* the next morning. He came around the desk and kissed Lottie on the cheek, dislodging her spectacles as he did so. 'I hope you will be very happy, my dear. Though I suppose this means I will have to find someone else to write "Home Notes".'

Lottie settled the spectacles back in their usual position on her nose. 'No,' she said, 'I will still be able to write them and send them to you, won't I?'

'How can you write on the fashions in Durham shops when you are in Newcastle? And your husband, a lawyer did you say? He will not like you working, my dear.'

'Thomas will not stop me writing.' Lottie looked down at her feet so that she did not betray the feeling of panic she felt at the idea. Jeremiah, however, was well aware of how she felt.

'Perhaps not,' he said gently.

'I can write about fashion as it is in Newcastle,' said Lottie. 'Some of the shops in Northumberland Street are very smart, almost as smart as London.' Though she had never been to London of course; she had read about it in *The Lady's Journal*.

'Well, we'll see how you get on.' Jeremiah smiled at the small figure before him. He remembered the first time she had come to his office, excited at having her short story printed in his paper. Oh, she had a talent this girl, she had indeed. She would become a household name if only she did not get bogged down with her marriage and children.

'Send me articles by all means,' he said. 'And remember, I am negotiating with your publisher to print excerpts from *The Clouds Stood Still.*'

Lottie said her goodbyes to George, the reporter, and Edward, the photographer and illustrator, and left the office with some regret. It had been a happy place for her, where she had been successful in beginning to realize her dream. She walked back to her little house in North End, where she intended to make a list of things she had to do before Thomas came at the weekend to take her back to Newcastle.

'*Post!*' The newsboy called raucously from the corner of the street. '*Durham Post!*'

Lottie looked up from her desk, where she was working at her novel. She had packed most of the things she was taking to Newcastle, but for the typewriter and a few sheets of foolscap, and now at last she was free to write for a few short hours before Thomas came for her. Jumping up, she hurried out to catch the boy before he went on to the next street. She liked to check her 'Home Notes' as soon as they came out, though by then of course it was too late to do anything about an error. Not that there were any errors, she thought as she held out her penny to the boy and took a copy from him.

Back in the house, she made tea and sat down at the kitchen table to read as she sipped. This afternoon, a man was coming to clear the house of furniture. First of all, she read her article, then turned to the page of local news.

### MURDER IN Durham City

A woman's body had been washed up on the banks of the river just below Prebends Bridge. *Poor soul*, thought Lottie, and read on.

The young woman, who was well advanced in pregnancy though she wore no wedding ring, was at first thought to have thrown herself off the bridge, but upon examination was found to have a stab wound to the heart. She has been identified as Elizabeth Bates, a servant at the house of Alfred Green in Sherburn Hill.

Mr Green is missing and the police would like to know his whereabouts. His son, Matthew, a hewer at Sherburn Hill Colliery, says he has not seen his father since he went on shift the night before last.

Lottie read it through three times, feeling as though she must have missed something. Hadn't Mattie gone to Australia? He must have come back. But that wasn't what filled her mind and shook her to the core. Guilt did that.

She had neglected Betty in the last few years. She should have gone to see the girl and made sure she was all right, indeed she should have done. Only, she hated to go back to that house where she had been so miserable. The house where Alf Green lived had such bad memories for her. Betty had been so adamant though that Alf was going to look after her; they were going to get wed. Only they had not and Lottie had always suspected they would not.

'I should have kept in touch,' she said aloud. Poor Betty, poor, poor Betty. She had had no life, no life at all. Sadly, Lottie folded the paper and laid it on the kitchen table. She was restless now, she could not settle to anything. She would like to go and see Mattie, to see how he was and find out what had happened to Betty's first baby. Maybe she would do that. There were hours to go before Thomas would come for her.

Impulsively, she got to her feet and pinned her hat to her head and put on her jacket. She would take the omnibus to Sherburn Hill, she thought. It would be take an hour or two to go there and back. She had seen the old hacks that pulled the omnibuses along the roads to the mining villages around the city, but she had the time.

It was mid-afternoon by the time she stood and knocked at the front door of the house where she had gone as a maid of all work when she was barely thirteen years old. She looked to the side where the window was close-curtained. Perhaps Mattie wasn't in, she thought.

'Now then, young woman, what do you want?'

The voice close to her ear made her jump and turn to stare. It was a policeman, a sergeant. She might have known they would be guarding the house.

'I . . . I used to work here, I read about the tragedy . . . ' she stammered. 'I wanted to see Matthew. He is a friend.'

'A friend is he? I don't know if he wants to see anyone. Who are you, Miss? I'll ask if he wants to see you. Wait here.'

'Lottie Lonsdale. I used to work here before Betty came.'

'You did? My sergeant may want a word with you.'

People passing by and those simply there from curiosity were gathering and he took Lottie's arm. 'Come with me around the back,' he said. 'Away from prying folk.'

Mattie was in the kitchen smoking a clay pipe by the fire. At first she thought it was his older brother, Noah, he seemed so grown up. But of course he would be, she told herself. How many years since she had seen him that day in Claypath? He, however, knew her immediately. He rose to his feet and took a step towards her.

'Lottie! You've come then. You heard about Betty?'

'I did, Mattie. I had to come.'

'I'm on my own now,' he said after the policeman went out in search of his sergeant and they sat down together. 'Poor Betty. She had a bad time of it, you know. Just a slip of a lass an' all.'

Mattie had been sitting there brooding for most of the night before and the morning. He was very agitated: lighting his pipe and putting it out again almost immediately, standing up and walking to the window then coming back and sitting down again. His eyes were red-rimmed and there were still flecks of coal dust in the lashes as though he had not washed properly after coming off shift. The fingers of one hand tapped out a silent tune on his knee, endlessly.

'Where are your brothers?'

'Long gone. Noah went to Australia, Freddie emigrated to Canada. I went to Australia but I came back. I couldn't help but think of Betty here with me da. Poor lass,' he said again. 'He was a sod, you know, Lottie. He didn't marry her neither, not when the first bairn died.'

'It died?'

'Stillborn. Then when she fell wrong again . . . Why did you not come to see us, Lottie?' He did not wait for an answer. 'She talked about you a lot, you know. I came looking for you again. It was when you had a story in *The Post*. I spoke to someone in the office but he said you didn't work there any more and anyway it wasn't policy to give out the addresses of their employees. An older man it was, talked like he had a mouthful of marbles.'

'By, Mattie, I'm sorry. I am, that sorry.'

'Aye,' said Mattie and lit his pipe for the fourth time. His hand holding the taper, which he lit from the flames in the grate, shook.

'I was always going to.'

It sounded lame even to her own ears. Why hadn't she? Because she was so caught up in the excitement of her new life? Because the time went by so fast until it felt as though it was too late? Shame washed over her once more.

'Lottie Lonsdale?'

The question came from a police sergeant, who stepped over the threshold of the open back door, removing his helmet at the same time.

'Charlotte Mitchell-Howe, actually,' Lottie replied. 'I'm sorry, I was just married a week ago. Sorry.' She had to force herself not to go on apologizing.

The sergeant, whose head almost reached the low ceiling of the kitchen, wrote something in his notebook. 'I would like to ask you some questions about your time here,' he said, before looking at Mattie. 'We will go into the front room if that's all right by you.'

Mattie nodded. 'Go on, Lottie,' he said.

Lottie rose meekly to her feet and followed the policeman into the front room; the room where, as a little maid straight from the workhouse, she had looked after Laura Green though her last illness. Her heart beat wildly as she walked down the short, narrow passage and went in.

# Twenty

'Where were you?' Thomas demanded.

She had seen him waiting for her as she turned the corner into the street. It was almost dark; the lamplighter had already been around to light the streetlights.

'I had to go to Sherburn after what happened,' Lottie replied. She was out of breath, for she had run almost all the way from the bus stop. She looked up at him as he stood in the doorway of her house in North End, hands on hips, legs astride, frowning and angry-looking.

'After what happened? What could happen that could be so important, more important than being here to meet me?'

'Let's go inside, Thomas, there's no need to talk out here on the street. It's cutting in cool now, there's a mist rising off the river.' Lottie shivered, as much from his anger as from the cold.

Thomas turned and stalked into the house and she followed. 'Now then,' he said, 'I'm waiting.'

'Yes,' Lottie replied. She looked at the cold grate, for of course the fire had been dead for hours. She could have done with a warm drink of tea, she thought, before turning back to Thomas.

'It was Betty, Betty Bates,' she said. 'I had to go to see Mattie.' She handed him the paper with the news item in it. 'Betty was my friend,' she went on and told him the full story. She was tired and sat down on a chair, propping her elbow on the table and resting her head on her hand. She found it a great effort to go over the story for him but she was sure he would understand. He did not.

'So, you went traipsing about even though you are with child,' said Thomas, and it was the only comment he made on the sad story.

'But Betty was my friend!' she protested. 'And Mattie too . . .'

'How were you helping Betty? Or Mattie either? The only man you should be thinking of is your husband! Or had you forgotten I was coming this afternoon?'

Lottie was stung into a hot reply. 'Of course not, I just couldn't get home any earlier! The police wanted to talk to me.'

'The police? What could you possibly know about what happened?' Thomas was standing over her, still very angry.

Lottie sighed. She didn't want to talk about it any more, especially when he was so unsympathetic. She had had a long day and she was still very emotional when she thought of poor Betty. The last time she had seen her, Betty had been so hopeful for the future even though Lottie had tried to persuade her that Alf Green was no good, that he would let her down. She should have tried harder, she knew that. The guilt rose again in her as she remembered how she had let Betty down, had not even visited her because of her contempt for and dislike of Alf.

She had relived her own time in the house in Sherburn to the police, telling all of it. Now she was older she could do that when she never could have before.

'Why did you not report the man at the time?' the sergeant had asked. 'It was against the law. You were underage and no doubt Betty Bates was too.'

The question was not really serious though, how could it have been? Everyone, even the police, would think the girl had led the man on.

'I did not think I would be believed. I'm sure Betty would think the same at first. Then when she was expecting her first baby, he promised to marry her. She believed him.'

'The baby she was carrying was not the first?'

'No. The first baby died.'

The policeman pursed his lips and wrote something down in his notebook. He had a look of distaste on his face, which he didn't bother to hide.

*What did he know of the wretched lives of workhouse foundlings*, she thought, *girls like Betty?*

'It's Alf Green you should be questioning. Have you found him? He's a murderer,' she said bitterly. 'What can a young girl do if she is sent to work in the house of a monster like him?'

The policeman gave her a level stare. 'You got out,' he said.

He closed his notebook and put it in his breast pocket, then stood up. 'That's all, Missus,' he went on and walked to the door, before turning back to her. 'We'll find him, Alf Green, and he'll be tried for murder at the assizes.'

'Lottie? Are you listening to me?'

She started, for of course she had not been listening at all; her mind had been going over the events of the afternoon.

'I'm sorry, I'm just tired.'

She was too, she realized; she was bone weary. 'What were you saying? Oh yes, the police. Well, I did work there for a while. They were asking me about Alf Green, how he treated me then.'

Thomas was horrified. 'Good God!' he cried. 'I certainly hope your involvement is not reported in the press. After all, in my position . . .'

'Your position! How can you think of that when there is a poor lass murdered?'

Thomas stared at her. 'My position is what is important to me,' he said coldly. 'I think the sooner we are away from here the better. We will return to Newcastle tonight. I am your husband and you will do as I say. Do you hear me, Lottie?'

Lottie paused for a moment before replying. This was not the boy she had used to know, she thought. Oh, his education had changed him all right. No doubt she was lucky he had condescended to marry her and she should be grateful for it.

Only she was beginning to realize what it meant to lose her independence.

'I hear you, I'm not deaf,' she replied. 'I'm ready to go.'

Thomas picked up her bags and followed her out of the door and waited as she gave the key to her neighbour. The house clearance man who was also the landlord was coming tomorrow and then the little house where she had been happy would be no longer hers. She did not look back; she couldn't bear to.

The first few weeks of her new life were busy and she had little time for her writing. Sometimes she found herself going over a plotline and working it out in her head, but she did little actual writing apart from her short articles for *The Durham Post*.

Thomas did not approve anyway.

'There is something here for you,' he said one morning as they sat over breakfast.

'Oh?'

'It's from that editor chap, the one you used to work for.'

'Jeremiah,' said Lottie. She felt a bit queasy as she watched Thomas load his fork with bacon and dip it into his egg yolk. The yolk was slightly underdone, as he liked it that way, and drops of brilliant yellow fell from the fork to the plate. She couldn't look away from it until he at last put it into his mouth. The room seemed to be dipping and swelling, dipping and swelling. She closed her eyes for a moment and when she opened them her vision was restored to normal but her nausea was rising.

'Shall I open it?'

'Em . . .' Lottie got to her feet and rushed out of the room to be sick in the newfangled water closet down the hall. She flushed it and wiped her mouth with the flannel.

Back at the dining table, Thomas had taken her permission for granted and opened the letter and taken out a cheque for one guinea. He was frowning.

'You don't need to do this,' he said, then belatedly asked if she was all right.

'I'm fine. I don't need to do what?'

'Be a newspaper hack any more. You are my wife. In any case, I think that man is altogether too familiar when he writes to you.'

'Familiar?' Lottie echoed.

'You know what I mean,' snapped Thomas, becoming angry. 'And I don't think it reflects well on me that people know you are doing this work. I can afford to keep my wife.'

'I like to do it.'

'Well, you will write and tell him you won't be doing it any more,' said Thomas with an air of finality. He blotted his lips with his napkin and got to his feet. 'I expect you to do that today,' he said. 'Now I have to go. I'm in court this morning.'

Rebellion seethed in Lottie's breast but she knew she had no choice. She called Janey, the girl Thomas had insisted on employing in the house, through to clear the breakfast things, then went upstairs and sat down at her dressing table. She opened a drawer and took out her writing case and began to write a letter to Jeremiah, telling him that owing to circumstances she would not be sending him any more articles. She read it through, and biting her lip, added 'for the time being' and signed her name.

Well, she would get on with her novel. Though it was a little cramped sitting at the dressing table working, but Thomas would not allow her near his desk or to have one of her own. Regretfully, she thought of her desk in Durham. She pictured it in her mind as it stood before the window overlooking the old city: the woods and the distant gleam of the river and the castle and cathedral seeming to be almost in the sky rather than on the ground.

Suddenly Lottie picked up her notebook and pencil and jumped to her feet. She ran down the stairs and into Thomas's study. His desk was a grand affair and stood before the window looking out on to the garden. The summer flowers were dead now but there were a few October daisies still showing purple against the hedge. It was not the view of Durham she loved but it was better than looking at herself in the looking-glass on her dressing table. What Thomas didn't know couldn't hurt him.

It was almost eleven when Janey knocked on the door and entered the room. Lottie was scribbling away in her notebook, developing a plotline she had thought of a couple of weeks before. She was completely lost in her story and Janey had to speak twice before she heard.

'Ma'am? Mrs Mitchell-Howe?'

It penetrated Lottie's thoughts at last. 'Yes? What is it, Janey?'

'There is a caller, Ma'am, Mrs Snape. Will I show her into the sitting room, Missus?' Janey had been told the correct forms of address when speaking to her employers by Thomas, but had regular lapses. Lottie thought of the time when she was a maid of all work in his mother's house. They had been friends, they still were.

What would Eliza make of Thomas's pretensions now? Lottie had a sudden wish to see her friend and talk things over with her.

'Do that please, Janey,' she said. 'And bring in a tea tray and a plate of those ginger biscuits I made yesterday.'

'Aye, I will,' said the girl, then corrected herself. 'Yes, Ma'am.'

Lottie smoothed her hair with her hands, then gave them a rueful look. It would take too long to get the ink stains off her fingers or to change her dress. Well, she would have to do. Leaving her work on Thomas's desk, she went through to her sitting room.

'Mrs Snape, how nice of you to call,' she said, as she held out her hand to her visitor. Mrs Snape was a large woman held in by a formidable corset. The resulting bulge over the top of the corset strained at the black silk bombazine of her dress. The hat sitting at an improbable angle on her glossy, black ringlets had a small bird perched on the brim as though preparing to fly the nest. Lottie tried not to stare at it but it drew her eyes.

'Please, do sit down,' she said and they sat down on the plumply cushioned chairs. Janey brought in the tea and Lottie poured it out, all the time conscious that Mrs Snape was looking at her hands with their black ink stains and from them to a lock of her hair that had fallen down over her forehead and over her spectacles. She felt awkward and then as she handed the tea to her guest the cup rattled in the saucer, spilling a drop or two.

'I'm sorry,' she said. 'I'll get you another cup.' She felt all fingers and thumbs. This was almost a repeat performance of the day that Mrs Brownlow Jun. came to call. Suddenly she giggled.

'Don't bother,' said Mrs Snape. 'This is fine, I have a napkin.'

Suppressing the fit of giggles that threatened to overwhelm her, Lottie looked up and saw that beneath the perched bird there was the merriest pair of brown eyes. She relaxed.

'I'm sorry I couldn't call earlier; I desperately wanted to talk to you about your work,' said Mrs Snape. 'Only I took the children to Lindisfarne for the summer. I like to get them away from the city, and Sidney came up at weekends.' She paused and smiled at Lottie. 'I do so envy you. It must be grand to have such a talent. I get bored writing a letter, never mind a whole book.'

Lottie had found a friend. In no time she was confiding that her novel, *The Clouds Stood Still*, was coming out the following week and how excited she was about it.

'Thomas must be very proud of you,' said Alice, for that was her name.

Lottie shook her head. 'I thought he was. But that was before we were wed. Now he disapproves of my "scribbling", as he calls it.'

'Hmm,' said Alice, pulling a face. 'Well, when you're famous he will most likely change his mind.'

She stayed much longer than the usual calling time of half an hour, talking about her children and asking about Lottie's life in Durham. 'You lived alone? In a house on your own?' she exclaimed. 'Oh, how daring of you! And going to work for a newspaper too. It's so exciting. I think women should be independent, don't you?' She took off her hat and placed it on the seat beside her. 'You don't mind, do you?'

Lottie shook her head. 'No, of course . . .'

'I don't know why we have to wear such concoctions,' Alice went on. 'But still, I'm fond of birds, aren't you?'

'I . . .'

It seemed that Alice wasn't really expecting an answer. She talked on and on and no doubt got on some people's nerves but not Lottie's. Lottie liked her. In fact, she was already imagining her as a character in her novel. She would fit in beautifully.

By the time Alice at last took her leave, after inviting Lottie to her 'At Home' the following Tuesday week, Lottie had cheered up immensely. She could make a friend of at least one of the partners' wives.

'Alice Snape?' said Thomas when he came in to dinner. 'I bet she talked you to death, that one.'

'I like her,' said Lottie as she served out the lamb chops and passed him the vegetable dish. She felt the need to defend her new friend.

Thomas shrugged. 'I would rather you made friends with the Brownlows,' he said, but did not pursue the subject. He tucked into his chops and afterwards made for his study. It was only then that Lottie remembered she had left her notebooks on his desk.

'Lottie! You've been in my study!'

He came striding back to the dining room with a face like thunder. He had the notebooks in his hand and he flung them down on the table so that they skidded over the polished surface and fell on to the floor. Lottie scrambled to pick them up. When she stood up again she was raging.

'Why shouldn't I? There's nowhere else I can work. It's not as though you were using the desk anyway.'

'You can give up your scribbling. It's not as though you are going to get anywhere with it, not really!'

He did not look at all like her Thomas, she thought, with his disdainful look and cruel tongue he was more like a stranger. She flushed. 'You think not, do you? Well it's just as well my publisher thinks otherwise, isn't it?'

'I've told you, I don't want my wife to write tuppence-ha'penny novels and gossipy pieces for the local newspaper. I told you to tell the editor you were finished with all that. You'll do as you are told, my lady!'

'Will I?' Lottie was as furious as he was. 'I'll leave you first!'

She pushed past him as he stood, open-mouthed at her threat. Leave him? How could she leave him? Of course she couldn't leave him. He started to go after her; he had to show her who was the master in this house. He stood at the bottom of the stairs, watching as she went up them. About halfway up she stopped and turned.

'Any road, you knew I was a writer when you married me! You didn't have to marry me! You didn't say I would have to give it up, either!' She bent forward and took her hand from the banister to shake it at him and make her point but as she did so she tripped over the hem of her skirt and fell. Thomas started forward but he was too late to catch her before she came down heavily on a stair and slid further. He was just in time to catch her before she finally fell to the floor.

# Twenty-One

'The women in our family seems to have a habit of falling down the stairs when we're expecting.'

The voice came in and out of Lottie's consciousness. It was a familiar voice but she couldn't quite place it. She tried but it was too much of an effort. She relapsed back into the grey nothingness.

'I thought she moved her eyelids there,' Eliza went on. She gazed at Lottie's white face on the pillow. 'The lass looks a bit vulnerable when she's not hiding behind her glasses.'

'Is she going to be all right, Mam? You should know.'

Thomas had been gazing unseeing out of the bedroom window at the street leading down to the river Tyne, hidden in the distance. Now he turned and approached the bed and stared down at his wife's face. A blue vein showed through the skin of her forehead and there was a small rosy bruise on one cheekbone. There was no other colour at all.

'You should ask the doctor that,' Eliza replied.

'But you should know,' Thomas insisted. 'You've nursed women in childbed long enough; ever since I can remember.'

Eliza didn't answer immediately. She was thinking of that long ago time when Thomas was born, when she had fallen down too. Only, thank God, Thomas had been born alive and well. It had not been at all the same as what was happening to Lottie now.

Oh aye, she had nursed plenty of women, young girls and middle-aged women, who had been in the same position as Lottie was in. Most of them had fallen or been knocked down by their men. More babies were lost that way . . .

'You didn't do it, did you Thomas?'

'Mam! I did not! How can you ask such a thing?' Thomas was shocked to the core.

'I'm sorry. I just had to hear you say it.'

Eliza wished that she were as close to her son as she had been when he was younger. Now he told her nothing about his life and it was hard for her to know what he was thinking. Perhaps that was natural when a lad grew into a man. She looked at the girl lying so still on the bed. So white she was and her skin so translucent. Not a picking on her, her mother would have said.

She put her hand under the bedclothes and felt Lottie's stomach. It was not hard, her skin was not hot; she mebbe would not be getting an infection. On the other hand, she had lost her baby. Her own grandchild. Eliza sighed.

'She won't die, I don't think,' she said. 'But she's but a slip of a lass, she'll take some nursing.' Lottie's tiny figure and narrow hips were the result of childhood deprivation; Eliza had seen it all too often. But she didn't say so to her Thomas. It didn't mean that the girl would not recover well. She was surprisingly tough, but then workhouse girls had to be to survive.

Thomas let out a sigh of relief. He felt guilty, for it had been his fault, he knew that. But why wouldn't she do as she was told? Women were supposed to obey their husbands, weren't they? And nothing good ever came of women working. Look at the times he had come in from school to an empty house and nothing but a cold tea set on the kitchen table. Then when he went to boarding school he had visited his friends' homes. Their mothers weren't dashing about the place all the time working, working, no, they had been waiting at home with fresh-cooked meals they had made themselves, even when they had a maid in the house.

Lottie had been the maid in their house, he thought. Not like Bertha who had carried on her own washing business and helped his mother out at the same time. When he was younger, Lottie had always done what he wanted her to do, tidied up after him, fetched and carried for him. But she had still been considered a friend by his mother.

'Why did you marry Lottie?' Eliza asked suddenly.

For a moment or two Thomas couldn't think of an answer. He had always liked Lottie, loved her even. Why was his mother asking such a thing? In her world a lad always married a lass if he impregnated her. 'Took her down', they called it.

'I'm surprised you don't say it was my duty.'

'Aye. Well it was. Do you love her though?'

'I do.'

'That's all right then. Lottie is a decent lass and she has a good brain an' all, she won't let you down.'

Thomas looked away, embarrassed by this unusually frank speech coming from his mother. He walked to the foot of the bed and looked again at Lottie's white face. 'I . . . We were arguing,' he said. 'I wanted her to stop working on her dratted writing.'

'Why?'

'She should have been spending more of her time on me and preparing for the baby, not scribbling away at rubbishy novels.'

'Aye, well.'

Eliza was quiet for a moment, gathering her thoughts. 'She needs her writing, man. Her stories are not rubbish. Haven't I just said she has a good brain?' she said eventually.

A sound from Lottie made them rush to the side of the bed. Lottie's eyes were open. She licked her lips and tried to speak. Eliza lifted her head from the pillow and gave her a few sips of water from the feeding cup on the bedside table.

'Take it easy, petal,' she said. 'You're going to be fine, you'll see.'

'I've lost the bairn?' Her eyes flickered to Thomas when Eliza nodded. 'I'm sorry,' she whispered.

'It wasn't your fault,' he replied as he stepped closer and took her hand in his. Eliza slipped from the room to give them time to themselves.


'A fanciful tale of a girl aspiring to enter the law profession,' said *The Review* when *The Clouds Stood Still* was published at the end of November. 'Nevertheless, it is quite entertaining.'

'Typical patronising remark,' said Lottie. 'I don't suppose it will sell very well without a good review.'

'If it doesn't, you have the satisfaction of knowing that you tried at least,' Thomas replied. He was reading the business page of *The Times*. There was an article about the fortunes to be made from investing in railways in the far-flung corners of the world. If he could only get in at the beginning, he could become a millionaire in no time at all. Excitement rose in him, the sort of excitement that took hold of him when he wagered money on an outsider at the racetrack and saw his horse romping home at the head of the field.

'My publisher thinks it will sell well. He should know, shouldn't he?' Lottie went over to the small table by the window where half a dozen copies of her book were on display between bookends. She picked up a copy and looked at it. It had a plain cover with a small illustration of a girl on the front. Just looking at it made her fill with pride.

'Alice really liked it. I gave her a copy,' Lottie went on. In fact, Alice had been filled with admiration for her work, which made up in some part for Thomas's uninterest. 'Alice says . . .'

'What? What are you going on about?' asked Thomas. He folded his paper and rose to his feet. 'I must go, I have things to do before I go to court,' he said. Forgetting to kiss her or even say goodbye, he swept out of the room.

Thomas was not interested in her work, Lottie thought sadly. Still, at least he was not so against it as he had been before she lost the baby. Surely if her book was popular and made money he would be more glad for her. Proud even.

'Can I clear the table, Missus?'

Janey had come into the room with her tray and Lottie nodded. 'I'm going out, Janey,' she said. 'I'm meeting Mrs Snape.'

'All right, Missus,' the girl replied.

As Lottie went upstairs to get ready for her morning with Alice, she kept her eyes averted from the stair where she had fallen that day. The memory of it brought such a feeling of guilt and depression to her. She blamed herself, oh aye, she did. She mourned for her baby too.

'When you're rich and famous, I'll tell everyone you are my friend,' Alice declared. They were in Alice's parlour drinking coffee, which was the fashion now in London, according to Mrs Brownlow, who had just returned from the capital. Lottie was not fond of it, not even as an after-dinner drink. It would never be as good as tea for slaking thirst or giving comfort in difficult times, she reckoned. It was bitter and left a nasty taste on the tongue, even with added sugar.

'Sometimes I just wish I was back in Durham sitting at my desk and scribbling away or pounding on the typewriter,' mused Lottie. Sometimes indeed, she thought but didn't say aloud, she wished she were back in West Stanley dashing the pit clothes against the wall in the yard or boiling pot pies for one of the lads coming in off shift.

Alice was shocked. 'You don't really wish you had not married Thomas, do you?' Alice was so happy in her own marriage. She couldn't imagine that her friend was not.

Lottie laughed. 'No, of course not,' she said. 'I'm happy with Thomas. I'm a lucky woman.' Alice would never understand her feelings. She couldn't understand them herself.

'Well, Lottie, I'm glad to hear it. Independence is nice in theory I suppose, but it does limit a woman's life. There are so many places we cannot go alone. The Playhouse for instance, and especially not at night. We are "the weaker vessel". Even if we do rail against it, it is a fact.'

'Alice!' cried Lottie as she stared at her friend. 'I didn't know you were so old-fashioned.'

Alice's cheeks became pink. 'I don't think it old-fashioned,' she replied stiffly. 'I think it all too easy for a young woman to get a bad reputation even if she has not done anything seriously wrong. It is enough that she is too free in her ways. She becomes hoydenish.'

It was enough for Lottie to realize that despite their friendship there was a huge gulf between them. Alice would never understand how she felt. Yet she couldn't resist a try.

'What about the women who have no man to depend on?' she asked.

'I'm sorry for them, of course,' said Alice. Her cheeks were red rather than pink now and she wished she had said nothing. Of course she knew that Lottie came from the lower classes; indeed, there was some question about Thomas too, but surely with a name like Mitchell-Howe his family must have good connections? To her relief, Lottie rose to her feet and brought the conversation to an end.

'Oh!' she exclaimed, glancing at the marble mantel clock. 'Is that the time? I'm sorry Alice, I've had a lovely morning but I promised Thomas I would be home when he comes in for the midday meal.'

\*  \*  \*

Thomas was not in court that morning. The client he was representing had withdrawn his action. So he was sitting at his desk supposedly working on another case but in reality dreaming of making a fortune from investing in a new railway in Uruguay.

There was just one catch to this scheme. He did not have enough capital. He cast about in his mind for ways to raise the two thousand pounds needed for the initial investment. This was the lowest amount the company was prepared to accept from someone wanting to buy in.

'An excellent opportunity' was the phrase used in the prospectus. Oh, indeed he had to find a way.

'I have had a complaint concerning you and the fact that you were late in court for the Prentiss brief. What have you to say for yourself? Mr Prentiss says it was because of your incompetence that the case was lost. What do you have to say about that?'

Thomas gave a start. He had not even heard Mr Brownlow senior come into the room. He rose to his feet. 'Mr Brownlow! I did my very best; I always do my best for my clients. But when the client's case is weak . . .' He let the sentence hang in the air for a moment. 'Mr Prentiss is, perhaps, looking for something or someone to blame it on. I will not be made a scapegoat.'

'And I will not have the reputation of the firm jeopardized in this manner,' Mr Brownlow replied sternly. 'I suggest you pay more attention to your work and less to your outside interests.' He turned on his heel and walked majestically out of the office. At the door, he turned.

'This is a warning, Thomas. Do you understand me? A friendly warning, but nevertheless a warning. There is unlikely to be a partnership on offer if this sort of thing is brought to my notice again.'

'Yes, Mr Brownlow.'

*Stuff your partnership*, Thomas said to himself savagely. A career in the law was not the great thing he had thought it to be, not at all. He sat back in his opulent leather chair and moved the swivel from side to side aimlessly. A career in the law was as dry as dust and not nearly as lucrative as he had been led to believe. Not in the early years, it was not.

When he had made his pile in South American railways he

would chuck it all in and spend his time in London, Paris or even Monte Carlo. All he needed was the money for the initial investment and he would be away.

There was Lottie, of course. He loved her, he did, but she didn't excite him as she had done at the beginning and it was not the same since she lost the baby. In a way she had been responsible for their inability to break into Newcastle society. It wasn't just her writing; in fact some women seemed to think more highly of her because of it. He had been wrong about that. No, it was her origins. His own had been overlain with his good schooling, which had given him a better accent, and the fact that he had some money, not much, but some, from his father's family in Alnwick. Lottie was a workhouse girl with the accent of the local working classes. He had not noticed it so much before, but it grated on him now.

Thomas sighed and looked at the case notes on his desk. Boring it was: two brothers fighting over the mineral rights on a hitherto worthless strip of land, but where a rich seam of coal had been discovered. Why could they not just share whatever came their way and be thankful for it?

Suddenly, Thomas closed the folder containing the notes and shoved it in his desk drawer. There was plenty of time for working but this was the last day of Sedgefield Races and he had a few good tips and a feeling that he might, he just might have the luck running with him. He straightened his tie before the looking-glass, smoothed back his hair, winked at his reflection (by, he was a handsome devil), and took his hat and overcoat from the stand in the corner behind the door of his office and put them on.

'I have to go out, Mr Thompson,' he said to the clerk who had looked up from his ledgers as Thomas's door opened. 'Take any messages for me, will you? I may not be back today.'

'Yes, Mr Mitchell-Howe,' the clerk replied.

Liberated, Thomas hailed a cab and went merrily on his way to the railway station for the train to Durham and then to Sedgefield. All his woes were forgotten in the excitement of going to the races. This was his lucky day, the day he made enough money to buy into a South American railway company. Oh yes, he would be a millionaire yet.

# Twenty-Two

'*The Clouds Stood Still* was a little slow to take off in the first few months, but I am pleased to inform you that sales from your book are now increasing steadily,' wrote Mr Bloom. There was a royalty cheque enclosed with the letter. Lottie stared at it. Nine pounds, seventeen shillings and sixpence. She said the amount out loud, though there was no one there to hear it. Thomas was rarely at home in these last few months. Often he spent the night at what he termed 'his club'. Lottie did not question it, for in some ways she was happy to be able to get on with her writing.

The cheque was for only a few pounds but it showed that the original advance had already been earned. It would take a hewer at the coalface a month or more at least to earn that sort of money. Lottie rose to her feet, moved to the window and gazed out at the February scene. Of course, she mused, the book had taken longer than a month to write.

Outside it was starting to snow: large flakes that quickly coated the ground and blew against the window in small swirls. On the street beyond the tiny garden, a couple were walking against the wind, the man holding a large black umbrella in front of the woman protectively. The woman's skirt was blowing against her legs and billowing out a little behind her. She had her hand tucked under the arm of the man and they hurried along together as one. It made her think of Thomas. The couple outside had something special, a closeness she did not have with Thomas.

It seemed to her that the only times he touched her nowadays were those when they were in bed together on the nights when he did come home. His need of her at these times seemed as strong as ever, yet he still stayed away for days at a time.

She had taken to inserting a ball of cotton wool soaked in vinegar into her vagina in the evening when he was at home.

It was the only way to stop conceiving that she had heard of and she couldn't bear the thought of going through the trauma of another miscarriage. Nor could she ask Eliza for advice. Eliza would be scandalized and she was, after all, Thomas's mother.

Sighing, she turned away from the window, sat down and stared at the neatly written sheet she had been working on. She inserted a sheet of foolscap into the typewriting machine and typed in the number of the page, 201, and the first line from the handwritten sheet, but she was unsettled, she couldn't carry on.

'I will go to the bank,' she said aloud, and rising to her feet, she put on her coat and hat, picked up her reticule with the cheque in it and went out into the wind.

The snow had turned into sleet and she had to bend her head into the wind as she walked up the street. She folded her umbrella and tucked it under her arm, for it was straining to turn inside out when she had it up. Yet the icy sleet, which was stinging her cheeks, was refreshing at first: it took her breath but lifted her mood.

In the bank, she paused for a moment to catch her breath, then took the cheque out of her reticule and handed it over to the clerk.

'Good morning,' she said pleasantly.

'Good morning, Mrs Mitchell-Howe,' he replied, as he picked it up. 'Do you wish to put this in your account? Or perhaps you would like it in cash?'

Lottie had had every intention of banking the cheque, but suddenly, without conscious thought, she changed her mind. The account was in Thomas's name of course, and once she countersigned it and it left her hand, only Thomas would have access to it.

'I'll take the cash, please,' she said. It was a long time since she had had any money in her purse apart from the house-keeping, and this week Thomas was late giving her that.

'Certainly, madam,' the clerk replied and opened his ledger. He scanned the appropriate page, then coughed, looked at her sitting across the desk from him, and then back down at his ledger. His lips moved soundlessly, then he looked up at her again.

'Excuse me, madam,' he said, slightly embarrassed. 'This

account is well overdrawn, I'm afraid. Are you sure your husband did not want you to deposit the cheque? He is late making this month's payment and I'm afraid our charges . . .'

'Oh, there must be some mistake!' Lottie stared at the clerk then at the ledger, trying to read it upside down. She couldn't quite make out the amount but it was written in red ink; at least the last few entries were. There was little doubt that Thomas was in debt and he had not told her anything about it. No wonder her housekeeping money was late! Though her first thought had been that it was a mistake, somehow she knew it was not. And the clerk was holding on to her cheque.

Rising to her feet, she said, 'My husband is not at home, he is away on business. I will have to speak to him about it.'

The clerk, a nice, well-mannered man who felt sorry for the girl – for she looked no more than that – stood too, still holding the cheque. 'I'm sure Mr Mitchell-Howe will straighten out this misunderstanding,' he murmured, though in fact the thought ran through his mind that he would like to be there when the gentleman tried. *Poor lass*, he thought, but the next minute she had snatched the cheque from him and was turning to go.

'Mrs Mitchell-Howe, I think that should go towards clearing your husband's debts . . .' he began, but Lottie was already at the door. He hesitated; after all, the cheque had been made out to the client's wife, and he might be on doubtful ground if he tried to get it back. These days there was such a lot of talk about women having the right to their own money and he had not as yet entered anything in his ledger.

The clerk glanced behind him at the door of the manager's office. It was firmly closed. No one would even know Mrs Mitchell-Howe had been there.

Lottie hurried down the street and around the corner and then around the next corner before slowing down. The cheque was clutched tightly in her gloved hand. She folded it and slipped it inside her glove until it rested against her palm. Then she walked on, more slowly this time. Slowly her whirling thoughts began to settle. She had to find out what was going on.

'Mrs Mitchell-Howe,' said Mr Brownlow senior as she was ushered into his chambers. 'Do sit down.'

He was not smiling but then, Lottie told herself, he was a dour sort of person, wasn't he? It did not mean much.

'I will not, thank you,' she replied. 'I came to see if you can tell me where my husband is, for I need to get in touch with him. It was careless of him, I know, but he went without telling me where he was going and how long he would be away. I need to contact him urgently.'

'Sit down please, Mrs Mitchell-Howe,' insisted Mr Brownlow. 'I think we have matters to discuss.'

Lottie's heart beat uncomfortably fast as she sat down in the chair by Mr Brownlow's desk. She took off her spectacles and rubbed at them with a handkerchief, before putting them back on her nose and fiddling nervously with the wire earpieces to get them comfortable.

'Do you have any idea at all where your husband is, Mrs Mitchell-Howe?' the barrister asked. He had a strange expression on his face; she couldn't make it out. He seemed embarrassed yet angry, unbelieving yet sorry for her.

'I do not,' she replied.

'How long is it since he was home?'

'A few days. What's this all about? Surely you know when and why he went? He was on a case, he said.'

'I do not, Mrs Mitchell-Howe. In fact I have no idea where he is. His behaviour has been erratic, to say the least, these last few weeks, even months.'

He paused and looked keenly at her as though to judge her reaction to this piece of information.

'What do you mean?' Lottie felt as though she were living a nightmare. All the certainties of her world were falling to bits. Where was Thomas? Where was he? The question thundered in her brain.

'Your husband has missed court appearances, let clients down and caused us a great deal of trouble in the past fortnight, Mrs Mitchell-Howe. At first I thought he must be truly ill; perhaps having a breakdown, I don't know. But I am afraid there is worse. There are discrepancies in the accounts. He has been claiming money for expenses, which he did not in fact incur. That is serious enough but we now find that there is a substantial sum of money missing from a client's account.'

Lottie sat frozen to immobility with the shock of his words. It could not be true; indeed, it was all a horrible mistake. It had to be. Yet was it? Thomas's increasingly erratic behaviour, his evasiveness when she asked him questions about what he was doing or where he was going, and then the incident at the bank today. These things showed that there was something wrong. If she had not been so wrapped up in her own work she would have seen it sooner.

Mr Brownlow was gazing at her with some concern. 'I'm sorry if all this has come as a shock to you, Mrs Mitchell-Howe,' he murmured. 'Would you like a few minutes to compose yourself? Perhaps a cup of tea?'

'No, no thank you,' Lottie replied. She rose to her feet. 'I am sure there must be some mistake. When my husband returns he will clear it up.'

She turned to the door, hardly able to see for the heat that had rushed to her face. Her spectacles had steamed up a little and she took them off and held them in her hand. Even so, she seemed to be seeing through a mist.

'I hope you are right, Mrs Mitchell-Howe,' said Mr Brownlow in a tone that implied he did not think she was. He held out a hand to shake hers, but she didn't see it. All she could think about was making it to the door and fresh air.

Once outside, she leaned against the solid stone of the building for support. She wiped her spectacles with her handkerchief and replaced them on her nose, settling them squarely. After a few moments her vision cleared. The wind blew strong and cold against her skin and she shivered suddenly. She had to go home. When Thomas came home (for he would come home, she knew it, he would not desert her), she needed to be there. She stood up straight, fastened her hat more securely and set off into the wind.

Thomas had not returned to the house. In her absence the second post had arrived, and there was a letter on the doormat, the address written in his sloping hand.

Inside the envelope was a single sheet of paper. The few words written on it jumped out at her.

*I'm sorry,* they read. *You will be better off without me. In any case, you have your writing. Thomas.*

Lottie stared at them. He had run away, he must have done. And he had been lying to her for God knows how long. He had emptied the bank account and left her with nothing. The advance money from *The Clouds Stood Still* and any other funds in the account had gone. All she had was the house contents. She sat down on the hall chair abruptly and put her hands to her face as the letter fluttered to the floor.

Through her gloved hand she felt the paper of the cheque and drew it out. Oh aye, she had nine pounds, seventeen shillings and sixpence. She laughed mirthlessly. Not completely destitute then. When she was younger, nine pounds, seventeen shillings and sixpence would have been like riches to her.

Lottie sat for a few minutes collecting her chaotic thoughts. Then she got to her feet, went upstairs and began to pack a Gladstone bag with clothes. She looked at her typewriting machine, but no, she could not take it, for it was too heavy and cumbersome. Still, she took the pile of typewritten sheets she had already done.

Downstairs again she looked in the mirror, straightened her hat, gave the hall one last look around and left the house. As she closed the door, the sudden swish of air took hold of the letter on the floor and it fluttered under the hall table and against the wall. Further up the street, Lottie hailed a passing cab and climbed in.

'The station, please,' she directed the cabbie. It was not until she was sitting in a third class carriage on the train going south, first stop Durham, that she allowed herself to think of Thomas again. Brought up as she had been in the workhouse, with the exigency of survival always having to come first, she was following her instincts.

Thomas, Thomas, she had thought he loved her.

'I thought his father loved me,' said Eliza sadly after Lottie told her the tale. Eliza was shocked and bitterly hurt, even more so than Lottie. Thomas, her golden boy, her little lad. 'I never thought he would turn out like his father, a gambler.'

'A gambler?'

Somehow, this explanation, that Thomas was a gambler, had not occurred to Lottie. In fact she had not thought about what he had done with the money, only that it was gone. She began to fill with anger and resentment. He had taken the money she had earned (*her money!*) to gamble with, to throw away like that evil Alf Green had on pitch and toss and the bookie's runner.

'His father threw himself off a cliff over gambling debts,' said Eliza. 'Oh, dear God, you don't think Thomas might do that?' Her face was white and despair shone from her eyes. 'He was such a good boy and he didn't show any interest in gambling. In fact, I used to impress on him what a mug's game it was.'

'Do you know where he is?' Lottie felt sorry for the older woman but she desperately wanted to find Thomas, even if all she got from him was some sort of explanation or apology or both.

Eliza looked at her hopelessly. 'How would I know? I never could find his father. Though he did go back to his family in Northumberland once. Alnwick, that is.' She was sitting on the hall chair, pleating and unpleating the skirt of her wrap-around apron. 'When Tot was a child he ran away and tried to reach them. Did I tell you about that?'

'Yes, I know.' Lottie felt deathly tired suddenly. 'Oh, never mind, Eliza, I'll be all right. At least there are no children to think about.'

What was she saying? The memory of the baby she'd lost rose to torment her. Tears pricked at her eyes. 'Can I stay here for a while, Eliza?' she asked.

'Well . . .' said Eliza, then noticed Lottie's expression. 'Yes, of course you can,' she went on quickly, although she did not really want Lottie to be there, constantly reminding her of her son. Tot, her lovely son who was so clever and had done so well; Thomas, the name he had reverted to when he trained as a lawyer. Anxiety rose in her. He wouldn't kill himself, would he? As his father had done?

'I will get my own place as soon as I'm able,' Lottie was saying. 'I'll go to see Mr Scott at *The Post*. He will give me work, I know. And I do have some money, to see me over until then.'

'Don't worry about it, Lottie,' said Eliza dully. She felt her heart was breaking. How could Lottie not feel that too? The lass was altogether too self-possessed. Why wasn't she weeping for her man? She should be, especially a man such as Thomas.

She should not have gone to her mother-in-law, Lottie realized as she unpacked her things in the small back bedroom of the house in Gilesgate. It was the bedroom she had been given when she first came back from Stanley all those years ago. She stared out of the window at the houses opposite, not really seeing them. Well, here she was, back to where she had been then. She had succeeded then and she would succeed again, she told herself. And the sooner she started the better.

# Twenty-Three

'Lottie! How good to see you,' said Mr Jeremiah. He had come out of his office to greet her as she climbed to the top of the stairs and she felt a rush of warmth because he had done so. 'Come in, do, and I'll order tea. You would like a cup of tea, wouldn't you?'

He smiled down at her and she was struck afresh by the deep blue of his eyes. His tawny hair had thinned a little and here and there was speckled with grey, but the effect was to make him look even more distinguished than she remembered him. As she offered him her hand and walked before him into his office it was almost like coming home, or at least back to a well-remembered and loved place. Her heart warmed a little for the first time since Thomas's desertion.

'Thank you for seeing me. I know this is a busy day for you,' Lottie murmured.

'Nonsense! I will always have time to see you,' he replied, before going to the door and calling, 'Jackson, are you there? Fetch some tea, will you? Oh, and get some of those little cakes from the baker's please.'

A voice answered from below and Mr Jeremiah turned back into the room. Up until then he had been having a humdrum sort of a day, but the sight of Lottie had brightened his mood considerably.

He sat down opposite Lottie. 'Well then, Lottie. I can still call you Lottie, can't I? Now you are a married lady?' he said, not waiting for a reply. 'How are you? Do you like living in Newcastle?' He paused, then went on, 'And Thomas, how is Thomas?'

'That I wouldn't know,' said Lottie steadily. She stared down at the black cotton gloves encasing her clasped hands before continuing. She felt embarrassed at telling Jeremiah that her man had left her. 'Thomas and I don't live together any more.'

'I'm sorry, Lottie,' he said quietly. No more than that, but she felt he understood that she didn't want to talk about it.

'Are you living back here then? In the same place?'

'With my mother-in-law for the minute. Then I want to find a place, a room at least, somewhere overlooking the Wear. By Prebends Bridge, for preference.'

'Well then,' he said. 'As it happens I am in dire need of a lady to do the job you were doing before you left. There have been one or two but they don't stay long. Most of them are just waiting until they get married.' He paused and looked at her closely. 'Are you interested in coming back?' he asked.

Lottie sighed with relief. She had steeled herself to ask him for work; it was almost as if he knew that. But then, Jeremiah had always seemed to know what she was thinking. She smiled.

'Oh, Mr Jeremiah,' she said, 'that is exactly why I am here.'

'It is? And there I thought you had come to see us for old time's sake.'

Lottie blushed. 'Oh well . . .' she began and then noticed his dark blue eyes were twinkling at her. 'It is lovely to be back but I do need some work.'

'You have not made your fortune writing books then?'

She laughed. 'Not yet. But I'm trying.'

'You have a lot of talent, Lottie.' He was silent for a moment, looking thoughtfully at her. 'Can you start today?' he asked eventually.

Lottie didn't hesitate. 'What do you want me to do?'

'There has been some unrest in the mining villages, even among the miners who live closer in to the city. The usual thing: the owners want to reduce wages and the pitmen want to reduce their hours of working. I want you to go out to West Stanley and find out the wives' point of view. Not just Stanley but one, maybe two of the other places. Do you think you can do that?'

Lottie stared at him. 'Do *you* think I can do it?' she asked eventually. It was such a big job, and she had done no reporting for such a long time. When would she get time to write her own book, the book Mr Bloom was expecting on his desk before the autumn?

'I wouldn't ask if I did not,' said Jeremiah with a half smile.

'It's an article, Lottie. Maybe two thousand words at the most. What do you think?'

An article, not so big a job. 'I can,' she said.

Jeremiah smiled. 'Good. You can take Edward with you, he will take photographs.'

There was a knock on the door and Jos came in with the tea tray. He smiled and nodded at Lottie as he put it down before her. 'Good to see you, Miss,' he said before going back out.

'Oh,' said Jeremiah. 'There are biscuits. You will do the honours, won't you, Lottie?'

As Lottie sipped tea and nibbled a biscuit she felt there was some constraint between them as she surreptitiously watched Jeremiah. He was as courteous, even friendly as ever, but not as free and easy as he had been. He looked older too: there were lines on his face that she couldn't remember being there before.

'Your father, is he well? And your wife . . .'

'My father is fine. He will be in later, you may see him,' Jeremiah said rather quickly. 'My wife is not well, I'm afraid.'

'I'm sorry.'

She put her cup and saucer back on the tray and rose to her feet. 'Well, I think I may as well start right now,' she said. 'It's early, I can catch the horse-bus to Stanley.'

'What are you going to do? I mean, do you have a plan?' Jeremiah rose to his feet too and came around the desk to show her to the door. He opened it and stood to one side to let her through. 'Do you know anyone in Stanley?'

'I do as it happens, I have friends there, a mining family. It will be nice to see them again.'

'Oh, that's all right then. Well, it's nice to see you again, Lottie,' he said and looking up at his face she could tell he really meant it. 'I've missed you, we all have.'

'Thank you. I've missed you too. The office, I mean,' she added quickly and Jeremiah held out his hand to shake. His handshake was warm and firm and reassuring.

'I will wait for you to get in touch then,' he said. 'Goodbye, Lottie.'

Lottie hesitated before answering. 'You know Thomas's stepfather is a union official don't you?' she asked. 'Some might think my views are influenced by him. His mother is a friend of mine and we keep in touch.'

'I'm sure you will be fair-minded, as you always were in your articles, Lottie,' Jeremiah answered.

As she walked along the street towards North Road where she could pick up the horse-bus to Stanley, she realized how true it was that she had missed Jeremiah. The image of Thomas had faded from her thoughts for the first time since he left. Not that it had dominated them but it had been there, never really out of her mind. The difference between the two men was so marked. Thomas was such a charming man when he wanted to be, but he was unreliable, dishonest and in the end, a gambler and a thief.

After the experiences she had endured during her early life, she needed an upright man, a rock, a man she could rely on. A man such as Jeremiah, she thought wistfully.

'Lottie Lonsdale, I don't believe it!'

Dora, Albert Teesdale's wife, sat back on her heels, with the black lead brush in her hand. The steel fire irons were to one side, already polished, and there were black smuts on Dora's hands and cheek and on the sacking apron she wore around her waist to protect her dress, instead of her usual white pinafore.

'Hallo, Dora,' said Lottie, as she stood in the open doorway to the kitchen/living room in West Stanley. She had been feeling unsure of her welcome and Dora's tone of voice stopped her walking straight in, as she would have done in normal circumstances. The kitchen looked much the same as when Mary Anne had reigned over it, except for the fact that the walls were no longer lime-washed but covered in a black wallpaper decorated with large cabbage roses. 'How are you doing?'

'Nay, I'm all right,' said Dora. 'Albert's not too grand. His chest.'

She pushed herself up with the help of the wooden cracket on which she had her cleaning gear. Dora was heavily pregnant. She looked pale and tired and her face was puffy.

'Mind, it's a bit since we saw you,' she said with emphasis on the 'you'. She looked hard at Lottie. 'Well, come in and sit down if you're coming,' she went on. 'Speak quietly though. Albert's in bed, he's on night shift.'

'Thank you.'

Lottie moved into the kitchen and pulled out a chair from

the square scrubbed table in the middle. It was one of two; she recognized them as the plain, unpolished chairs sold by the Co-operative stores that had been varnished by Mary Anne. There was a long form at the other end of the table for the children to sit on. It too was varnished to a dark, almost black colour.

'I'll put the kettle on but you'll have to wait until the fire gets built up. I let it go down while I did the fireplace.'

'Don't worry about it,' said Lottie. Now she was here, she felt some constraint about broaching her reason for coming. 'I wouldn't mind a cup myself.'

Dora mended the fire with the aid of a few sticks and small lumps of coal. When it blazed up to her satisfaction she pushed the iron kettle back from the bar on to it.

As they waited for the water to boil, Albert came down the stairs in his stocking feet. His braces hung down over his trousers and his shirt was collarless. He stared at Lottie, unsmiling.

'Mind, we are honoured,' he said. 'We haven't seen you for a year or two. We might have been dead and gone for all you cared. What's all the bloody racket any road? When a man's been down the pit all night he should get a bit of peace in his bed after.'

'Albert,' said Dora.

'Albert what? I've said nowt but the truth, have I?'

'Hello, Albert,' Lottie intervened. 'How are you? I'm sorry if we woke you, I thought we were being quiet.'

'What do you care how I am, or any of us for that matter? My mam gave you a home when you were out on your arse and what did she get back? Eh? Eh?'

'Albert!' Dora said again.

'Aw, don't Albert me, she wouldn't be here if she wasn't after something, would she?' He glared at his wife. The kettle lid began to lift and fall as the water boiled. 'Well, are you making tea or not? If not, I'll away down the club for a pint of ale. I'll get no more sleep the day with a strange voice nattering on all the time.'

'I'll be going soon,' said Lottie. 'I just came to see how you were getting on.'

She couldn't talk about her article now, not with Albert there.

'What about the tea?' asked Dora.

'Let her go, she's not interested in us, Dora man!'

Lottie hurriedly said goodbye and backed to the door. She could hear Albert's voice shouting at Dora as she went off down the street, glad when it eventually faded away.

There was a corner shop on the end of the street which sold just about everything that the families might run out of before the Co-op store cart came around on Fridays. Inside there were a few housewives, shopping baskets in hand, waiting their turn to be served. Lottie recognized one or two of them as her neighbours when she had lived with the Teesdales. They turned around to inspect the newcomer as she opened the door and the bell jangled above her.

'Eeh, it's little Lottie!' cried one. 'What are you doing back here, Lottie? The last I heard you were living in Durham or Newcastle and were a famous writer!'

The speaker was Dot Turner, who lived a few doors along from the Teesdales. She was a blowsy woman with untidy fair hair, blue eyes and red cheeks, and she stood with her arms folded across her ample bosom and grinned at Lottie. Lottie smiled back at her. Dot was a woman who said whatever came into her head without thinking about it first, but there was no real harm in her.

'I don't know about the famous bit,' she replied. 'I have written a book and it has been published but I don't know how well it will do.'

'Get away, lass,' Dot declared. 'That's more than anyone here as done. Most of us cannot write our own names, man!'

'You've written some bits for *The Durham Post* though, haven't you?'

This came from the shopkeeper, who seemed to have abandoned her serving in her interest in the newcomer.

Lottie admitted this was true.

'Are you going to write about us, now?' asked Dot.

This was so near the truth that Lottie was surprised for a minute. 'I'm hoping to write an article about miners' wives,' she admitted.

'Aye well, I reckoned it had to be something brought you back,' a thin woman with a grubby shawl said, nodding her head in emphasis. 'You wouldn't be slumming here otherwise.'

'Aw, get along wi' ye, the lass has family here,' Dot asserted.

'Didn't she marry Eliza Teesdale's lad? Anyway, pet, what do you want to know?'

'The editor wants me to ask the opinions of the miners' wives about the present dispute between the owners and the men,' said Lottie. The women began to laugh.

'By, you're as good as a turn, Lottie Lonsdale,' said Dot. 'Don't you think so, Meggie?' Meggie, the shopkeeper nodded her agreement.

'The dispute between the owners and the men? Don't you mean the owners trying to get the pitmen to work all hours for nowt and the men determined to stop them and get paid a decent wage?'

'I reckon you could say that,' Lottie admitted. Even this small interchange had given her some idea of the women's opinions, she thought. 'All right, yes, that's what I mean. I'm just trying to be even-handed for the readers of *The Post*. It's a city paper and there are a lot of readers who are against the men causing trouble in the workplace.'

There, she'd done it again, she realized as soon as she uttered it. She had been away from the miners and their families too long. They would never use language like that. They would think she was against them. The women had stopped smiling and were looking at her with suspicion.

'By, Lottie Lonsdale,' said Meggie. 'You *have* changed. You're on the side of the bosses now, aren't you? Well, you'll get nowt out of us, I'm telling you.' Meggie's man was a shot-firer down the pit.

There was a murmur of agreement among the women. 'You'll away back to Durham if you know what's good for you,' one of them said, her voice rising to a shout. 'An' you married to the union man's lad. Shame on you.'

'No!' Lottie protested. 'I'm not on the side of the bosses! I was just saying what some people think, that's all. I'm for the ten-hour day, I am. Especially for the lads. I just wanted your opinion that's all. *The Post* reports things fairly, they do. It's just . . .'

'Aw, hadaway, will you lass. You're not making things any better,' said Dot. 'If you don't know what we think by now, after all the time you spent among the pit folk, you've been going around with your eyes and ears shut.'

'Aye, I'll go.'

Lottie turned to the door, then turned back. 'But I think I can say that feelings are running high in West Stanley any road. I promise I'll put the case as best I can.'

'I'm sure,' said Meggie drily. 'Well, a man working down the pit is worth a fair wage, that's all we're saying.'

# Twenty-Four

'You've been to West Stanley?' said Eliza. 'By, I wish I'd have known, I would have come with you. I'm worried about Da. Did you see him?'

Lottie had to admit she hadn't even thought of Tommy or Harry when she was in the mining village. 'I think they must have been on shift,' she said. 'I saw Albert and Dora though, they were all right.'

'It's time Da was out of the pit,' said Eliza. 'I thought he should come to live with us here. I could keep an eye on him. His chest is worse since he went on datal work.' She did not mention that with Lottie in the house there was not really space for Tommy, but Lottie was well aware of it.

She would move out to make room for Eliza's father, Lottie thought to herself, though Eliza would not ask it of her. It was time to look for a place on her own again and she thought of the little house where she had lived before going to Newcastle with Thomas. She regretted leaving it now, oh yes she did indeed.

'Tommy will be fine,' she said, trying to reassure Eliza. 'Harry will let you know if he isn't, even if Albert does not. You know your father is independent. He'll want to work as long as he can.'

'Still, he's into his seventies now. He's worked in the pit since he was nine years old.' Eliza bit her lip. 'Then there's Thomas. I wonder where Thomas is. What is he doing? Surely he'll get in touch soon,' she said. 'He's a good lad really, Lottie, you know he is. He'll have a good reason for staying away, you'll see.'

Lottie looked at her mother-in-law. What could she say? Poor Eliza was worn down with worry, what with her son and her father, though she didn't know the true extent of the trouble Thomas was in and Lottie hadn't the heart to tell her.

'Perhaps you're right,' she replied, then excused herself to go and write up her notes.

The following day she visited some of the local pit wives before going to see Mr Jeremiah in the early afternoon to show him her notes, which still needed some knocking into shape before she wrote the final article. She was a little unsure of herself; after all, it was a long time since she had worked on the paper. His smile as he rose from his desk as she went into his office was heart-warming.

'Lottie! How are you? I must say you look blooming. I think living in Durham suits you better than living in Newcastle did.'

Lottie smiled back and relaxed. 'Hello,' she said. 'I've brought you my notes on the article . . .'

'Yes, about the views of the women folk. I'm looking forward to seeing them.'

He barely glanced over them before handing them back to her.

'Come on, Lottie, you're an experienced journalist, you don't need me to supervise you,' he said. 'Write the article.'

He sat back in his chair and smiled at her and she was struck anew by what a nice man he was. His eyes were such a deep, friendly blue (were they really so much deeper and more expressive than Thomas's?), his voice so gentle and kind. She found herself comparing him with her husband. Oh, how had she let herself think she loved Thomas? He wasn't the man she had thought he was. He had let both her and his mother down so badly.

'Well, Lottie what do you say?'

Lottie started, realizing that Jeremiah had asked her a question twice.

'Sorry, Mr Jeremiah?'

'I was talking about the article though I'm sure you were thinking of something completely different.' He smiled again, his eyes wrinkling up at the corners. 'Call me Jeremiah – Jerry if you want to. In private, of course.'

Lottie blushed. 'Oh, I couldn't!'

'As you wish, Mrs Mitchell-Howe,' said Jeremiah formally, the smile leaving his face. He rose to his feet to escort her to the door. She glanced at him anxiously, fearing she had offended him, but he was smiling again.

'I'll bring the article in good time,' she reassured him.

'I'm sure you will, my dear,' he replied. Oh, he was a lovely man, she thought to herself. If only Thomas had been like him. She began to imagine what it might be like to be married to someone like Jeremiah – Jerry, as he had asked her to call him. It would be so different . . . She caught herself up. She was a married woman already and this was foolish, scandalous even. She stole a glance at him as he was closing the door after her. If he knew what she was thinking she would be mortified. She went on down the staircase, and out. The cold, fresh air cooled her cheeks, which were suddenly burning. What a fool she was, she thought as she went on down Northgate.

Thomas had only been gone a few weeks and here she was thinking romantically of someone else. An abandoned woman she was and if Jeremiah knew what she was thinking he would be horrified, him being a Quaker an' all.

'I think you would find the women are united behind their men,' Peter remarked when he heard what it was she was writing. He sat beside the kitchen fire in the rocking chair with the newly-bathed Anne on his knee, gently rocking. Opposite him, Eliza was darning socks, stretching the heel with the hole in it over a wooden 'mushroom' as she threaded the wool across and back. It was a common domestic scene, thought Lottie wistfully. Eliza had been fortunate in her second marriage, there was no doubt about that. She brought her thoughts back to what Peter was saying.

'Yes, they are loyal,' she replied to him.

'Not only that, the men have a fair case,' said Peter. 'But at least the women don't work in the pit, not as they do in other places. In Durham we have avoided that. But the owners say they can't make a profit as things are. Why don't they realize that if only conditions were better, if the lads especially could have their hours cut, production would go up?'

He stood up, holding the now sleeping Anne against his shoulder. 'I'll take her up now, Eliza,' he said, then as an aside to Lottie, 'Think on it.'

'I have done,' said Lottie. 'Now I'd best get on with writing the article.'

Union business was ever on Peter's mind, she thought as she settled down to work in her bedroom. She worked well into the night, breaking only for supper with Peter and Eliza. It was so long since she had worked on anything for the paper that she felt unsure of herself, redoing the article twice before she was satisfied with it. The bells of the cathedral were ringing out the midnight hour before she finally climbed into bed.

There was a lot of interest generated by Lottie's story of the women in the pit villages. Some of it was sympathetic to the cause of the miners, but quite a lot was not. On the whole, the tradespeople of the town were on the side of the owners. There were letters about the miners 'biting the hands that fed them', of them 'not knowing their place'. But there were also letters making the point that such dirty, dangerous work should be properly rewarded. 'There should be laws against boys as young as nine working in the pit,' one reverend gentleman asserted. 'Jesus said, "Suffer the little children."' The debate ran on for weeks, even though there were few letters from the mining villages.

'Most of them can't read properly anyway,' Mr Scott senior said.

'A lot can,' said Lottie. 'Now that the National Schools are open. In any case, a lot of them were taught by the Methodists before that.' She was feeling ruffled. Usually she found Mr Scott to be more understanding of the miners. 'And now there are classes in the Workingmen's Institutes.'

'I think Lottie is right, Father,' Jeremiah said, glancing at Lottie's pink face.

'Hmm,' said Mr Scott.

'Well, it can only be a good thing for the paper when there is such interest in an article in the ladies section,' said his son, then he changed the subject firmly. 'Lottie, I would like you to visit more of the mining villages around and try to gauge the support the men are getting from their womenfolk,' he said. 'Just two or three – perhaps Sherburn and Haswell – though you can decide which ones for yourself. You should get enough data for a follow-up article.'

'I'd love to!' Lottie replied. She had very little money left, though she was still to be paid for her article. Oh, she would manage, it would only be short for a while. She would not let the lack of money stop her doing this.

'I'll give you some expenses,' said Jeremiah, almost as though he had heard what she was thinking.

'I'll start tomorrow,' she said eagerly and Jeremiah smiled.

'In your own time,' he said. 'I'll give you a chit to get expense money at the cash desk downstairs.'

'Thank you. I'm so grateful, Mr Jeremiah, I really am,' said Lottie as she moved towards the door, her mind already planning the day ahead.


Lottie was filled with the old fervour for her work as she travelled around the isolated mining villages talking to the women. Mostly she had to follow them about as they hung out washing on lines across the street or down back gardens or working on other household chores. Sometimes they were reluctant to talk to her, viewing her as an outsider and therefore someone under suspicion.

By the end of the day she had a notebook almost filled with her descriptions of the women, the ways they had of helping each other and combating the harshness of their surroundings.

'You're late,' remarked Eliza as Lottie opened the back door and let herself into the house. Eliza was bathing Anne in the tin bath before the fire in the kitchen. She helped the little girl climb out and wrapped her in a towel. Anne looked over her mother's shoulder solemnly at Lottie. Her eyes were the same blue as Thomas's, Lottie thought distractedly.

'I've been over Auckland way,' she said. 'I had to wait for a train back.' She glanced at the wall clock hanging to one side of the fireplace. It was half past seven already and she had to write up her notes to take in to the office the following morning at the latest if her article was to get into the weekend edition of *The Post*.

'Well, there's your dinner in the oven. If you're hungry enough you will be able to eat it, though it's likely dried up by now.' If Eliza sounded sharp, it was no doubt because she hated to waste good food, Lottie told herself.

'I'm sorry, Eliza,' she said contritely and suddenly yawned, as fatigue took hold of her along, with the heat of the kitchen.

'Aye, well,' said Eliza as she pulled Anne's nightgown over her head.

Lottie watched them both as Eliza gave Anne her supper of bread and milk broily with a grating of nutmeg on the top.

'You've been very good to me, Eliza,' she said. 'Taking me in an' all.'

Eliza looked up. 'Why wouldn't I be? You are family, aren't you?'

'Yes, but . . .' Lottie paused for a moment, think fleetingly of Thomas. She would probably never see him again and he was her only real connection to the family. Blood was blood and she was reminded that Eliza wanted to bring her father to live with them. Only she, Lottie, was in the way.

'I am going to see about renting a little house tomorrow,' she resumed, coming to a sudden decision. 'I can manage the rent now. I don't need anything big. I saw one or two for rent over by Prebends Bridge and I've always fancied living there. Besides, I know you need the room for your father.'

Eliza didn't make any objection, simply nodded her head. 'Well,' she said, 'you must do what you want to do. I don't deny I want Da here where I can keep an eye on him. Mind, I'll have to persuade him to leave the pit.'

Later, as Lottie was in her room, sitting cross-legged on the bed and putting her notes in order ready to type them out, she reflected on the new coolness in her relationship with Eliza, who had been such a friend to her when she was in dire need of one. Oh, she could understand it, Thomas was Eliza's son and in her heart Eliza must blame her for Thomas disappearing as he did. But she would find a place of her own, tomorrow if she could. It was not so hard to find a place in the city.

Within a few weeks Lottie was in a tiny cottage overlooking the Wear, almost close enough to hear the running of the water. It had a single cold tap in the pantry, which stuck out into the tiny backyard from the even tinier back kitchen, but it was space enough for her on her own. There was one bedroom and a box room, which was large enough to take a table with her typewriter and a small bookcase besides. The small window looked out on to the yard rather than the river, but still it was adequate for what she wanted.

Lottie sat at the table one morning typing up the notes she had taken at the meeting of the Ladies' Temperance Society. The society met once a month in an upstairs room in the Town Hall and the proceedings were just about the same month after month. Nevertheless, the members expected to see a full report in *The Post*.

Finishing at last, she sat back with a sigh, rubbing at her forehead where an incipient headache threatened and pushing her spectacles further up her nose. Her thoughts wandered to Jeremiah, as they did so often lately. What must it be like to be his wife? Wonderful, she thought dreamily, then pulled herself up sharply.

How could she think that? Jeremiah never mentioned his wife, at least not to her, but then he would not, would he? No, but his father had, only the day before.

Lottie had been in the room at the back of the front office when Jeremiah came in much later than usual.

'Did you go up the dale to Stanhope?' Mr Scott, who was standing behind the counter reading a copy of *The Observer*, asked him. 'How is your wife?'

'Not good I'm afraid,' Jeremiah replied. 'I was summoned by her doctor yesterday evening. I'm afraid she is very weak now.'

In the back room Lottie dithered, not wanting to listen but not wanting to show herself either when the men were talking privately. The problem was resolved for her as the doorbell jangled and David, a recently appointed office boy, came in.

'Look after the desk for a few minutes please, David,' said Mr Scott. 'I won't be long, Mr Jeremiah and I are just going upstairs for a short while. The others are about somewhere. Ring the bell if anyone comes in.'

Lottie waited – skulked, she thought to herself wryly – until the men's voices receded before coming out. 'Good morning, David,' she said brightly.

David looked surprised. 'Oh, Miss,' he replied. 'I didn't know you were there.'

'I've been through to the store room,' she explained, though why she should need to she did not know.

The scene ran through her mind as she pushed a small kettle on to the fire in the grate, steadying it on the bar. She was sorry if Jeremiah's wife was ill, of course she was. And why she had hid herself when the Scotts were talking in the office she did not know. She was an absolute fool at times, she told herself.

She took the cup she kept on the small mantelshelf and spooned mint tea and a little sugar into it. When the kettle boiled she took her tea through to her bedroom, where she had an armchair by the window overlooking the bridge over the Wear. Lottie always found this view so peaceful. It calmed her when she was agitated, and lifted her spirits when she was low. The Wear, she thought dreamily, watching a cleric walk over the bridge, his black gown billowing slightly in the wind. The river had been called the Wear throughout its history but spelt differently. The Wiir it had been in early Saxon times, there were documents in the cathedral library. She often spent time in the library.

Lottie was sitting there when she saw another figure of a man crossing the bridge, and the man looked familiar somehow. She leaned forward and watched him, but he was a distance away and she couldn't quite make him out. Or at least she couldn't believe it. He disappeared up the path, which was shrouded with trees leading up the bank to the houses above.

Lottie stood up and took her cup back into her small office. Her heart beat uncomfortably fast as she sat down once more and looked down at the typewritten sheets before her. It couldn't be, she told herself. Of course it couldn't be. Just then there was a loud knocking at the front door of the little house.

# Twenty-Five

A month earlier, Thomas had been walking aimlessly through the streets of Montevideo with no particular plan in mind. In fact, his mind was a blank, as much through shock as that he had not been to bed for three nights. He had lost everything he had in a last game of poker. He did not have the means to get out of the city even. For where would he go? Not back to England, unless he wanted to risk a prison sentence. Why did he always have such bad luck?

He turned down a narrow alley, which offered him some protection from the searchers who might be on his trail. Who were almost certainly on his trail, for they wanted revenge, not to mention their money back. He didn't think of where the alley might lead, only that it offered him anonymity. Eventually, he came on to the riverfront lined with docks. Coming out of the dark alley into the light of the early morning sun blinded him for a moment and he hesitated.

'Mind, you're in a bad way with yourself!'

Thomas started with alarm and took a step back into the shadows. The voice was English; the words not merely English but spoken with an accent that came straight from the banks of the Tyne. The searchers had caught him, they would exact revenge for – what? Last night's gambling fiasco? The money he owed to the last lodging house he had stayed in? Or worse? Money he owed back home? That was most likely, considering this man's accent. His tormented thoughts were interrupted as the Geordie grabbed hold of his arm with a fist of iron and stopped him easily.

'Let me go!' shouted Thomas, pulling ineffectually away.

'What's the matter wi' you? Is somebody after you? Weel, it's not me, man, I've just got off the boat.'

'I-I'm sorry . . .' Thomas mumbled, recovering himself. This man wasn't a searcher, thank God. Now he wasn't panicking his brain began to race. This was his chance to get away from whoever was following him. At least if he stuck to the seaman he would have backup, for a Geordie would help another if he was in trouble.

'I was attacked last night, like, and I thought it was all happening again.'

'Robbed, were you? Bastards! Well, I haven't seen anybody about except me shipmates. You look as though you're down on your luck. Howay along wi' me, there's a decent bar near here where we can get a pie and a pint. It's a Welshman as runs it.'

The seaman was a middle-aged man with brawny arms and shoulders and a face that was burnt mahogany brown with the sun. But he was smiling at Thomas in understanding and Thomas responded to the first kind words he had heard in weeks.

'Thanks, I think I will,' he said and fell into step with the seaman. He put his hand in his pocket and felt the few coins there. Were they enough?

'My name is Jonty, by the way,' the seaman said. 'Jonty Polson from Shields. And you?'

'Tommy. I'm from Northumberland, Alnwick way.' It was best to be cautious, he thought.

'Mind you don't sound Northumbrian,' Jonty said as he led the way into a crowded bar-cum-restaurant. 'I'd have said Durham or mebbe Sunderland.'

'I was brought up in Durham,' Thomas said but Jonty had lost interest. 'I'll get the food. Meat pie all right wi' you? Hey, take that empty table afore someone else does.'

He went up to the bar as Thomas slid into a seat by the wall, which gave him a good view of the room and the door to the street. He felt safer now – surely no one would be after him, it was almost day. The lights in the street were going out, along with those from the boats and the one or two ramshackle houses. He put his forearms on the rough wooden table and leaned his weight on them. Dear God, he was weary to death!

'Here we are then lad, get that down you, it'll put a lining on your stomach.'

Jonty plonked a plate of pie in front of Thomas and a flagon of ale beside it. The smell of the pie made Thomas feel faint and his mouth watered. Jonty hooked a stool to the table with one foot and sat down opposite him. He watched as Thomas attacked his pie, shovelling it down with his fork.

'Mind, you're a bit peckish,' said Jonty.

Thomas hesitated. 'I haven't eaten all day,' he admitted.

'Nor yesterday neither, I'd say. Well lad, get it down you.'

Thomas slowed down a little. At least the ravening hunger was settling down a bit.

'You want a billet? You can have one on the Mary Jane. We're a bit short on this trip: one of the stokers has been taken off here. Something wrong with his gut, he's in a bad way. It would get you back to North Shields and a few bob in your pocket but mind, it's a hard slog.'

Thomas paused with his ale halfway to his mouth. 'I-I don't know . . .' he said. What if he were taken up by the bobbies as soon as they docked? Would they be looking for him or would it all be forgotten? By, but it would be grand to get back to England though, it would an' all!

'Aye well, if you don't want to,' said Jonty. 'But the way I look at you and the way you're expecting trouble, you'd be best off coming wi' us.'

'Go with you? Are you authorized to take on men?' Thomas asked.

Jonty stared, then laughed. 'You swallowed a dictionary have you? It sounds like it. What do you do when you're at home? Not labouring, I would bet. Mebbe you're not the man for the job.'

'I've worked hard in my time!' snapped Thomas. 'I'll do it an' all, you'll see if I'm up to it.'

'Howay then. You'll have to be signed on and the sooner the better, before they find someone else.'

Jonty got to his feet, swilled back the last of his ale and led the way out of the bar. 'You got anything you want to pick up?'

'Nothing that matters,' Thomas admitted.

'Howay then, let's away. We're off on the next tide.'

Life aboard the steamer was hard, harder than anything Thomas had done before, and the work of a stoker the hardest of all. His hands cracked and blistered and coal dust got into the cracks so that they began to look like a miner's hands, only they were not hardened to it and he felt they never would be. But the work did not really occupy his brain and his thoughts went over the events of the last months, even years.

If only he had had that big win, how different his life might have been. If only he had not put everything into the last gamble, the South American railway scheme that would have made his fortune, aye and Lottie's too. Hadn't he only taken the money from the firm so that he could give Lottie a better life? Didn't she deserve it after all she had been through? Oh, Lottie, he agonized. He had to see her again, he had to. As the days went by, filled with hard slog and indifferent food, the turmoil in his brain seemed to fuse with the ache in his muscles and the stinging pain in his hands.

'If I get through this I'll never gamble again, I swear to God,' he mumbled to himself as he came off shift one day and fell into his hammock.

'What's that? Who the hell is that talking? Can a man not have a minute's peace?' an irate voice asked out of the gloom. 'Shut your flaming face!'

Thomas didn't hear it because he was already in an exhausted sleep.

It wasn't until they were but two days out of North Shields that Thomas began to worry about how he was going to manage to see Lottie and yet keep hidden from the law. Where was she? Had she gone back to Durham? He would have to find out before he risked going there himself. There was one thing for sure though, he would keep well away from Newcastle. Brownlow, Brownlow and Snape would have had to make good the client's money he had taken. Though he had only borrowed it really; he had meant to pay it back. He was no thief. He would have repaid it were it not for the bad luck that dogged him. He would go to his mother's house. Even if she had heard what he had done she would take him in. After all, it was a while ago now.

'Oh Thomas, Thomas.' Eliza wept to see him standing on her doorstep. 'I thought you were dead; Lottie thought you were dead.'

She was unable to move for shock, standing there on the back doorstep, for he had come in through the yard. She felt she was seeing things. He looked twenty years older than when she had last seen him and he was dressed in dirty old clothes like a common labourer.

'Well, can I come in, Mother?' Thomas asked. Maybe she didn't want him in, he thought. *Had* she heard what he had done in Newcastle? She had evidently been in touch with Lottie.

'Aye, come in, come in,' she said, standing back from the door and wiping her eyes with the corner of her pinny. She put her hand on his arm as he brushed past her, almost as though to reassure herself he was real. She gazed up into his face. 'You're so brown, lad,' she said, though what she wanted to do was shout and rage at him for leaving as he did without so much as a word.

'Mam,' he said and put his arms around her and kissed her cheek and suddenly they were both overcome by the emotion of the moment. Her body felt small and frail and he was shocked at how much she seemed to have aged. Awkwardly they went into the kitchen and she pushed the kettle on to the coals automatically and put the teapot to warm.

'Does Lottie know you're back?' Eliza had her back to him as she asked the question.

'No, I don't know where she is,' he said and she swung around to face him. 'I reckoned you might.'

'I do. I know my responsibilities even if you do not,' snapped Eliza. She dumped the teapot on the table with such force that drops of tea welled up through the spout and spilled on to the scrubbed bare wood. She made no attempt to get cups or milk and sugar; she forgot about the tea.

'Where is she, Mam?' Thomas asked patiently. He did not sit down, just stood there by the table.

'Over by Prebends Bridge, she has a cottage there,' said Eliza. 'Well, she couldn't stay in Newcastle waiting for you to come home, could she? Poor lass, she must have been ashamed and devastated an' all to have her man run away like you did.'

Thomas did not respond to her remark. What was there to say? 'Give me her address, Mam?' he repeated.

'I'll have to, I suppose. But don't you think she's gone through enough? By, you were never brought up to run away from your responsibilities, Thomas, you make me ashamed, you do an' all.'

'I know, Mam, I'm sorry. But give me her address, please.'

'All right, all right! You stay away for God knows how long and then you cannot spend a few minutes talking to your mother. You're not going right now, are you?' Eliza remembered the tea and gestured towards it. 'Stay and have a bite and a cup. By, lad you look that thin and poorly. Let me look at your poor hands, I can see they're not right. By, what have you been doing to them? Slaving and skivvying by the look of them. Thomas . . .'

'Mam, please, if you don't tell me I'll find out for myself somehow. Don't worry, I'll come back, I promise I will.' Thomas turned to the door impatiently, then looked back again to his mother.

'It's 54 George Street, I told you I would give it to you. Go on, then, go.'

'I'll come back, Mam, I will,' said Thomas. 'But I have to see Lottie, you can see that, can't you?'

'Aye. Go then.'

She watched through the kitchen window as her son went down the yard, pulling the gate to after himself. *His poor hands*, she thought dully. When he came back, if he came back, she would mix an ointment of boracic and petroleum jelly to poultice them.

Well, she had work to do. Anne would be coming in for her tea and Peter too. She would make some panacklty. She went into the pantry for potatoes and onions, then cut some pieces of bacon from the slab on the cold shelf.

# Twenty-Six

'Afternoon, Lottie,' said Thomas.

She leaned forward the better to see him, for she couldn't trust her eyes. Her glasses were on a string around her neck and her fingers shook as she put them on. His image swam into focus. It was Thomas's face, albeit an older Thomas with greying hair and a furrowed face, and it was definitely Thomas's voice. But still . . .

'Thomas?' she said.

'None other,' he replied, smiling the old smile. 'Aren't you glad to see me?'

'Where have you been?' she asked, for all the world as though he had stepped out for a paper and taken longer than she had expected.

'Ask me in and I'll tell you,' he said with a small laugh. 'Or am I to stand here all day?'

She stood back and pushed the bridge of her glasses up her nose in an unconscious gesture. Her thoughts whirled. Thomas stepped over the threshold and closed the door behind him. He was still smiling as he put his arms around her, but the smile faded as she stiffened, then shrank away.

'Hey, now that's not nice, Lottie,' he said. 'Here I've come home after being gone so long and you don't want me to touch you. I'm your husband, Lottie, and you are my wedded wife.'

'You ran away from me, remember,' said Lottie. 'You ran away and didn't care what happened to me.'

'Well, I had to get away,' said Thomas reasonably. 'I would have sent for you; I intended to send for you but the right time just didn't come. Are you not going to even ask me how I am?' He gave her a mocking smile as he walked past her and into the small sitting room without waiting for an answer. 'Make a cup of tea, will you, lass? It's a while since I had a decent cup of tea.'

Lottie stared after him, unable to believe what was happening. She followed him into the sitting room. He was sitting on the only armchair there, taking off his shabby boots. Stretching out his legs and putting his feet on the steel fender, he sat back in the chair, and closed his eyes for a minute.

'By, that feels good,' he said. 'I've dreamed of this all the way back from that hellhole I've been in. A room with a proper armchair to sit in and my dear wife by my side.'

Lottie saw red. She went over to him and kicked his feet from the fender, then leaned over him and slapped him across the face with all her might.

'God damn you, Thomas Mitchell!' she screamed at him. 'Where have you been, I said? Where? You've ruined my life! You rotten excuse for a man, you swine . . .'

She got no further, for Thomas jumped up from the chair, caught both her hands in one of his and hit her so hard that her head rocked from side to side and waves of blackness swamped her brain. He swore as he pushed her down on to the hard, stone-flagged floor and tore the buttons from her shirtwaister in one movement, as he took it by the neck and wrenched it open.

Her head bumped painfully against the stone and she was incapable of any resistance as he dragged up her skirt and forced her legs apart with his knee. He held her there as he unbuttoned his trousers and forced himself inside her. He had loosed her hands by now but they were pinned between her body and his. When she finally got one arm free, she managed to rake his face with her nails, yet he hardly seemed to feel it. He simply knocked her hand away and grasped her breast with a horny hand, squeezing and twisting at the soft flesh until he gave one last grunting thrust and collapsed on top of her. She lay there, barely conscious, unable to breathe until he rolled off her, panting heavily.

Eventually, he got to his feet and buttoned up his trousers, before sitting back in his chair and put his feet back on the fender, crossing them negligently. Steam rose from his socks with the heat of the fire and the smell of him filled the air to the extent that she felt suffocated. Her vision cleared gradually and she sat up, pulling her shirtwaister together, wincing as her breast throbbed even more when she brushed it with her arm. Her thighs ached, her belly ached, there was a stabbing

pain in her groin and a throbbing in her head. She pulled ineffectually at her skirt but it wouldn't go down properly until
she got to her feet.

He turned his head and looked at her and she stared back
with utter loathing.

'You filthy beast,' she said and paused, for her head was
swimming again now she was upright. She sat down abruptly
on a hard-backed chair she had bought at the second-hand
market in Durham marketplace. It was the only other chair
besides his in the room and had a carved back, which dug
into her bruises, but she had to get off her feet before she fell
down again.

'Aye, well you don't get a lot of opportunity to wash on a
tramp steamer. Nor time either.'

'You stink! God forgive you for what you've just done to
me.'

'Hey! I'm your husband aren't I? And you are my wife. I
did nothing I hadn't a perfect right to do, I did not.'

Thomas was smiling now, a cold smile. She could hardly
recognize him for the man she had married. There was nothing
in him at all of the boy she had known before then. How
could a man change so much? His personality was totally
different. He was a stranger in Thomas's body.

'You raped me,' she said, with no expression in her voice.

'A man cannot rape his own wife, Lottie,' he said, smiling
in amusement. 'Did you not know that? Well, you can believe
me, I'm a lawyer.'

'Well, you don't look like one.'

Suddenly Lottie couldn't bear to remain in the same room
as he was. She rose to her feet and went out of the room,
though every step gave her pain. She went into the kitchen
and felt the water in the set-pot boiler; it was barely warm
but it would have to do, for she was desperate to wash off
the stale male smell of him. Bringing in the tin bath from its
nail in the yard wall, she used the ladle tin to empty the water
from the boiler into the bath and began to take off her clothes.

Hearing a noise from the other room she stopped undressing
abruptly and took a chair and propped it under the handle of
the door to hold it closed, before taking off the rest of her
clothes and stepping into the bath. She scrubbed herself clean
with lye soap and would have done it again but for the fact

that she was worried he would manage to find a way through. She jumped uncontrollably as she heard his footsteps and again when he tried the door handle, rattling it angrily.

'Lottie, let me in or it will be the worse for you,' he said.

'I will not!'

Lottie hurriedly climbed out of the bath and rubbed at herself with a towel before pulling on her clothes over her still damp body. What she really wanted to do was throw the lot on to the fire but her clean clothes were upstairs in the bedroom closet.

He had stopped rattling the doorknob, had he given up? As she hesitated, she heard a noise behind her.

'Now then, Lottie, have you got the kettle on yet? I'm fair parched for a cup of tea.'

She whirled to see him right behind her. He must have gone out of the front door and around the street and in through the backyard. Oh, why hadn't she locked the back door?

'Don't touch me,' she warned, backing away from him and picking up the brass poker from the fireplace. 'I swear if you do, I'll swing for you.'

Thomas laughed and took a step forward. 'Now Lottie, you know you won't use that on me.'

'I will, I will indeed,' she said as she took a tighter grip on the poker. The pain in her breast deepened and her heartbeat raced. She began to feel dizzy again and it took all of her willpower to stay upright.

Thomas hesitated, gazing at her uncertainly, then he shook his head. 'No, you won't do that, Lottie,' he said and stepped closer.

It was done in a minute. She didn't even think about it. She brought the poker up to hit him and he sidestepped away from the blow. His foot caught in the clippie rag mat Lottie had laid as a hearthrug and he fell on to the unemptied tin bath which was sitting there. His head hit the side handle, slipped from there to the fender and he lay, stunned. Lottie dropped the poker and it clattered on the tin hearthplate, resounding over and over.

She had killed him. She had killed him. The phrase repeated and repeated in her head. *God help me*, she thought. She could hear herself screaming in her brain but nothing was coming out. She stepped back from the clippie mat and sat down by the table. The water was still sloshing in the bath, what was left in the bath. The rest was soaking into the mat, some sizzling on the hot hearthplate, a trickle running over a flag-stone to a groove then along the groove to the next one. Some of it was pink. Why was it pink? Was there blood in it?

He was so still, she thought – one thought amongst a chaotic jumble of thoughts. She couldn't remember whether she had hit him with the poker or not. No, of course she hadn't. Had she? Whether she had or not, she would have to tell the polis.

She would swing for him, she had said. But she had not meant it, no, she had not. She was defending herself . . .

Thomas groaned and she jumped into the air in shock and her heart beat even more wildly. Was it her imagination? She stared at him. His hand moved – he brought it up to touch his face, hold his forehead. She leaned over him and saw that his eyes were open and he was staring back at her.

'Well woman, I thought you were going to go for me there. Come on, come on, help me up, my head's fit to burst.'

'I will not.'

Thomas pushed himself into a sitting position using the fender as a prop. He breathed out heavily and groaned. 'My head is fit to burst, Lottie,' he said and suddenly he sounded just like the old Thomas to her so that she moved towards him, hesitated for only a second or two, then helped him up and into the fireside chair. He leaned back, his head on the bentwood frame that held the rails together. He closed his eyes and seemed to slip into sleep.

Lottie watched him for several minutes but he did not move. After a while she emptied what was left of the water from the bath into a bucket and took it into the yard and poured it down the drain, then took out the bath itself and hung it on the nail in the wall. She took the soaking mat outside too and dried up the water slopping about on the stone flags. In all the time it took her to clear the mess in the kitchen he did not wake up.

It took all her will power to make herself touch him. She felt his forehead; it was cold and clammy but not icy. There was a pulse beating at his temple. She felt quite detached somehow, as though he really were a stranger, a tramp who had wandered into the house. Stepping back from him, for the smell was overpowering now with the heat of the fire drying out his clothes, she pondered what to do about him. Eventually, she went upstairs to her bedroom and changed her clothes.

Downstairs again, she saw he had moved only a little and seemed to be in an even deeper sleep.

She would fetch Eliza, she thought. Eliza was a Nightingale nurse besides being his mother; she would know what to do. She covered him with a blanket and left him.

It took twenty minutes for her to get to Eliza's house, and only ten for them to get back, for they came in Eliza's trap. On the way, Lottie gave her mother-in-law an edited version of what had happened, with no mention of the rape.

'But how did he fall? Surely he hadn't been drinking?'

'No, at least I don't think so. He tripped over the clippie mat and hit his head,' replied Lottie.

By this time they were pulling up in the street outside Lottie's little house and Eliza couldn't ask her anything more. They climbed down from the trap and Eliza put the nosebag on the pony.

'He's in the kitchen,' said Lottie. 'I couldn't move him on my own.'

'No, of course not,' Eliza replied as she hurried in front of Lottie through the house to the kitchen at the back. 'Where? Where is he?' she asked.

'In the chair by the fire,' said Lottie, surprised she should have to ask. She pushed past Eliza and stared. The kitchen was empty. There was no one there, no one at all.

'Where is he?'' she echoed Eliza.

'He must have wandered off,' Eliza said, more to herself than Lottie. 'He must have been suffering from concussion and when he woke up didn't know where he was. We have to find him. You go the back way and I'll go the front.' She started back the way she had come but when she looked back, Lottie had not moved.

'Howay, Lottie! Goodness knows what he'll do, where he'll go, don't you realize that? He could get himself hurt; killed even, if what you said was true.'

'Aye. Yes, I'm going.'

Lottie ran out to the backyard gate and looked up and down the back lane. The only things in sight were a couple of lines

of washing strung across the lane, for there were only two
more cottages along this way. But there was a coal merchant's
cart going along the end road and she hurried to catch it up.

'Have you seen a man going along here?' she asked.

'A man? I've seen a few, Missus, but not going along here.
Will I not do for you?' He grinned to show he was joking.

'Oh, don't be soft, this is serious,' said Lottie, her voice
breaking into a shout in her anxiety.

'Aye. Well if your man's ran away from you I'm not
surprised, Missus. I bet you gave him hell.' He was offended
but she couldn't take time to placate him now. She turned and
ran the other way and down towards Prebends Bridge. *Please
God, don't let him have fallen into the Wear*, she prayed.

There was no sign of Thomas in among the trees and bushes
that lined the river. Nor on the footpath, which ran alongside
it. She went over on to the opposite bank but there was nothing
there either, not that she could see. There were a few people
walking along and a lone fisherman with rod and line sitting
on a stool.

'Have you seen a man coming along here?' she asked
everyone she met but most stared at her as though she were
mad, which made her realize that it was a daft question to
ask. 'A man dressed like a tramp?' she added.

'You been robbed, pet?' one man asked.

Lottie shook her head and carried along the path for a short
distance before turning back to the bridge and crossing over
again. She climbed the bankside towards the cottage. Perhaps
Eliza had found him.

'Did you see him?'

As Lottie turned into the lane she met Eliza, who was
wringing her hands, frantic with worry. 'Eeh, man,' she went
on when Lottie shook her head. 'Why did you leave him on
his own when he'd hurt his head? I thought you had more
sense, Lottie. I should have come with him. I could have
driven him over in the trap. I'm his mother, I would have
known he wasn't right, not well.'

'He was asleep,' Lottie replied. 'It wasn't my fault, it wasn't.'
She was sorely tempted to tell Eliza the whole story about
her precious son. But she could not, of course she couldn't.
How do you tell a mother that her son is a wastrel and a rapist
besides being a thief? And Eliza had been so good to her.

Eliza and her whole family had been good to her. Even if she told her mother-in-law, Eliza would not believe her.

'You could have asked a neighbour to look in,' said Eliza. 'Why didn't you? If anything has happened, anything worse to my Tot, it will be all your fault. It will, it will!'

She had thought he was dead and today he had come back and despite everything she had been so glad to see him. It was a load lifted from her heart. But now he had gone again and goodness knows what might happen to him. It was all the fault of this lass she had taken into her heart and home and this was how she repaid her.

Lottie was stricken with remorse. It was true she should not have left Thomas by himself. If he had concussion he could be wandering anywhere, falling down the bank or worse, off a bridge. There were so many bridges in Durham. By this time he could have been swept away to Sunderland and the North Sea.

'I'm sorry,' she said. 'I really am sorry, Eliza.'

'It's no good being sorry now, is it? You're an ungrateful little bitch, you are. Why Thomas married you I don't know. You've ruined his life.'

'I ruined his life! Why if you knew . . .'

Lottie stopped. It was senseless, the two of them fighting like this. What they had to do was find Thomas.

'If I knew what?'

'Nothing. Look we must find Thomas. He could have gone over to your house. It's worth looking. Why don't you go there and I'll look elsewhere, around the town. He can't have gone far.'

Eliza nodded. 'Aye, you're right. I'll go now. You fetch Peter, will you? And if you don't find him in half an hour go to the polis. Or no, maybe I should go to the bobbies now.'

'No, don't get the polis,' said Lottie. 'Not yet, any road.'

Eliza glanced keenly at her. 'Why not?'

'Well, you know there was a misunderstanding with the law firm in Newcastle. I don't think Thomas would want the polis.'

'Aw, getaway, it cannot have been anything much. I brought Thomas up to be honest.'

'Still, I'll get the polis but not until I have to. Any road, we might find him any minute. He's probably just sitting down nursing his headache, somewhere by the Wear.'

Oh God, she shouldn't have said that, Eliza would be imagining him falling in the Wear. But Eliza agreed to Lottie's suggestions and agreed to seek Thomas at home. The two women pulled on their shawls and went out looking for Thomas once again.

# Twenty-Seven

It was the police who found Thomas almost three weeks later. Lottie had scoured Durham City and its environs, looking for him from first light until the dark of night made it impossible for her to see. She searched the riverbanks in all their twists and turns and she searched the streets and the outskirts, even the mining villages close to the city. Peter and Eliza searched too, and when they didn't find him, advertised in *The Northern Echo* for him but with no result.

'I am going to the police,' Eliza said to Peter. 'I don't care what happens. I have to know where his is and whether he is alive or not.'

'I'll find him. I've asked all the girls at school to keep a lookout for him and you know, they come from all over Durham,' said Anne, then a thought struck her. 'You don't think his head got better, do you? He might have joined the army or run away to sea or taken himself off to Australia . . .'

'Anne! Of course he hasn't,' snapped her mother. 'He must be hurt, that's what. He could be anywhere, lying hurt. He would have got in touch with me at least, if he was going away.'

'He didn't last time,' said Anne.

'Anne!' Peter said sternly.

'Well he didn't . . .'

'Go to bed, Anne,' said Peter. 'It's past your bedtime any way.'

Next morning there was a headline in *The Durham Post* and also in *The Sunderland Echo*. *Man found drowned in the Wear at Chester-le-Street*, it read.

*The body of an unknown man who appeared to be a tramp has been found washed up in reeds by the side of the River Wear at Chester-le-Street. The coroner has been informed.*

'I know it is Thomas,' said Eliza.

'You do not know, how can you?' Peter replied, trying to calm her down, for she sounded hysterical. She was at the end of her tether, he thought, so white and strained looking. He tried to reason with her. 'It could be any one of a number of tramps who go from workhouse to workhouse looking for a bed. You know they do.'

'No, it's Thomas. I can feel it in my bones. It says here he is in the mortuary at Chester-le-Street. I have to go and find out for myself.'

'I'll come with you if you insist on going,' said Peter with a sigh.

'No, you go to work. I'll see Anne off to school and then I'll go round for Lottie. I'm sure she'll want to come.'

'Well if it is him, she's the next of kin. She'll have to identify him.'

'Aye, legally she is. But who could be closer to him than his mother?'

Wisely, Peter simply shrugged for an answer.

Eliza and Lottie drove to Chester-le-Street in the trap. They said little on the way, for all their thoughts were concentrated on what lay ahead. Lottie told herself that she hoped it was not Thomas lying in the mortuary, that he had recovered and gone off, left the country forever, taken a berth on a ship going out of Seaham Harbour or Hartlepool or somewhere else along the coast. She did not want it to be Thomas lying dead on a slab in a mortuary. Of course she did not, she repeated to herself. Yet the bruises on her thighs and breast were in the colours of the rainbow now and she wore a high-necked shirtwaister to cover up the bruises on her neck. At least the throbbing inside her had quietened down.

'Dear God, don't let it be my Thomas, my little Tot,' breathed Eliza as they stopped in front of the mortuary and climbed down from the trap, yet she was sure it was. She put the nosebag over the head of the pony and he began munching quietly, used to waiting outside a house for his mistress.

The mortuary was locked up but there was a small notice on the door indicating that the keyholder lived close by, and Lottie went in search of him.

'He's a tramp, Missus,' he said, 'Still, you can look, make sure it's not your man.'

'It is my man though,' Lottie mumbled to herself as she stood and gazed down at the corpse on the table. His face was mottled a pale blue and yellow like a waxwork and totally expressionless. Behind her, Eliza stood in the doorway, dreading to come any closer and have her fears confirmed.

'What? What do you say?'

Lottie was unable to speak or to answer Eliza for a moment or two. She could not even look up; her eyes were glued to Thomas's face.

'Tell me! Tell me, damn you!' Eliza shouted and the mortuary attendant drew nearer.

'Now Missus . . .' he began and put a hand on her arm. She shrugged it off as she finally found the strength to move forward and look down on the face of her son.

'Thomas,' she said quietly, seeming to shrink into herself, swaying. Lottie had to grab her quickly before she slid to the ground.

'Now then, Eliza,' she said. 'Hold up.' But she had to take her mother-in-law's whole weight for a minute or two.

The attendant led them to the outer office where there were chairs for them to sit down. Neither woman was crying.

'It was because of his father,' said Eliza. 'My poor lad, if only his father had been different. Thomas didn't deserve to die like this, though. He was such a good lad, Lottie, he was.'

'I know, Eliza, I know,' Lottie answered, though she was barely following what her mother-in-law was saying. In truth, Lottie felt quite numb. She desperately wanted to get out into the fresh air; she felt she could hardly breath. But there were papers to sign and questions to answer before the two of them could get away. Then at last they were free to climb back into the trap to return to Durham City. Lottie took the reins, turning the pony around and setting off down the road while Eliza lapsed into a dumb misery.

It was only after Lottie had left Eliza with Peter and gone back to her own little house and closed the door behind her that she could give way to her own feelings and mourn for Thomas and what might have been. She wept for a while, then dried her eyes, heated water for a bath and sat in it before the fire, her knees drawn up to her chin. The fire flickered in the darkening day, then died to a steady red glow, which warmed her bare shoulders and back.

The water cooled and the fire died down and still she sat there. It was only when the crust of cinders fell into the ashes with a small crash that she started out of her reverie. She had not realized how cold she had become: she was shivering and her teeth chattered. Stiffly, she stood up and pulled the towel from the brass line above the fire, before stepping out of the tin bath and towelling herself dry. She pulled on her flannel nightgown and walked upstairs in her bare feet, then climbed into bed and curled herself into a ball.

She even welcomed the iciness of the sheets as she lay there full of guilt for she knew not what. Some of what had happened must have been her fault. She could have done something to help Thomas, to save him from himself.

Eventually the bed warmed and Lottie's shivering stopped. It was quite dark as her eyes closed and she fell into an exhausted sleep, too deep for dreams.

The funeral was a low-key affair held at the Methodist Chapel in Old Elvet. It was a large church and the few mourners occupied only the front two pews. Five minutes into the service a couple entered the church quietly and sat down at the back. It was only as the people were following the coffin out of the church that Lottie lifted her head and saw that Mr and Mrs Snape were standing quietly to one side. She felt a rush of gratitude that they had come all the way from Newcastle to Thomas's funeral in spite of the fact that he had besmirched the reputation of the firm.

'Thank you for coming,' Lottie said to Alice and her husband quietly as they moved away from the open grave later, after the interment. She nodded towards Eliza and Peter, walking with Anne between them a short distance in front. 'His parents will appreciate it, as I do.'

'Oh, Lottie, we are so sorry for your trouble,' said Alice.

'I know, Alice,' Lottie replied. 'You were a good friend to me when I needed a friend. I am grateful to you.' She paused and glanced at Mr Snape. 'Won't you both come to the funeral tea? It's just in the chapel schoolroom. I daresay you could do with some tea.'

Alice glanced at her husband, who shook his head imperceptibly. 'If you don't mind, Lottie, we won't,' she said. 'We must get back.'

Lottie nodded, understanding that it would have been just a step too far after what Thomas had done to the firm.

'Do come up and see us soon, Lottie,' Alice said as their carriage approached. Lottie did not miss the look of alarm on Mr Snape's face nor the obvious relief when she murmured a non-committal reply. She waited until the carriage moved away, then turned to where Bertha and Charlie Carr were standing with Peter and Eliza. She doubted if she would want to go back to Newcastle for a very long time.

It took quite a time for Lottie to settle down to the routine she had just begun to establish since she had returned to Durham from Newcastle. She had nightmares; dreadful terrifying nightmares, all involving Thomas returning from the grave and climbing into her bed. She would wake, screaming, as she visualized him reaching out to her, forcing her to do what he wanted, raping her again. There was no one she could talk to. Eliza was her confidante, and how could she tell such things to Thomas's mother?

Eventually, she began to work again. She resumed the 'Home Notes' page for *The Durham Post* and took her turn at reporting cases at the magistrates' court and even at the assizes.

'Lottie? What are you doing still here?'

Jeremiah Scott put his head around the door of the small room where she was typing up her notes one evening. Lottie had had a busy day. Not only had she attended court but she had had to finish off her 'Home Notes' page, for tomorrow was Friday and the paper would be going to press.

'Oh! I'm just about finished now,' she replied, pulling the foolscap sheet from the typewriter and putting it on the growing pile by the side. She rose from her chair, feeling a little flustered, and promptly staggered and would have fallen were it not for the fact that Jerry stepped forward quickly and caught hold of her.

'Are you not well, Lottie?'

He looked down at her, his concern evident in his expression. He was still holding her; she could feel his arms around her warm and comforting. She felt she could have stayed there forever. If only . . . Lottie shocked herself by the turn her thoughts were taking. She pulled herself up quickly and backed away from Jeremiah.

His expression changed and his hands dropped to his sides.

'I'm sorry,' he said, sounding stilted. 'I did not mean to be too familiar.'

'No, of course not, ' she said. 'Please don't apologise! You were being kind, you are always kind to me.'

Lottie could still feel where his arms had been on her; she blushed like a schoolgirl and looked down at her work in an effort to hide it. With agitated hands, she picked up the pile of typescript and began to straighten it on the surface of the desk, in the process dropping half of the pages on the floor.

'Oh Lottie,' Jerry exclaimed, dropping to his hands and knees just as she did the same, and beginning to help her pick up the scattered pages. 'For heaven's sake!'

His fingers brushed hers and suddenly he took hold of her hand and pulled her to him. The carefully typed pages dropped yet again, but they were forgotten as he drew Lottie to him and smothered her with kisses.

Lottie forgot everything but the overwhelming feelings he was arousing in her. She sank to the floor with him and let herself drown in them. In fact, she was incapable of doing anything else. It was the most natural thing in the world and not at all wrong or sinful.

'My love,' he whispered and exhilaration swept through her. He lifted her and carried her to the couch before the fire. It was narrow and meant only to accommodate one lying down, but somehow this time it did not seem too narrow for them both but perfectly comfortable.

Afterwards they lay together, glorying in each other, but of course it could not last, she knew in her heart it could not last. His grip on her slackened. Without speaking, he got to his feet and turned his back on her as he adjusted his clothing. Her heart beat fast as she watched him for a moment or two, then she began to straighten her skirt and shirtwaister, fiddling clumsily with the buttons. Suddenly he spoke.

'I'm sorry,' he said. 'I should not have let that happen.'

Lottie bit her lip. 'No,' she said. He was going to say he did not want to see her again, she knew he was. Anyone so upright as he was must be shocked out of his mind and of course he was simply being polite. He must blame her; it was always the woman's fault wasn't it? Ever since Adam. Her sense of loss was as great as that she had felt when Thomas first went. More.

'I'll go,' he said and she nodded. She could not trust herself to look at him, let alone speak.

Jerry turned and looked at her. 'Lottie,' he said softly. 'Lottie.'

She did not look up. 'You were going,' she said. He went to the door and opened it, went out and turned back. He had to see her again.

'You will bring in your copy tomorrow?' he asked, meaning only that she would come to the office and he would see her again, somehow make things right between them.

Lottie jumped up, her aroused feelings turning into a blind rage that shone from her eyes. She spluttered as she shouted at him, 'Get out! Get out!' When she heard the front door close behind him and she could almost hear the thick silence he left behind, she walked up and down the room, unable to keep still as her chaotic thoughts jumbled up in her mind.

Men! Flaming men! He was as bad as Thomas had been. He was worse, bloody Jeremiah the God-fearing Quaker! A married man and his wife up in Weardale in a sanatorium an' all. And all he was worried about was his newspaper. That was all.

# Twenty-Eight

Lottie put off taking her copy into the newspaper office until the very last minute the following day. She shrank from facing Jeremiah. She had railed at him the day before but really she knew she had been as much at fault as he had, just as eager a lover. She had acted shamelessly, she had indeed, she told herself. Only . . . it had not felt shameless or wrong or anything but the most natural thing in the world to her at the time. No matter what the consequences, she could not be sorry it had happened. But still, she was aware that other people would frown on it. And Jeremiah, was he regretting it? So it was with some trepidation that she walked up North Road and entered the offices of *The Durham Post*.

Mr Scott was in the front office talking to Jos. They both stopped talking and turned sober faces to her as she entered. For a panicky moment she thought Mr Scott knew what had happened between her and his son and she could feel the heat rising in her cheeks.

'Lottie, my dear!' said Mr Scott. 'I'm afraid you have come at a bad time. Do you wish to see my son?'

Jos nodded at her and retreated to the print room, closing the door behind him.

'Good afternoon, Mr Scott,' said Lottie. 'Yes, I do. I've brought in my copy for Mr Jeremiah.'

'I'm afraid he is not here, my dear.' He hesitated a moment, then went on, 'Can I give it to him when he gets back? He has had to go into Weardale, a family matter.'

Lottie had keyed herself up to facing Jeremiah again. She had been dreading it but now she felt irrationally let down, an almost physical feeling.

'You look a little unwell, Lottie.' Mr Scott's expression changed to one of concern. 'Come along into my office and sit down.' He took her arm and led her into the small room he used as an office since he had turned the paper over to his son. 'Jackson!' he called from the door. 'Be so good as fetch tea, if you will.' Closing the door, he sat her down on the scuffed leather armchair he had in there and often used for a nap in the afternoons as age began to take its toll.

'Now then, Lottie, tell me what the matter is,' he said. 'I can see there is something wrong.'

'No, nothing, really.' She took a handkerchief out of her reticule and dabbed at her cheeks. 'It's just a little airless in here, don't you think?'

Mr Scott crossed to the window and opened it. 'Is that better?'

'Yes, thank you,' she replied in a low voice.

He studied her for a moment and was about to speak, but fortunately there was a knock at the door and Jos came in with a tray of tea. By the time he had gone back out Lottie had composed herself and Mr Scott must have decided to ask no more questions. They drank the tea and Lottie stood up to leave.

'I'll call later in the week,' she said. 'Thank you for the tea and for being so kind.'

'I'll tell my son you called,' said Mr Scott. 'If he has any queries about the copy I'm sure he will be in touch.' He paused for a moment, studying her expressive face before continuing. 'Lottie, are you all right? I sense there is something wrong.'

Lottie forced a smile. 'There's nothing wrong, really,' she assured him.

Mr Scott hit his forehead with the palm of his hand. 'Of course my dear, you are still mourning your husband. How could I be so insensitive?'

Lottie murmured something non-committal and left the office. Mr Scott watched her progress down North Road before turning back to the work he was doing. Sometimes he thought his son looked at her with a certain expression he didn't care to analyse. Perhaps it was just as well Jeremiah had been out somewhere when she called. The lad had enough complications in his life with Harriet, his poor wife. He did not need more. But perhaps he was worrying about nothing. Jeremiah was an upright, honest man.

Jeremiah was in Weardale, in a nursing home high on the moors above the town. It had been a hunting lodge initially, but had been given over to the treatment of lung disease because the air there was pure and untainted, for there was no industry near it. He sat beside his wife's bed, watching her sleep. She was propped up on pillows and a backrest but still her breathing was shallow and laboured, her skin white and translucent except for the hectic patches of colour on her cheeks. Jeremiah held her hand loosely, for the bones felt fragile; they showed through the thin skin.

It was just a matter of time, he knew that, for Dr James had called him on the new telephone in the office of the newspaper. Of course he had come immediately, travelling on the train. But Harriet hardly seemed to be aware that he was there. Her hand lay passively in his. Sometimes her eyes opened partly and she looked at him but with no recognition. Indeed, he realized she was not really looking at him at all, but gazing at something not of this world. The rise and fall of the bedclothes was so slight as to be easily missed altogether. A nurse stood quietly by, watching. He barely noticed when she moved to the door and went out.

Jeremiah was so lost in his own thoughts that he started when the door opened and the nurse returned with Dr James.

'Ah, Matron said you were here, Mr Scott,' he said. 'I hoped you would get here in time.'

'In time?'

For a second or two Jeremiah couldn't think what the doctor meant. In time for what? Of course! He meant before Harriet slipped away altogether. This time she really was dying. The good doctor had rung him up at the office and was very pessimistic about Harriet's chances of pulling through this latest relapse. But he had been gravely concerned before and she had rallied. Somehow in the back of his mind, Jeremiah had found it hard to believe.

'I mean . . . you think . . . this is the end?'

'I do.'

Jeremiah gazed at Harriet; she seemed little different to him than she had that morning. There was still a slight flush on her cheeks, her eyes were still half-closed. Was she breathing? He rose to his feet and leaned over her, loosed a hand from hers and leaned closer to see.

Dr James put a hand on his shoulder. 'Come, Mr Scott,' he said. 'Sit down in my office. I'm afraid she's gone. I'm very sorry.' He nodded to the nurse and led Jeremiah away as she pulled the sheet up over Harriet's face.

Jeremiah felt numb when he finally left the grounds of the hospital. He wondered why he felt nothing. Surely he should be grieving? So he turned on to the road over the high moor that led to Stanhope and strode along it, with the wind freshening the higher he climbed, until he had to bend into it to make any progress. Gradually, as the day began to fade, memories of his wife as she had been – the girl he had fallen in love with, the woman who had spent all of her adult life looking after him and loving him – came back to him, and images of those days flashed through his thoughts. Grief overwhelmed him. He sat down on a stone road marker and cried.

Eventually he rose, dried his eyes, and carried on his way to Stanhope railway station. There were things to be done, Harriet's sisters and brothers to be informed of her death, arrangements for the funeral to be made.

'Lottie, I've been waiting for you to tell me you're having a bairn,' said Eliza. She and Lottie were in the marketplace in Durham, having bumped into each other while shopping. It was market day and there were covered stalls selling vegetables and meat and boots and shoes and miner's boots hanging by leather laces, with steel toecaps and studs glinting in the sunlight.

Lottie bit her lip. 'I wanted to be absolutely sure,' she said. 'I didn't want you to get your hopes up and then be disappointed.'

'It's my grandchild, too,' Eliza continued.

Lottie couldn't think what to say. 'I'm sorry, Eliza,' she mumbled.

'Well then,' Eliza said in reply. 'Let's away home now. I could do with a nice cup of tea.'

Lottie followed her mother-in-law to where the trap was parked in a side street, with the pony still munching on the hay in the nosebag. Eliza took the bag from him and put it on the floor in the trap and climbed up on to the driving seat. Lottie sat down beside her. Eliza glanced at her as she picked up the reins.

'Move on,' she said softly and clicked her tongue at the pony, and they set off.

'You'll stay and have some tea, won't you, Lottie?'

It was the last thing Lottie wanted to do but she couldn't say that to Eliza. Eliza, who was still mourning her son. 'I will,' she replied. 'But I can't stay very long after that. I have work to do for the paper. Writing up notes . . .' Her voice faded away as they went into the familiar kitchen. She simply couldn't think of anything more to say.

'Oh, what are they on?'

Eliza had her back to Lottie as she mended the fire and settled the kettle on the coals. Lottie looked at the clippy mat laid before the fire.

'Oh, just the usual,' she said.

Luckily Eliza was setting the table, reaching cups and saucers down from the dresser. By the time she was sitting down at the table beside her daughter-in-law, she had lost interest in Lottie's work.

'When do you reckon the baby is due?' she asked.

'I'm not sure,' Lottie mumbled.

'Well, I reckon it must be soon after Christmas. After all, my Thomas was only home for a short while, wasn't he? It doesn't leave much leeway. Oh, Lottie I'm sorry! I didn't mean to go on, I know you must be hurting as much as I am myself!'

Eliza made herself busy pouring tea and adding milk and sugar, but her hand trembled and the spoon hit the side of the cup and a little spilled into the saucer.

'I'm sorry,' she said.

'Oh, Eliza, don't apologise to me!' exclaimed Lottie. She took the cup and saucer and blotted the few drops in the saucer with her handkerchief. 'Come and sit down, do. Drink your tea and you'll feel better.'

'But how are you managing? Do you feel all right? No morning sickness or anything like that?'

'No, I feel fine. Very well in myself, in fact.'

As Lottie said it, she realized it was true. She did feel very well, despite her recent unhappiness and her preoccupation with Jeremiah. And as she thought this, the child within her moved. She had felt slight tremors over the last week or two but this time it was a definite move, though perhaps not quite a kick.

'Eliza!' she cried. 'He moved, really he did! Give me your hand, quick.'

She took hold of her mother-in-law's hand and laid it on her belly and obligingly, the baby moved once again.

Eliza laughed. 'It's a fit one, that's for sure, and strong an' all. Oh Lottie, thank you for this. My little Tot's bairn! Though maybe it's a girl; you seem very sure it's a lad.'

'I don't know, I just think it is,' replied Lottie. Her eyes took on a faraway look, which Eliza had seen in so many mothers at a time like this.

'It must be four and a half months, Lottie,' she said softly. 'You're halfway there.'

'Yes, that's true and past the time of losing it, aren't I, Eliza?'

'I think so, I hope so, pet.'

The child could not be Jeremiah's then, thought Lottie. Was she pleased or sorry? Pleased of course, she admonished herself silently. In her imagination she had thought he just might be; sometimes she ached that he should be. By, she was a stupid, foolish girl. She finished her tea, before standing and reaching for her jacket, which she had hung over a chair.

'I must go now, Eliza,' she said and bent to kiss her. 'I like to get home before dark and besides, I have things to do. Tomorrow I want to get a start on my new book. Give my love to Peter, will you?'

'Of course I will. What is this book going to be about?'

'Oh, I have a few ideas,' Lottie replied. 'I'll tell you when I've sorted them out in my mind.'

'Well, give me some warning if you write about bossy mothers-in-law, won't you? Otherwise I'll sue you,' Eliza said lightly. She also rose to her feet and walked out to the street with Lottie. 'You will come back soon, won't you?' she asked. 'I couldn't bear to lose touch with you now.'

'I will, of course I will,' Lottie assured her.

She walked quickly off down the street, turning at the corner to wave, but Eliza had already gone in and closed the door. She walked on to her little house by Prebends Bridge and let herself in, closing the door behind her. It was cold indoors; the fire in the grate had died out. She shivered as she went through to the yard and collected kindling and filled the coal scuttle, ready to mend the fire. Once it was ablaze she sat before it in the gathering dusk and stared into the flames. Oh, she was tired – tired and lonely. The house was incredibly quiet, with no sounds penetrating from the outside. She put an arm across her stomach. Was it swelling now with the new life she carried? She waited, barely breathing, for the baby to kick or make any sort of movement, but he did not. For the moment she almost thought she had imagined his presence there inside her. But of course she had not. In four or five months he would be a living, breathing reality, her very own, and she would never be lonely again.

Lottie lit the lamp on her desk and closed the curtains so that she was enclosed in a little world focused on her desk. She opened her notebook and inserted a sheet of foolscap into her typewriter and after a moment's thought, started to type. She had only a few pages to do to finish the chapter she was on and she was determined to get them finished. To do that she had to forget about everything else – the baby, Jeremiah, her mother-in-law – everything and everybody, and she succeeded in doing just that.

It was almost ten o'clock when she finally took the last sheet out of the typewriter and laid it on top of the others. She sat back in her chair and stretched her arms above her head and yawned largely. Immediately thoughts of Jeremiah crowded in on her. Oh he was a lovely man, he was indeed. A lovely *married* man and there was no way of getting over that fact.

Jeremiah was also sitting by himself in his office, his lamp being the only one lit in the building. He felt enormous guilt as he thought of poor Harriet. She was his wife and he had let her down. Thank the Lord she would never know how badly he had let her down.

The office was cold; the fire in the small grate had gone out while he was editing the weekend's edition of the paper. His eyes ached and he felt deathly tired. He should have done as his father had advised and gone home long since. He would, but first he would close his eyes for a short while.

It was almost eleven o'clock when he woke up, shivering and absolutely freezing cold and feeling even more guilty, for he had been dreaming of Lottie. How she was, the feel of her in his arms. It had to stop.

# Twenty-Nine

L ottie plucked the sheet of foolscap from the typewriter, read it through and frowned. What was she thinking of? The words sounded stilted in her head. No one reading them would want to read on to find out what came next, nobody at all. She crumpled the page in her hand, rolled it into a ball and threw it on the back of the fire.

What she needed was a break and a breath of fresh air – maybe that would stimulate her ideas. Maybe she was writing the wrong book. The doubt plagued her. Her story was loosely based on the story of her own mother: Minnie her name had been. Not that Lottie knew much about her mother or where she had come from, but what she knew of her she had used her imagination to add to. Mainly it was the stories she had made up as a little girl about her mother: how she was really from a well-to-do family, landed gentry perhaps, and how she had run away with a penniless orphan and what had happened to her as a consequence. A story of melodrama and tragedy.

Now she could see it was silly and worthless and she had been wasting her time on it. Readers wanted happy endings, not tales full of woe. She would have to change it. Not now though. She would have to think it out properly and just now she was finding it hard to think about anything but Jeremiah, even though she had not seen him for months.

She had read all about his wife's death of course; her funeral too. She had thought about sending a note of sympathy but agonized over what to write, and in the end wrote nothing. As time went by the opportunity slipped away, until it was just too late. The weeks turned into months, until it was almost time for her baby to be born and she was occupied with her new novel and preparations for the birth. Eliza was her mainstay.

As the weather grew colder, her thoughts wandered back to Jeremiah, as they did so often these days. Depression fell on her like a blanket of snow: cold and all-pervasive. She had not been in to the office for weeks; she could not bear for him to see how swollen her belly was or how drawn her face was. And though her belly was swollen, her arms and legs were like sticks. She looked an absolute fright, she did indeed. She stared at herself in the mirror over the mantelpiece one day. She had to pull herself together, she thought; feeling sorry for herself never worked.

A knock at the door made her start. She went down the stairs and stood behind the front door thinking, hoping, he might have come to see her, though why she should think that, he never came to see her nowadays.

It would be the postman. Of course it would be the postman, who else would come knocking at her door at that time of the morning? It was barely seven o'clock, the cathedral bells were chiming the hour. Her hair was still plaited loosely, with the plait over one shoulder, but that didn't matter when it was just the postman. She drew the bolt on the front door and opened it.

It wasn't the postman, it was Jeremiah standing there. Taking off his hat and tipping his head so very politely. And there she had always thought it was Quakers who did not remove their hats for anyone except the Lord. Though what that had to do with anything, she couldn't think.

'I'm sorry to call so early in the morning,' he said. 'I was passing by as it happens . . .'

Lottie's mouth had dropped open when she saw him but now she collected herself and closed it. Where on earth could he be going, passing her door so early in the morning? She thought it even as she opened the door wider and stood to one side.

'Do come in,' she said. Her face felt hot. She was sure it must be red as fire and she was very conscious of her untidy hair and the old shirtwaister dress she had pulled on before she came downstairs, just until she had cleaned up the house a little.

Jeremiah walked past her through to the kitchen-cum-living room and stood on the clippie mat before the fire, with his hands behind him.

'Lottie,' he said, gazing keenly at her with his dark blue eyes, which seemed to be able to see right into her mind.

'Yes, Mr Scott?'

'I want the truth now, do you hear me?'

'There is nothing wrong with my hearing,' she replied. She pushed her spectacles up over the bridge of her nose, before folding her arms over the bulge under her apron. Standing before him, she had to look up at him, which was a distinct disadvantage. So she gestured towards a chair.

'Sit down, do,' she said and sat down in the rocker. Jeremiah hesitated for a split second, then sat down himself.

'I want to know the truth,' he said. 'Is the baby mine?'

Lottie was very tempted to say yes it was; she even opened her mouth to say so. But how could she? She couldn't lie to him. In any case, the baby's birth would prove it wasn't true, no matter how much she wished it were.

It was all over now, she thought dismally. He would never feel for her as she did for him. If only it had been his baby! Lottie got to her feet and walked to the window, staring blindly down the yard. 'The baby's father is . . .' she began, then suddenly a pain shot through her and she doubled up with a low cry. Jeremiah moved with such speed that he caught her as she fell.

'It's the baby,' she cried. 'Help me!'

'I'll help you upstairs,' he replied, turning with her in his arms, but Lottie shook her head.

'There's no time,' she gasped. 'He's coming.'

'What? The doctor?'

'The baby, you fool! Put me down on the mat!'

There was indeed no time. No time to get a doctor or a midwife or even the woman from next door. Jeremiah Scott found himself delivering the child, a little girl, on the clippie mat before the kitchen fire. And after the first numbing shock, he was automatically acting on the instructions Lottie panted to him between pains, which were coming ever faster, until one pain was running into the next and the baby came into his hands.

Then his own common sense and natural instinct made him wrap the child in a warmed towel, which was hanging over the brass rail above the fireplace, and give her to Lottie, still with the cord attached. Or rather he laid her on her mother's stomach, for Lottie had fallen back, totally exhausted.

'I'll get help,' he said. 'Will you be all right? Lottie?'

'Jane from next door,' Lottie said faintly. She felt she could not move to hold the baby yet, but she reached down and put a hand on her tiny shoulder. Jeremiah ran to the door, then hesitated.

'You will be all right?'

'Go on, fetch Jane,' she cried and he fled up the yard.

It seemed like an age, but in fact it could not have been much more than a minute before he was back with her neighbour, who took in the situation at a glance and bent over Lottie and the baby.

'There's a sharp knife in the table drawer?' she asked, but he was already taking one out before Lottie could answer. 'You have a binder ready?'

As Lottie nodded towards the drawer of the press, Jane, knife in hand, looked towards Jeremiah. 'Go on, this no place for you,' she said quietly. 'I'll call you when she's decent.'

'Thank you,' he said. 'I'll walk up the lane. I'll not go far.'

Jane nodded and turned back to Lottie. 'It shouldn't take long now, I'm well used to helping out when a woman's time comes. I'll have you comfortable in two shakes of a dog's tail. Mind, I'll get the midwife to have a look at you and the babby, just to make sure.'

Lottie murmured something, but she was tired and shaken by the speed of it all. She was happy to leave it to her neighbour, who soon had the tiny girl wrapped in a shawl and lying on a pillow in a drawer from the kitchen press and Lottie herself washed and sitting propped up by pillows and drinking a cup of tea sweetened with two spoons of sugar.

Outside, Jeremiah walked to the end of the lane and back again, hesitated, and then walked to the other end. He stood for a while looking out over the River Wear and the far bank, rising as it did above the city. Beyond, it was possible to see the ancient stone tower of the cathedral and the battlements of the castle. He stared at them for a few moments, thinking of the tiny baby in the cottage. Was she his baby? Maybe not, but it felt as though she were. After all, he had brought her into the world, and though it might be illogical he felt a responsibility towards her. He stood, gazing unseeing into the brown peaty water as a boat with the university rowing team bending over the oars went by, the coach on his bicycle calling the strokes through a loudhailer.

The feel of the baby in his arms had been like a miracle, he mused.

Smiling, he turned and made his way back to Lottie's back gate, and after a moment Jane waved from the kitchen window for him to go back into the house.

Lottie was lying on the settee with the baby, still in the press drawer, on a chair beside her. Jane hovered by her; after all, even if he had actually delivered the baby, it was not fitting to leave him alone with the new mother.

'We have to send someone for the nurse, Sister Mitchell,' Jane said. 'I could send my lad, or mebbe you would go, Mr Scott? Then my man goes on shift soon and I have to fix him a sandwich or something for his bait tin.'

'You go, I'll stay with her until she comes,' Jeremiah said blandly, though he was entirely aware of Jane's dilemma. He pulled a kitchen chair out from the table and took it over to the settee and sat down.

'Well . . .'

Jane hesitated, but in the end went out to get her son to run for Eliza.

'I fear we have shocked your neighbour, Lottie,' he said and she nodded, smiling.

'I don't know what I would have done without you, though,' she replied. 'Thank you, Jerry . . . Mr Scott.'

'Oh I think Jerry will do. I like it, no one else calls me Jerry.'

Lottie hesitated. She had to say something before Eliza arrived. 'She is Thomas's baby,' she blurted at last.

'I know,' he said, then after a pause, 'But I helped her into the world. I feel she is mine.'

'I am going to have her baptized Thomasina.' Lottie plucked at the blanket that Jane had put over her. 'Eliza, Sister Mitchell, is my mother-in-law. The baby's grandmother.'

Jeremiah said nothing.

There was a silence for a few minutes. Lottie lay against the raised end of the old settee. Jeremiah was restless. He sat for a while, then got up and walked through to the front of the house and watched the road for the arrival of the nurse, Lottie's mother-in-law. His feelings were in turmoil. How could she be so sure it wasn't his baby? The child could have been early, he knew it happened sometimes. He yearned for the tiny girl to be his.

The road was empty. He turned and walked back along the passage to the kitchen. As he did so, he heard the sound of a horse and trap and stopped, then went to open the front door just as Eliza knocked.

'Hello, are you there?' Eliza called, then stopped short as she saw Jeremiah.

She was in her nurse's uniform and cape and was carrying her nurse's bag. 'Oh,' she went on, 'I thought Jane from next door would be here.'

'She had things to attend to,' he said. 'I'm Jeremiah Scott, editor of *The Durham Post*. Lottie . . . Mrs Mitchell-Howe worked for the paper.'

'I'm well aware that my daughter-in-law wrote pieces for *The Post*,' said Eliza sharply. 'But obviously she cannot be writing *now*. I thank you for staying with her, but I think you should be on your way, young man.'

'I could wait in the other room to make sure I am not needed any more.' Jeremiah's face was a picture to behold: pink with embarrassment. He felt like a naughty schoolboy.

'I dinna think so,' said Eliza, lapsing into the local idiom. 'What will people think? Any road, I have to see to her. Close the door on your way out.'

Jeremiah found himself led to the door and out on to the street without quite knowing how it happened. He stood for a moment, then walked away. His own horse was whickering to Eliza's pony on the opposite side of the road, where tufts of lush grass were pushing through the holes in the fence. Swinging up into the saddle, he trotted off towards North Road and the office.

'Did I hear you talking to Mr Scott just then?' asked Lottie, as she settled down after Eliza had bathed her and the baby. They were in the front room by now, with Lottie in a single bed brought down by Jane's husband and son.

Eliza shook her head disapprovingly. 'You did, lass. I never heard anything like it, a strange man delivering a baby. Was there not a woman about at all? What was he doing here, any road?'

'He just came by,' said Lottie lamely.

'Aye, well, it's a good job Jane was in,' said Eliza.

Lottie gave her a quick glance. Was Eliza thinking something must be going on? No, of course not, she thought when she saw her mother-in-law's bland expression. Eliza had picked up the baby from the dresser drawer and now she started cooing over her.

'What are you going to call the bairn? Charlotte, after you? Or, what was your mother's name?'

'Minnie,' Lottie replied. 'But I've decided on Thomasina.'

'Thomasina, eh? It's mebbe a bit outlandish,' Eliza commented but she couldn't hide the fact that she was pleased. 'There's not been a Thomasina round here that I know of. It's nice though. Like a name from a fairy tale.' She smiled fondly at the baby before handing her over to Lottie to suckle. 'She has a look of our Thomas though.'

Lottie yawned widely and Eliza immediately became the professional nurse-midwife again. She tucked a bedjacket around Lottie's shoulders, before checking Thomasina was suckling correctly.

'Not that she'll get much nourishment at first, but it will help your milk to come,' she commented. 'Now, I'll send Jane's lad, Jackie is it? I'll send him for Mrs Corner.' Eliza moved towards the door. 'You'll be all right for a little while on your own?'

Lottie lay quietly, communing with her baby. Thomasina's eyes were a medium blue, but then most newborn babies had blue eyes. They might turn brown like her own or as dark blue as Thomas's. Or Jeremiah's either, she thought drowsily. Mother and baby drifted off to sleep. Eliza came back and lifted the baby gently from Lottie's arms and laid her in her makeshift cradle. When Lottie awoke, Mrs Corner, the monthly nurse she had engaged for her lying-in, was already there and Eliza had gone.

'She said she'd call in the morrow,' Mrs Corner volunteered. 'She had patients to see. Now, I bet you could take a nice drop of broth and a cup of tea, my dear.'

Mrs Corner was a plump, white-haired woman in her fifties and a widow. She had brought up six children since her husband had been killed by choke damp in the pit, but now they were married and away she did it for the love of it. Each job lasted a month, helping out new mothers until they were properly on their feet again. Lottie watched as she bustled around, noticing things that needed doing and doing them.

She felt extremely happy and content as Thomasina lay close by, making the occasional snuffling noise.

Surely nothing could spoil her contentment, her hopes for the future now? She had her baby and Thomasina was healthy. And Jeremiah knew the truth and loved her.

# Thirty

The bells of the old cathedral were ringing out the last hours of the old year as Ina, holding tightly to her mother's hand, skipped along the pavement to where the horse-bus stood in the marketplace of Durham City. Her mother carried a basket covered with a cloth and they were going to her grandma's house in North Road to see in the New Year. It was the only night of the year when Ina was allowed to stay up until midnight and for all it was so late and the sky so dark the marketplace was lit up with the lights from the shops, which were still open, and the Christmas tree from Norway still stood in the centre by the statue of Lord Londonderry on his horse, and it too was lit up. She tugged at her mother's hand in her excitement and Lottie almost fell over as she stepped down from the kerb.

'Ina!' Lottie cried. 'You nearly made me drop the basket!'

'Sorry Mam,' said Ina, slowing to a walk. They didn't want to lose anything from the basket. It had all the goodies in it to celebrate bringing in the New Year. There was a fruit cake and fudge and a stone bottle of dandelion and burdock pop and a bottle of home-made ginger wine.

'Lottie! How nice to see you! And you too, Thomasina. What are you doing out so late?'

It was the nice man, the one who sometimes gave her mother money for the stories she wrote. She liked him; his name was Mr Scott and he always spoke to her nicely and sometimes gave her a threepenny bit. She could buy three separate things with a threepenny bit: sweets and chocolate and a penny lucky bag.

Ina looked up at her mother, who had that funny look on her face she sometimes had when she met Mr Scott. Her face was sort of pinkish, and she had a faraway look in her eyes. Ina decided she had better answer him herself.

'Hello, Mr Scott. We're going to Grandma's to see in the New Year. And I can stay up until after midnight but I can't go first-footing.' She frowned as she thought of the first-footing. Only lads were able to go first-footing and it wasn't fair.

'I'm not allowed,' she said sorrowfully. 'I'm a girl.'

'I hope you are allowed to accept a New Year's gift,' said Jeremiah. He dug into the pocket of his waistcoat and brought out a sixpence, then looked enquiringly at Lottie.

'You shouldn't,' said Lottie. 'You'll spoil her.'

'Oh, I don't know, it is a special occasion surely, the turn of the year, is it not?' Jeremiah smiled down at the two of them, the little girl with shining blue eyes in a face that was full of excitement, and the woman he found himself thinking about more and more. It was more than four years since the day that he and Lottie had come together, and he still remembered every second of it. It was almost four years since he had delivered the child, Thomasina, on the clippie mat by the kitchen fire, and that too was etched on his mind. He could remember the smell of the woollen clippie strips, the sound of ash falling through the bars of the fire, the heat of the fire on his face.

He brought his mind back to the present with a wrench.

'I'm meeting my father in half an hour but I have a little time to spare. May I walk along with you? Or I can give you a lift to where your mother-in-law lives, near North Road, isn't it?'

'It is.'

'Here, give me your basket.'

They fell into step, walking side by side with the little girl between them, her hand in the pocket of her pinafore clutching the sixpence he had given her. Ina was quiet, thinking of whether to spend it all today or keep threepence for tomorrow. She was so absorbed with the problem that she didn't even hear the conversation between her mother and Mr Scott.

Lottie was surprised. In the time since Ina was born, he had rarely spoken to her except formally or in connection with her articles. In fact, she had often gone home feeling hurt because he had seemed so distant. He regretted what had been between them, she had decided. It had hurt at first but she had gradually got used to it. In any case, she was finished with men, they brought her nothing but grief. She and Ina could get on fine without a man.

Her books were doing well enough and providing a modest income, enough to live on. And there was a little extra from *The Durham Post,* enough for the odd treat for Ina and still some to save for emergencies.

'How are you, Lottie?' His question broke the growing silence between them.

'It is so long since I spoke to you as . . . as a friend.'

'It is.' She glanced up at him, surprised. 'I'm in good health, thank you for asking,' she answered his question.

'Good.'

They were walking down Silver Street by now, almost to Framwellgate Bridge over the Wear at the bottom. They paused for a moment, unwilling to part, and Ina stood on tiptoe and peered over the wall at the black waters below. Jeremiah put out a restraining hand in case she leaned over too far.

'Careful,' he said.

Ina was affronted. 'I'm not a baby,' she declared.

'Indeed, you are not,' he replied gravely. He looked over her head to her mother and smiled. 'Perhaps I could call to see you tomorrow,' he said, surprising her.

He rarely came to her little house nowadays. In fact, it must be months since he had. She felt as confused as a young girl asked out for the first time, which was quite ridiculous. But then, perhaps it was in the line of business he was coming; she shouldn't read anything into it. Though she usually saw him in his office in that case.

'Of course,' she replied. 'I'll be home about ten. We're staying to see the New Year in at Eliza's tonight.'

'I'll call at eleven. I'm looking forward to it.' His smile enveloped and warmed her. 'Now,' he continued, 'the pony and trap are just over the bridge at the blacksmith's yard.'

They walked over the bridge, swinging Ina between them, just like any parents with a young child might. It was as though the intervening years had never been, thought Lottie; yet she couldn't put her finger on what exactly had changed between them.

They drove up to the home of Peter and Eliza with Ina between them chattering away, complaining again that girls couldn't go first-footing and it wasn't fair but then she forgot about that particular injustice as she told Jeremiah of the doll Father Christmas had brought her with eyes that opened and closed. He nodded or shook his head and grunted at the appropriate moments, which was all she seemed to need or want.

It was but a short journey until the pony was stopping outside Eliza's house and Jeremiah got down and swung both of them to the ground, leaving Lottie breathless and Ina giggling.

'I'll see you tomorrow,' he said again. 'Happy New Year!'

They stood by the gate as he climbed back on to the trap and handed down Lottie's basket. He picked up the reins and was off, back down the hill and up the opposite side to the marketplace.

'Mr Scott is a nice man, isn't he?' said Ina. 'Is he someone else's daddy?'

'No, he isn't,' her mother replied. Ina gazed after the pony and trap until it was out of sight. It wasn't hard to tell what she was thinking. 'Howay, Ina,' Lottie said sharply. 'Come on in, your grandma's waiting.'

Jeremiah drove back to the blacksmiths at the bottom of Silver Street, hung a nosebag of hay around the pony's head and turned him over to the care of the blacksmith's boy, before walking up the steep road which led to the marketplace. He was lost in his own thoughts, barely noticing the thinning crowd, the shops already putting up their shutters.

In the last few years, he had managed to keep his feelings for Lottie pretty well bottled up. He did not admit them even to himself. After all, they were not fitting when his wife was so recently dead. There had to be a decent period of mourning for Harriet, he owed her that. But seeing how Ina had grown, he had realized that that time of mourning must be coming to an end in anyone's eyes.

Only that morning, his father had asked him if he knew when Lottie's new novel was coming out and he had had to say he did not. 'Though it surely cannot be long now,' said Jeremiah.

'Lottie must be earning a fair income from her books by this time,' Mr Scott senior had speculated. 'I wonder she still finds time to write articles on local current affairs for a newspaper such as ours. What do you think, Jeremiah?'

'I have no idea how much Mrs Mitchell-Howe earns,' Jeremiah had replied stiffly.

'Perhaps she just likes our people here?'

'Perhaps she does.'

The elder Mr Scott gazed at his son. 'And that is all you have to say? Righto then, that's all right.' He had walked over to the window and stood gazing out at the Durham plain, which was just visible, rising over the tops of the houses. 'I will wait until you have something to say.'

'Father, I don't know what you are talking about.'

'No, of course not. But it is almost five years since poor Harriet died,' his father said, before quickly leaving the room and going back down to the front desk.

Had the way he felt about Lottie been obvious after all, at least to his father? Jeremiah wondered as he strode to the top of the narrow medieval street, and up to the bank where he had said he would meet his father.

It was almost as if the meeting with Lottie and little Thomasina was meant to be. Though it was just a coincidence of course, he told himself. But he had at last come to the place where he could ask Lottie to marry him. Today he had finally believed that she might feel for him as he felt for her.

The next day Lottie was up early, even though they had stayed up until midnight to see in the New Year and she had spent the night tossing and turning in her bed, unable to sleep. For no matter how many times she told herself that he most likely wanted to discuss a new article he wanted her to write, the wild hope that it was something more personal he wanted to talk about would not go away. She tidied and cleaned the little sitting room and had the kettle singing on the hob in the kitchen so that she could offer him tea.

'Why are we wearing our best dresses, Mam?' asked Ina.

'Because it is New Year,' Lottie replied. 'Mind you keep yours clean now. Go on upstairs and play with your new dolly. We'll go for a walk this afternoon, if you like.'

Ina pulled a face but went upstairs anyway to find her doll, while Lottie sat down before the fire and gave herself up to daydreaming. Whether it was the warmth from the fire or the lack of sleep the night before, the next thing she knew she awoke with a start and jumped up, as she realized there was the dark outline of a man between the window and herself.

'Who's that?' she cried, completely disoriented, then, 'Oh Jerry, it's you.'

'I'm sorry Lottie, I knocked but you didn't hear and as the door was unlocked I came in. I should not have startled you, but you looked so sweet sitting there with your glasses falling off your nose and your cheeks pink from the fire that I just stepped forward to watch for a moment.'

He caught hold of her hand and held it to his chest. 'Lottie, I did wrong by you those years ago but now I have come to put it right. I was not free before, but now . . .' He paused, realizing that had not been what he meant to say. 'I don't mean that is the reason I am asking you to marry me, Lottie, oh no it is not.'

'You are asking me to marry you?'

Lottie left her hand in his as she gazed up at him. She couldn't make out his expression, not properly, until she realized it was her twisted glasses and put up her other hand to straighten them. Oh, his eyes were such a deep blue and his expression so open and honest. He was a straightforward man – a lovely man, as Thomas had never been.

His hand tightened on hers as he took a deep breath and said, 'I am. Yes, I am. Though of course you don't have to answer me yet, I don't want to rush you . . .'

'I will. I will, of course I will. I thought you wouldn't ask, I thought it was too late for us, I really did. Oh, Jerry! I love you.'

He gathered her up in his arms, knocking her glasses askew once again, and kissed her, a long and lingering kiss. From behind her came Ina's voice.

'Mr Scott, if you marry my mammy, will you be my daddy?' she asked.

'I will, Thomasina, I will,' he replied fervently.